Big
Trouble
in Little
Greektown

The Goddess of Greene St. Mysteries
by Kate Collins

Statue of Limitations

A Big Fat Greek Murder

Big Trouble in Little Greektown

Big Trouble in Little Greektown

Kate Collins

KENSINGTON
PUBLISHING CORP.

www.kensingtonbooks.com

KENSINGTON BOOKS are published by

Kensington Publishing Corp.
119 West 40th Street
New York, NY 10018

All Kensington titles, imprints, and distributed lines are available at special quantity discounts for bulk purchases for sales promotion, premiums, fund-raising, educational, or institutional use.

Special book excerpts or customized printings can also be created to fit specific needs. For details, write or phone the office of the Kensington Sales Manager: Attn.: Sales Department. Kensington Publishing Corp., 119 West 40th Street, New York, NY 10018. Phone: 1-800-221-2647.

The K logo is a trademark of Kensington Publishing Corp.

First Printing: December 2021
ISBN: 978-1-4967-2437-3

ISBN: 978-1-4967-2438-0 (ebook)

10 9 8 7 6 5 4 3 2 1

Printed in the United States of America

This book is dedicated to all of the fans of the Flower Shop Mysteries and now to the Goddess of Greene St. mysteries, as well. Thank you for believing in me and my stories.

This is also dedicated to my wonderful assistant, Jason Eberhardt, whom I know will one day have a loyal following of readers, too.

And as always, this is dedicated to my daughter Julia, who listens when I need an encouraging ear.

PROLOGUE

Saturday, 10:45 a.m.

"Let's walk and talk." He smiled.

A friendly smile. Nothing to worry about. Hugo took it as a good sign. His plan was working.

The sand fell away as they left the dunes area and started up the forested path. Hugo was sweating in his short-sleeved shirt, long pants, and heavy shoes. He knew he should've worn shorts and sandals, but they didn't look professional, and he'd wanted to look especially professional today. He adjusted the camera strap around his neck where it was chafing and walked on.

They wove their way among the giant, thickly branched trees, leaving behind the bright June sun, the fluffy white clouds, leaving behind the noise of the festival, the smells of popcorn and taffy apples. They strolled up the winding path, the sun barely filtering through the leaves overhead, passing thick bushes and tall grasses until the man stopped, turned toward him, and smiled again.

"Now let's see those photographs."

CHAPTER ONE

Saturday, 10 a.m.

"Popcorn. Get your caramel-coated popcorn right here."

"Let's stop," I said to Case, pushing up the strap of my sundress. "It smells delicious."

"Athena, fifteen minutes ago you told me not to let you ruin your lunch."

"I forgot about the popcorn." I gave him a sheepish smile. "Just one bag and I'll behave. It'll be my treat."

We stopped at the popcorn stand, bought a bag of the sweet/salty stuff, and took stock of our surroundings: arts and crafts booths, food booths, a lovely woodland area, sand dunes, a view of Lake Michigan, and happy people enjoying a perfectly sunny Saturday morning. It had been so long since I'd taken a Saturday off, I'd almost forgotten how enjoyable my little tourist town could be.

The June sun was streaming down in beams through the voluminous puffy clouds, raising the temperature above 80 degrees, making sundresses and shorts a necessity. I had my long brown hair up in a ponytail and had on an aqua-colored sundress, a flowy style just perfect for a warm day. Case was wearing sandals, khaki shorts, and a dark green T-shirt that brought out the green flecks in his light brown eyes. He'd met me at the pier where his houseboat was docked, and even though I'd promised he'd find the art festival interesting, I'd had to practically drag him there.

Sequoia, Michigan was well-known for its weekend festivities, drawing people from all over the western side of the state as well as from northern Indiana and Chicago. I was glad to see the festival had already attracted a huge number of locals as well as tourists.

Entitled Art for the Park, the festival was well underway by the time we arrived.

The rambling, old Victorian mansion that hosted the event sat at the southern end of Greene Street, a corner lot on a wide expanse of land that had been all but forgotten until the historic home had been repurposed. From the porch hung a large sign that read *The Studios of Sequoia* and listed the services they offered: painting lessons, private art rooms, art sales, and studios for rent. This was the first time the Studios of Sequoia had sponsored a festival, and so far, it looked like a huge success.

A woman was standing on the wraparound porch giving a tour to a small group. Case and I passed by the house and wandered through the crowd into the backyard, a magnificent expanse of land with a perfect view of Lake Michigan. The back of the house had a large ce-

ment patio big enough to host painting classes or enter-
tain guests.

"Shall we look around?" I asked Case as he munched
on a handful of the sweet-smelling caramel corn.

Behind the mansion's property was a large tract of
dune fronting Lake Michigan, as well as a forested area
with hiking trails. The land had once been a beautiful
public park, but time and lack of funds had turned it into
an eyesore.

Case pointed to one of the banners strung across the
yard. "Save Our Dunes," he read. "Save them from what?"

"The dunes have been off-limits because of erosion." I
picked up a pamphlet sitting on a nearby booth. "'Art for
the Park,'" I read aloud. "'All profits will go to help save
our dunes from destruction.' Save Our Dunes—we call it
SOD—was started to raise awareness and education about
Sequoia's treasured strip of natural dune land."

Case grabbed a second handful of popcorn. With his
dark, handsome good looks and athletic build, I wasn't
sure which looked yummier, him or the popcorn. "Looks
like they have a lot of support."

We passed more booths and tables set up in a wide
square on the expansive back lawn, people selling jewelry, hooked rugs, brightly colored pottery, drawings,
even sculptures. Anything considered art was fair game at
this festival.

I flipped through a selection of vintage movie posters
as Case continued to eat the popcorn. "So, this is what
you call interesting?" he asked.

I snatched the bag from him. "You just lost popcorn
privileges."

A deep voice to my left caught my attention. "Hello,
Goddess of Greene Street."

I swung around and came face-to-face with Hugo Lukan, the photographer who'd taken my picture with the now-famous *Treasure of Athena* statue that graced the entrance to my father's business, Spencer's Garden Center. The *Treasure of Athena* and I had made quite a splash in the newspaper after I'd helped solve a double homicide that centered around the six-foot-tall statue of the goddess Athena. That investigation had earned me the title the *Goddess of Greene Street*.

"Hello, Hugo."

Hugo was a lean, nervous, forty-something man who was always on the move. With prematurely white hair, he took photographs for the daily newspaper and also sold his photos to magazines and advertisers. Now on his third divorce, Hugo was known around town for his penchant for flirting and his scandalous lack of scruples.

He shook my hand and then Case's. "You're a hard man to reach, Donnelly."

"I've been busy," Case said. He eyed the professional camera hanging around Hugo's neck. "Are you here on official business?"

Hugo did a quick sweep of the crowd. "I guess you could say that. Let's have you two stand closer and smile for me."

We did as he suggested, and he took our photograph. "It's always nice to see a celebrity mingling with the common folk," he teased.

"You're lucky I'm in a good mood," I teased back.

"You get your private eye business up and running yet?" he asked Case.

"Still working on it," Case replied.

Hugo glanced around again as though checking for

someone. "You'd better hurry," he said, suddenly serious. "You and I have a lot to discuss."

"What do you two have to discuss?" I asked, feeling suspiciously left out of the loop.

He lowered his voice. "I can't talk about it here, but I do need Case's expertise. Watch your mail."

"Are you selling any of your photography today?" Case asked, changing the subject.

"Are you kidding?" Hugo rolled his eyes. "This festival is a waste of time. The Save Our Dunes group wanted me to donate some of my photos for the park renovation project, but what I'm working on now will help their cause more than any donation could. Just wait and see."

"Wait for what?" I asked.

As though he hadn't heard me, Hugo glanced around again. "There's Pearson Reed. If you'll excuse me, I need to speak with him, so I'll let you get on with your day. Enjoy the festival." Hugo turned and practically trotted away.

"A celebrity, are you?" Case asked, putting an arm around my shoulders.

"No autographs, please. This celebrity is officially off-duty. Now, if you'll do me the honor of filling me in."

"Don't mind Hugo," Case said. "I met him last week at a bar. He was going on about some conspiracy within the city council and asked for my help. I told him it'd have to wait until I got my private investigator's license. He wasn't too happy about that."

"I don't trust him, Case. He does exceptional photography, but otherwise doesn't have a very good reputation."

"That's why I've been avoiding him."

"He sounded very serious."

"He said wait and see. I guess that's all we can do."

We kept walking down the aisles of booths, my eyes focused on Hugo as he followed Pearson through the crowd. "Pearson Reed is on the city council," I told Case. "His wife is a friend of mine. Maybe we should look into this conspiracy Hugo mentioned."

"Not until I get my P.I. license. I don't want to jeopardize my career before it starts."

We passed by a beverage booth sponsored by Sequoia Savings and Loan, where I waved to my friend Darlene, a senior vice president at the bank. We saw a face-painting booth for kids, a booth selling artisan cheeses, and another selling goat milk soaps and lotions. We stopped at one called Jewel's Jewels, explored a booth selling watercolor art, and browsed a long table of homemade desserts sponsored by the Women of St. Jacob's Greek Orthodox Church. They had baklava, *kourabiedes*, and my favorite, *galaktobourekos*, among others. To go with it they were offering Greek coffee, a sweet, strong, pressed coffee that was dessert in itself.

"We have to stop here," I said. "I want you to try the *galaktobourekos*."

"I can't even pronounce it. Why would I want to try it?"

"Do you like custard? Because these are heavenly little squares of custard pie with honey drizzled on top."

Case motioned toward the empty bag of popcorn in my hand. "I promised to keep you from ruining your lunch."

"And I promised you this art fair would be interesting."

"Touché."

"Buy one for me!" I heard and glanced down to the

next booth to see my youngest sister, Delphi, sitting behind the table. With her dark, curly hair pulled back in a ponytail, she had on a deep teal T-shirt and tie-dyed harem pants in teal and gold with her ever-present flip-flops, those also in gold.

"What are you doing here?" I asked, moving down to stand in front of her.

"Raising money." She smiled up at me. "Check out our sign."

I glanced up and saw a sign that read: *Mind, Body, Spirit.* And in smaller letters underneath: *Reiki Healer, Psychic Medium, Massage Therapist, Tea Leaf Reader.*

"Delphi, you don't do tea leaf readings." And her coffee ground readings were iffy at best.

"Go away, then," she said with a pout. "You'll ruin business."

"Athena, are you causing trouble?" I heard, and turned to my left to see my mother standing inside the Greek church's booth, arms crossed, shaking her head, an amused look on her face. Next to her stood my older sister Selene, my younger sister Maia, and my ten-year-old son, Nicholas.

"Look at that," Case whispered in my ear. "It's a family affair."

"Hi, Mom," said Nicholas, or Niko, as he preferred to be called now. "Can I have a piece of custard, too?"

"Not now, honey," I said. "You'll ruin your lunch."

"There's the pot calling the kettle black," Case said quietly, earning him another poke in the shoulder.

I came from a big, zany, half-Greek, half-English family of two parents, four sisters, a Greek grandmother and grandfather, and lots of aunts, uncles, and cousins. Like my sisters Maia and Selene, I was named after a Greek goddess. Delphi was named after the Oracle of Delphi, which she assumed made her an oracle, too. Unlike my sisters, however, I took after my father in looks, while my three sisters took after my mother, with long, dark, curly hair, rounder faces, olive complexions, and sturdier bodies than our willowy, fair-haired, English relatives.

"Athena," my mom said, snapping her fingers beneath my chin, causing the gold bracelets on her arm to clatter.

"Sorry, I was just thinking."

"Leave Delphi alone," Mom said. "She's making money for SOD."

In lieu of sticking out her tongue, Delphi wrinkled her nose at me. I wrinkled my nose back and turned away. I usually tried to monitor her coffee ground readings when she did them for customers at Spencer's. Amazingly, although she often put her foot in her mouth, now and then she actually got her readings right. She claimed a 75 percent success rate, which I highly doubted.

"Nice to see you, Case," my mom said. "Athena, let your son have a small square. He's been good all morning."

"I think Athena wants some Greek custard, too," Case said, pulling out his wallet. He eyed the luscious custard squares and added, "Make that three."

"Coming right up." Selene turned to dish three squares onto heavy cardboard plates.

Case picked up our desserts, passed one to Nicholas with a wink, and we moved on to the booth after Delphi's, where the sign said: *Save Our Dunes Nature Walk*.

"Today we're giving a short lecture on the native plants as we hike a portion of the trail," a man in matching khaki shirt and pants told the crowd. "If you enjoy nature, you'll enjoy this. Our first walk starts in half an hour."

"Let's sign up," I said to Case.

He looked dubious. "It's hot today. Are you sure you want to hike?"

He was looking for a way out. "Come on, this will actually be interesting," I said, writing our names on the list. "And we'll have time to eat our dessert beforehand. Let's go find a place to sit."

"Interesting?" Case muttered. "Right."

"What?"

"Tables are *right* over there." Case pointed across the wide lawn to a grouping of bright green wooden picnic tables.

As we sat down at an empty table facing the water, Case held his hand up to shield his eyes from the bright late-morning sun and glanced around. "This *is* beautiful land."

"You should have seen it twenty years ago. My family used to come down here with a picnic lunch on Sunday afternoons. I have fond memories of playing in the sand and swimming in the lake with my sisters. I'd really hate to see it destroyed."

As Case took a bite of the soft custard dessert, I asked, "How is the *galaktobourekos*, by the way?"

"You were right. It's delicious. But I'm not even going to try to pronounce that."

"Just say *Gah-lacto-burekos*." I finished my dessert and sat back with a sigh. "The Greek language is a challenge, which is why I skipped a lot of Greek school."

"I have an idea," Case said, sliding his arm around my waist. "Why don't we skip the nature hike and take the boat out? Just you and me. Out on the water. Alone."

The idea was tempting. It seemed as though Case and I hadn't been able to spend any quality time together in weeks. Ever since he'd started working toward his P.I. license, all of his free time was spent studying, researching, and taking classes. Not only that, but the summer rush was in full swing at the garden center. Between that and spending time with my son and family, there wasn't much room for romance.

"Athena!" someone called. I looked around and saw Elissa Petros Reed, a talented artist and wife of city councilman Pearson Reed, walking toward us.

"Hold that thought," I said to Case.

A full-blooded Greek, Elissa was a petite woman with thick, short dark hair, an olive complexion, dark brown eyes, and a generous mouth. After inheriting the Victorian house and property from her father, Elissa and her husband were responsible for renovating the mansion and turning it into a well-regarded art studio and tourist attraction.

I'd known Elissa since we were both gawky preteens. We'd become friends through summer camp and had stayed friends until college, when our paths took us in different directions. Now that our sons had become friends, we looked forward to seeing each other regularly. "It's good to see you," I said.

"You, too. And who is this handsome gentleman?"

I introduced her to Case and told her we had signed up for the nature walk. "Case is really excited about it."

He stared at me as though to say, *I am?*

"Good," she said. "You'll understand why we love this land so much. In fact, my husband and I are the ones who started the Save Our Dunes group. I hope you two will join. We need more members."

"I'd love to join," I said. "I'm all for turning the lakeside back into a park."

As Case ate the last bite of the soft custard dessert, he glanced past the dunes to where the trees started. "What about the forested area?"

"If a business bought the land," Elissa explained, "it could be razed or ignored. Either way it'd be a shame to see it go to waste, and it would completely ruin the view from our studios. That's why Save Our Dunes was created, to convince the city council this land should be rehabbed as a public park again."

"What's the latest word from the city council?" I asked.

"According to my husband," she said, "there's a company that wants to build on the land, with a parking lot on the southern end and an industrial driveway that would run alongside the property here. Supposedly it would bring in a good chunk of money in tax revenue for the city. Unfortunately, it would also devastate the dunes and more than likely put my studios out of business."

"That'd be awful," I said. "This is such a beautiful property and a great old house."

"Yes, it would be awful," she said. "This is one of the oldest homes in Sequoia. Have you taken Case inside?"

"Actually, we have time to do that now. The nature walk doesn't start for another twenty minutes."

"Then I'll leave you to it," she said with a smile. "Let's meet for lunch soon and catch up." Then she turned to talk to someone else.

"Let's go," I said, dragging Case from the bench. "We'll have just enough time to take a fast tour."

"Am I excited about that, too?"

We walked around to the front of the huge Victorian mansion and went up the stairs to the spacious front porch. Inside the foyer we found a list of artists who

rented space in the building to create and sell their artwork. We took the staircase to the second floor and
toured the former bedrooms that were now studios. Just
as we were about to start down the curving staircase,
Elissa's eleven-year-old son, Denis, came trotting up, out
of breath, his bookbag bouncing heavily on his shoulders.

"Hello, Denis," I said.

He seemed surprised to see me and muttered a quick,
red-faced hi.

"Niko's at the Saint Jacob's booth. If you're looking
for something to do, why don't you go find him?"

"Thanks. I will," he said, and kept going up the staircase to the third floor.

Case and I did a fast sweep-through of the main floor
and exited just in time to walk back to the nature trail
booth and join the group. Our guide was a tall, solemn-
faced man in his forties who introduced himself as a pro-
fessor at the local community college. "Does anyone
know why native plants are so important to a region?" he
asked as we hiked over the dunes toward the woodland
area.

"Because they're more resistant to disease?" I answered.

"Very good. That's one reason. Actually, native plants
require less water, less fertilizer, less pesticide, and less
care and maintenance. They also provide a habitat and
food for many birds, insects, mammals, and other wild-
life. This is why we're so dedicated to preserving this
land. We don't want to lose all the benefits of this beautiful sanctuary."

He paused to point out some thorny shrubs. "Please be
mindful of these barberry bushes. You'll find them all

over the woodland. They can cut into your clothing and
your skin very easily."

As we walked along, he pointed out flowers, shrubs,
and trees that were native to west Michigan. We also saw
perennials such as butterfly weed, black-eyed Susans,
showy goldenrod, and blue coneflower, as well as an as-
sortment of ferns.

"This is more than I wanted to know," Case said quietly as we walked along.

"I think it's interesting."

"That makes one of us."

"Over here we have a perfect specimen of a black
cherry tree," our guide said. "And on your right a type of
bush called the—" He stopped suddenly and then gasped.
As everyone crowded forward to see why, he pulled out
his phone, putting out one arm to hold us back.

I craned my neck to see what everyone was staring at
and saw a pair of a man's legs sticking out of the under-
brush.

"Yes, hello," the guide said. "I have an emergency."

"Oh my God," someone cried.

Case pushed through the crowd to get a closer look,
and I followed. "It's Hugo," Case said, "and it looks like
he's dead."

While everyone stood around gawking, I took out my
cell phone and quickly snapped some photos.

"We'll have to stay here until the police arrive," our
guide said after ending the call. "Let's move back to the
dune area to wait."

As we followed the guide back up the trail, Case said,
"*Now* it's getting interesting."

CHAPTER TWO

The police arrived within minutes, along with a pair of EMTs and the county coroner. Among the police was my friend and former high school classmate Bob Maguire, who was sweet on my kid sister Delphi. I also recognized Detective Bill Walters from the last two homicide investigations I'd worked on. We weren't friends, but he had found that Case and I deserved respect for the work we'd done in solving three murders.

As he passed us by, he gave Case a slight nod. He eyed me warily as he trudged through the sand in his dark jacket and heavy black shoes back to the area where Hugo lay.

As we sat on the dunes with the rest of our tour group, I couldn't help but reflect on Hugo. "To think we saw him alive and well just a while ago."

"Isn't it awful?" I heard. I glanced over and saw a former classmate, Marylou Porter, settle in the sand close by. Her husband sat next to her, caressing her shoulder as though she was upset.

"Did you know Hugo?" I asked.

"Casually," she said. "We just saw him earlier."

"Same here," I said.

"Athena," Bob Maguire said, coming over to squat in the sand near where Case and I sat. "Case, how are you?"

"Let's just say it's been an interesting morning," Case replied.

"Were you able to determine how Hugo died?" I asked. "Heart attack? Stroke?"

One benefit of a police officer having a crush on Delphi was getting inside information.

"Strictly off-the-record," Maguire said quietly, "I can't give you any verified facts yet, but from what I've gathered, his body was moved, and there are deep ligature marks around his neck."

I glanced at Case in surprise, no doubt thinking the same thing. "He was strangled?"

Maguire neither denied nor confirmed it, so I said, "Was his camera strap used to kill him?"

Maguire looked puzzled. "I haven't heard any mention of a camera or a strap."

"He was taking photos of the festival, Bob. The camera was hanging around his neck. If it's not there now, someone must have taken it."

"They still have to search the area, but I'll let the detectives know." Maguire pulled out a pocket tape recorder. "I need to get statements from you." He spoke our names and contact information into the device, then asked us routine questions, such as, did we know the victim? Had we spoken with him today? Did he seem in any distress?

Did he mention anyone in conversation? To that, I answered that Hugo had told us he needed to speak with Pearson Reed. Since that was the limit of our knowledge, we were released to return to the festival, and Maguire moved on to talk to the others.

I rose and brushed off my skirt. "Hugo was murdered, Case."

"We don't know that for sure."

"Ligature marks around his neck. Missing camera. Moved body. The question is, why would someone kill him?"

Case thought for a minute. "He said he wanted to talk to Pearson, and Pearson is on the city council. Maybe he was working on his conspiracy theory."

"Pearson Reed is not a killer," I said. "Trust me. I've known the Reeds for a long time. But we should look for him. Maybe he knows something. We should also see if—"

"Here we go," Case muttered. "She's off and running."

I ignored his comment and finished, "See if we can find the other members of the city council. But then the question is, how did Hugo end up in the woods?"

Case put his arm around my shoulders. "Let's let the detectives sort it out."

Well, that was no fun. And besides, it was too late. My mind was already spinning with questions. Like, why did Hugo want to speak with Pearson Reed? And had Hugo wanted to speak with anyone other than Pearson? Had the conversation led to an argument, which led to murder? Which was now leading my mind into overdrive. I had to stop it.

As we trudged back up the sandy hill toward the festival, we passed by several other officers taking information from members of our group. Apparently, word of Hugo's death had spread. A large number of people were standing at the edge of the mansion's property waiting to hear what had happened. Unfortunately, the commotion had taken its toll on the art fair. Most of the tourists had left, the dunes tours were cancelled, and many of the artists were quietly packing up their goods.

The crowd grew silent when the EMTs brought the covered body up on a gurney, taking it to the waiting ambulance. A man with a medical bag followed, his navy windbreaker emblazoned on the back with the word *CORONER*. Unlike the former county coroner, who was now sitting in prison thanks to Case and me, this man was tall, youthful, and physically fit. Officer Juan Gomez walked behind the coroner, leading the remaining witnesses with him.

"Nothing more to see here, folks," Officer Gomez called, causing the crowd to disperse. "That means you, too," he said to me.

I narrowed my eyes at Gomez, who had never fully accepted that I'd lied to him about hiding a fugitive from the police. Even after Case had been cleared of the charges, Gomez and I'd had remained at odds. Luckily, Gomez had changed partners, so I didn't have to see him when Maguire stopped by to visit Delphi.

"I can't stop thinking about the conversation I had with Hugo the last time I met him," Case said as we reached the lawn and began to walk toward the booths, winding our way through the crowd.

"About the conspiracy?"

"Yes. He told me he had something to show me and needed advice from someone he trusted. He wouldn't tell me more except that he wanted to meet with me."

"And then he ends up dead after chasing down a member of the city council."

As we passed by the Sequoia Savings and Loan's booth, I saw Pearson having an animated conversation with a man I didn't recognize.

"There's Pearson Reed," I said.

Case paused, partially concealing himself behind a booth, and motioned for me to stand near him. We watched for a moment as the two men conversed in lowered voices and angry gestures. Suddenly, the man Pearson was talking with grabbed a few items from the booth and stormed away from the festival grounds. Pearson watched him leave before making his way toward the mansion.

"Who was the other man?" Case asked.

"I don't know, but I'm guessing he works for the bank."

Case took my hand, and we continued walking. "Tell me about Pearson."

"He's a great guy. I've known him since seventh grade. He and Elissa were childhood sweethearts who married while they were in college. They couldn't have children of their own, so they adopted Denis. Pearson owns a printing company downtown and has been on the city council for a long time. In fact, he was the only member who fought alongside the Greek Merchants' Association to stop Grayson Talbot from destroying Little Greece. What more can I say? He's not a murderer."

Case was quiet for a few moments as we strolled along, rubbing his chin as if deep in thought. "If Hugo had information that would help the Save Our Dunes group, then he must've known something that could help save the lakefront land."

"True."

"And since Pearson helped start SOD, then he and Hugo would have been on the same side."

"Then that would eliminate Pearson as the killer," I said happily.

"Let's not get ahead of ourselves." He put an arm around me. "We're still only assuming."

As we drew near the St. Jacob's booth, I spotted Elissa Reed at the Mind Body Spirit booth sitting opposite my sister. "Oh, great. Delphi is reading her coffee grounds."

We watched from afar as Elissa's expression went from pleasant to confused to angry. She thanked Delphi and stalked away like a woman on a mission. I strode over to the table and sat down in the chair she'd vacated. "What did you say to Elissa?"

"I told her what I saw," Delphi replied defensively.

"Which was?"

"At first, I saw the letter *C*, which meant nothing to her. Then after a few more swirls I saw the letters *BK*, which isn't good because it's my symbol for a black knight. That means someone close to her is involved in shady dealings."

"Is that why she stormed off?"

"She said she didn't know what it meant and wanted to ask her husband."

"Because her husband is involved in shady dealings?"

"You'll have to ask her that, Athena, and stop looking so put out. It's supposed to be fun."

"Did Elissa *look* like she was having fun?"

"Hey, Mom," I heard Nicholas call. I turned to see him coming toward me. He wrapped his arm around my waist. "Want any more dessert? We couldn't sell it all. Everyone left after the guy was murdered in the woods."

"Who said anything about murder?" I asked him.

He glanced over at Delphi, who quickly looked away. "Grandma is gonna take me to the garden center after we're done cleaning up. It's time to feed Oscar."

"Honey, I know you love that little raccoon, but I doubt that he's depending on you to feed him."

"Then you don't know Oscar very well," Nicholas replied. "He'll be waiting for me."

"We're going to be leaving soon, too," I said, "so I'll see you back at the house."

I'd almost said back at Spencer's. I was so used to working at the garden center every day that it was hard to believe I could actually take a Saturday off now. In addition to my dad and Delphi working there, we'd recently hired my cousin Drew, which gave me a little more freedom. We'd also started letting Nicholas work there since he was out of school for the summer.

Nicholas gave me a hug and then jumped up to give Case a very high five. "Are you coming to Sunday dinner tomorrow?"

"Not this time, kiddo," Case replied. "I'll be spending the rest of the weekend studying."

"You're welcome any time," Mama told him. "In fact, why don't you come over to the diner for lunch once in a while? Get off that stuffy boat."

"Mom, look," Nicholas said as two police officers escorted Pearson Reed into the mansion through the back door. "That's Denis's father."

They were followed by Bob Maguire and Detective Walters. Elissa followed behind, wringing her hands, but stopped short of going inside.

Delphi came up behind us and said softly, "The Black Knight."

"This is going to be the talk of town," my mother said, coming to stand with us.

I couldn't help but feel responsible. Was it my statement that had marked Pearson Reed as a suspect?

Sundays were devoted to family, with my mom and all of us sisters helping prepare a big, traditional Greek dinner of lamb, roasted potatoes, lemon chicken, rice, two types of salad, and of course, dessert. Uncle Konstantine and Aunt Talia, Uncle Giannis, Aunt Rachel, cousins Drew and Michael, my Greek grandparents, and our whole family were in attendance. It was a loud, laughter-filled, argumentative at times, and thoroughly enjoyable way to spend several hours on a lazy Sunday.

Nicholas opted to sit with his cooler, older cousins, so we pulled out the card table and let the boys sit together. Drew and Nicholas had become close since working together at the garden center. Nicholas looked to Drew as an older brother and enjoyed the comradery, something that he had been missing when we'd lived in Chicago.

As I sat with my family at the long, hand-crafted olive-wood table, I couldn't imagine myself anywhere else. My *pappoús* and my dad sat at opposite ends, with my *yiayiá* and mother sitting next to the kitchen door. I had chosen the seat beside my mother, which put me between her and Uncle Giannis, who was known for his unseemly and often flat-out rude dinner etiquette. Across from me sat Delphi, and next to her Maia and Selene.

I hadn't always been so willing to embrace my Greek heritage. At the age of twenty-four, I'd moved to Chicago, gotten a job at a newspaper, married a non-Greek man, and had a baby boy.

Ten years later, I'd been forced back to my hometown of Sequoia, Michigan, by finances. My marriage was in shambles, my son needed a supportive family, and I needed to get out of the city and back to a calmer life, all of which my mother had predicted, much to my chagrin.

Since being back, I had made a name for myself by helping Case Donnelly, then a stranger, beat a murder charge, and in the process, catch two murderers. Case had come to Sequoia to collect his family's statue of Athena the warrior goddess and ended up helping me solve a double homicide case. Now Case was looking into getting his private investigator's license and had already decided to stay in Sequoia instead of returning home to Pittsburgh. And that was fine by me.

Tall, dark-haired, and handsome, Case had admitted to staying in Sequoia because of me, even going so far as to say he wanted me to be a partner in his detective agency when it opened. That was fine by me, too, since my job working for my dad at our family-owned-and-operated Spencer's Garden Center didn't satisfy my investigative reporter's instincts. After weeks of studying and preparing, Case was almost ready to take his exams, and I was ready for a new challenge.

"Your mom was telling me about the Save Our Dunes project," Uncle Giannis said, snapping my attention back to the adult table. "I remember taking you kids to the dunes' park when you were little. This was before the boys were born. I'd take you all down to the beach to play, and you'd come home with sand everywhere."

"I don't remember that," Delphi said.

"Sure," Uncle Giannis said. "In fact, one whole summer I watched you girls while your parents worked."

"I remember taking the boat out with Pappoús," Delphi said, "but I don't remember the dunes."

"Of course not," Giannis said with a mouthful of lamb. "No one remembers having fun with old Uncle Giannis. I wasn't always old and fat, you know."

"Giannis," my mom scolded her brother, "you're neither old nor fat. Delphi was just too young to remember. And for heaven's sake, close your mouth."

He shrugged.

"I remember, Uncle Giannis," I said. "One time Maia fell into the bushes and got stuck in the thorns."

Selene laughed. "Her shirt almost ripped in two from us trying to get her out."

"I don't remember any of this," Delphi said with a pout.

"It was the year before Pappoús got his boat," Dad said. "You girls were still very young, but you had a great time."

"You were little water babies," Mom said. "We couldn't get you out of the lake."

"I hope they don't tear all that land up," Aunt Rachel said. "I've got a lot of good memories with our boys at those dunes, too."

"That's why I want to help save the dunes," I said. "And I could use all of your help spreading the word."

"I'd be happy to help," Aunt Talia offered, and the rest chimed in their support.

"I knew I could count on you." I smiled, relieved that we could come to an agreement on at least one subject.

Yiayiá was the first one up from the table, as always, having nibbled at her smaller portions. She returned with a carafe of sweet Greek coffee, announcing the dessert menu as she filled each cup. "We have baklava and *kourabiedes* today."

I loved baklava, but the dainty almond shortbread cookies known as *kourabiedes* came in a close second.

Uncle Giannis picked up his coffee, and to my great annoyance, noisily slurped the hot liquid. Delphi must have noticed my irritated look because she smiled impishly across from me and sipped her coffee with her pinkie raised. But I wasn't about to let her have the last laugh.

"I'll help Yiayiá bring out the desserts," I said to my mother, easing her back down into her seat.

"Thank you, *glykiá mou*," Mama said. *Sweetheart.*

"Oh, and Uncle G., why don't you tell Delphi some stories about the dunes?" I looked at my sister, one eyebrow raised devilishly. "Here, Delph, you can have my seat."

That evening, after I'd read Nicholas another chapter in *Harry Potter and the Sorcerer's Stone* and tucked him into bed, I went to my room to write my blog. I stared at the screen for ten minutes, for the first time in ages unsure of what to write. Normally my blog was a vent for my frustrations, a rant about my shortcomings, but as I sat on my bed with my fingers on the keyboard, I had none of those feelings.

After being beaten down by a job I wasn't passionate about and run into ruin by a selfish husband, I'd never expected to feel such hope again. Sure, I had moved back to Sequoia with the intent of starting over, but this was a new feeling. I actually *had* started over, and now I was hoping for more than just getting back on my feet. My son was the happiest I'd ever seen him, my family was prosperous in their businesses, and I had found a man who had not only helped me to my feet but was encouraging me to run.

I wasn't scared anymore. I wasn't worried about my future. I wasn't overly frustrated by my crazy Greek family like I'd once been, although they were the same crazy Greek family I'd always known. Either I was becoming just as crazy as they were, or the crazy was just becoming normal. Whichever, I still had to think of something to write. My blog was really popular, and my readers would be expecting a new post. I looked at the clock and realized that I was normally finishing my blog just about now. Bedtime was soon.

I laughed at myself, a grown woman, counting down until bedtime.

Aha!

IT'S ALL GREEK TO ME
Blog by Goddess Anon

TICKTOCK, TIME FOR BED!
Do you live by the clock? Are you the kind of person who stops what s/he's doing at noon to eat lunch, or at 6 p.m. to have dinner? My family is, hence, I've become one of "those" people, too.

I've read that bodies crave routine and feel out of sync when the routine is thrown off. That's certainly true for my family. They like to have breakfast at a certain time, lunch at a certain time, and even climb into bed at a certain time. Days off are always enjoyable for me, but for them they're a challenge. And too many days of irregular schedules, especially when we're on vacation, make them feel unsettled. Everyone starts snapping at each other, and when the next workday rolls around, they heave a big sigh of relief.

What I realized recently is that I used to be the kind of person who rolled with the punches, but as I get older, I'm finding myself falling into the same habits as my family. Yowsers! What happened to my spirit of adventure? Am I turning into my mother?

What kind of person are you, a routine craver or a routine hater? Leave your comments below. And as always, speak your truth.

Adio sas. *Or good-bye for those of you who are new to my blog.*

Goddess Anon

I wrote and published the blog anonymously so my family wouldn't know because often it was about them. The funny part was that my mom and sisters were fans of Goddess Anon and had no idea it was me. My dad had found out only because I'd left the blog up on the computer at work which had given me away. Fortunately, he'd promised not to tell anyone.

When I finished, I posted the blog to run in the morning, then went to bed, satisfied that the rest of the family would never figure it out.

CHAPTER THREE

"Athena, are you Goddess Anon?"

I almost choked on my coffee. Delphi stared at me unblinking.

That Monday morning Nicholas and I had started out with a stop at my grandparents' diner, the Parthenon, Nicholas for a breakfast of scrambled eggs and bacon, and me for hot oatmeal and Greek coffee. As usual, when I walked in, the diner was full of hungry members of the Greek community, Yiayiá and Pappoús were busy churning out delicious dishes from the kitchen, and my mother and sisters were gathered around a laptop computer at a table reading the latest Goddess Anon blog and discussing it among themselves.

I looked at Delphi in shock. "Who?"

"You know who I'm talking about." She stared at me steadily. "Are you her?"

"Do you mean, Miss Routine Hater herself?" my mom asked, elbowing my sister Selene, which made them all titter with laughter.

My mom was wearing her standard hostess outfit—a blue blouse "the color of the Ionian Sea" with black slacks and flats and her stack of gold bracelets. All the waitresses wore the same color blouses with black skirts or slacks, complementing the blue background of the Parthenon's murals. Each of the two side walls had a huge Greek mural on it, one of the Parthenon itself, the other of the Acropolis.

Deep red booths lined the dark golden walls, and ancient black-and-white linoleum covered the floor. The long, faded yellow lunch counter with its red leather–cushioned stools separated the diner into two halves, each side with booths and tables that were almost all full. Behind the yellow counter was a wide pass-through window that showed Yiayiá and Pappoús hard at work in the galley kitchen at the back.

"Delphi, have you ever seen Athena enjoy a day off?" my sister Maia asked.

"Yes," Delphi said, getting huffy.

"Well, Goddess Anon craves routine," Selene said. "She alluded to that at the end of her blog."

"What are you all reading?" I asked, trying to throw them off the scent. "That silly blog again?"

Normally, my mom would reserve the back-corner table for us, but the diner was crowded that morning, so Nicholas and I had cozied up to the counter instead of crowding my sisters at their nearby table. We were still close enough to converse, but not close enough to converse in private.

"That blog is not silly," Mrs. Galopodis said. She was

sitting at the next table with her group of Red Hat ladies, unabashedly eavesdropping on our conversation. "This Anon woman is very insightful. In fact, her blog today describes us perfectly, especially Goddess Delma here."

A similar yet more reserved titter of laughter escaped some of the ladies' lips, except for Delma, who huffed indignantly, crossed her arms, and looked away, causing the long, dark red feather on her hat to brush one of the diners sitting at the table behind her.

The Red Hat Society was famous around town for their stylish dress and their strict schedule. They were also well-known at the diner for feuding amongst themselves, an activity they actually seemed to enjoy.

Mama sidled up next to Delma and refilled her coffee, successfully squelching the brewing feud. "You're not alone, Delma, darling," Mama said. "I know quite a few people whom that blog describes perfectly."

My sister Selene spoke up. "Like Mama and vacations."

"Wait just a minute," Mama said. "I don't get crabby on vacation. I love vacations, especially to the Greek Isles."

"Mama, you know by the last day you can't wait to get back," Maia said, sipping her coffee.

Delphi glared at me. "I have a very strong sense about this Goddess Anon."

I ignored her. As my mother placed Nicholas's eggs in front of him, I stuck a spoonful of oatmeal in my mouth, avoiding my sister's eye. But Delphi continued, "And when I have a sense of something, it's almost always right."

"I have a sense, too," Mama interjected. "My Athena is too reserved to share her inner thoughts with the world."

"The blog is anonymous," Delphi said. "That's the whole point."

"Even so," Mama said, jangling her bangles as she

waved away the thought, "I know it's not her, but I do think it could be someone we know, someone from our Greek community. It could even be someone sitting right here in this diner."

"It *is* someone we know," Delphi said in a rising voice, "and she's sitting right *there*. Why doesn't anyone ever listen to me?"

I kept quiet and so did my sisters while Mama calmly walked to the serving station to refill her coffeepot. Delphi groaned loudly, then snatched her purse from the booth and stomped out of the diner.

"What's wrong with Delphi this morning?" I asked, trying to shift the subject. But more importantly, something definitely *was* wrong with Delphi. She was usually the free spirit of the family, always following her bliss, but at the moment it seemed as though her bliss was struggling to keep up. Was she really this mad over Goddess Anon, or was something else going on?

My sisters kept their mouths closed but were clearly thinking along the same lines. Maia gave Selene a look, and they transferred it over to me. I took their looks as a hint to find out if Delphi was having relationship troubles with her secret romance, Bob Maguire. Mama caught my sisters' glances and looked my way as well, but I simply lifted my shoulders and pretended to puzzle over Delphi's behavior. We all knew better than to mention any kind of relationship, secret or otherwise, around Mama.

"What are you keeping from me?" Mama asked.

"Finish your eggs," I said quietly to Nicholas. He shoved the last two bites in his mouth and pushed off the stool.

"Don't you girls keep secrets from me," Mama warned. "I know something is going on."

Yiayiá handed me a to-go bag for Drew, and I gave her a peck on the cheek. Nicholas and I waved good-bye to Pappoús and slid away from the counter while Mama and my sisters surveyed the diner, no doubt making their guesses as to who the anonymous blogger could be.

When we arrived at the garden center that morning, we entered through the big red door into what used to be a large barn. My grandfather, Sam Spencer, had taken the old barn and retrofitted it with a new arched ceiling, lots of windows, fresh paint on the walls, and aisles for all the gardening supplies anyone could ever want. Besides the gardening supplies, Spencer's had flower and vegetable plants, and all the way at the back, sets of patio furniture, including a long, oak plank table that we used for the Greek Merchants' Association meetings that met monthly at Spencer's.

Directly in front of us was the statue, *Treasure of Athena*, a beautiful, six-foot-tall female warrior who beckoned to everyone who walked in the door. To the left was the checkout counter, and behind it was a door that led to the office. A short hallway led to a bathroom, conference room, and kitchenette, where we ate our lunches in inclement weather. Otherwise, we took our food out the back door into the open patio area, a large cement pad outlined by a string of white lights and swaying paper lanterns where more outdoor furniture was displayed. There was also an outdoor cabinet for supplies, including a jar of peanuts and a few shiny toys we kept on hand for Oscar.

Beyond the patio area were rows of shrubs, roses, large landscape plants, and saplings, filling the one-acre space all the way back to the fence. The fence separated Spencer's from a lane that ran behind all the shops on Greene Street and was where the trash containers were kept.

Spencer's sat at the northern end of Greene Street, the main thoroughfare through town. It was a street filled with tourist shops, art shops, restaurants, bars, ice cream and yogurt shops, and clothing boutiques. It also included a section called Little Greece, a block filled with all things Greek, including the Parthenon, my grandparents' diner.

I had to stop for a moment to reflect on all the changes in the newly remodeled barn since I'd come back home. I'd convinced my dad to hire cousin Drew for the summer to handle the extra business we always had from May through September, I'd rearranged the aisles to be more practical, and I'd accessorized the outdoor furniture area to stage the setting for potential buyers. And even though I'd also taken over the accounting and purchasing end of the business, it hadn't been enough to keep my curious mind occupied. I couldn't wait for Case to get his private investigator's license so I could really get busy.

I caught sight of my younger cousin coming in from the outdoor area. "Morning, Drew." I handed him the steaming-hot to-go bag and could practically see the drool forming. For a skinny college boy, he could eat like a grown man twice his size.

Drew traded his garden shears for the breakfast platter and turned to Niko. "Guess what, buddy? You're taking over my project while I eat." With that, Niko and Drew disappeared into the barn.

"We're here, Pops," I called to my father as I headed toward the office.

Dad stopped unloading bags of fertilizer to say, "Morning, Thenie. And before I forget, there's a message for you on the desk. Where's Delphi?"

"I don't know," I said. "I was just about to ask you that."

"I'm here," she called as she dragged a huge, brightly decorated garden pot through the front door. "Look what someone was getting rid of. Just tossed away. Forgotten." She looked right at me as if I was to draw some sort of double meaning. "Where's Drew? I need someone I can *trust* to lend me a hand."

I left that conversation for later and walked into the office, a generously sized room filled with a big oak desk, two wooden chairs that faced the desk, a console table against the opposite wall that held a Keurig coffee machine, and a mini fridge for coffee creamer, water, and snacks. I made myself a cup of coffee, poured in some vanilla creamer, and got comfortable behind the desk. I spotted the pink message slip and read it: *Elissa Reed will be stopping by midmorning to see you. She said it's urgent.*

My stomach knotted. Did Elissa know about my statement to the police?

Two hours later, there was a soft rap on the office door and Elissa stuck her head in. "Are you busy?"

"Just finishing up. Come on in."

My mind was put at ease when Elissa entered with a wide smile. I had expected the worst, that she'd found out I had caused the police to question her husband. I had even prepared an apology. Instead, an apology was offered to me.

"I'm so sorry everyone saw the police take my husband in for questioning," she said. Her dark hair was pulled back by a red bandanna, and her loose top and capris were speckled with paint. "Pearson said it was all just a misunderstanding."

"Is your husband okay?"

"Okay but embarrassed. The police let him go after a few hours. Thank God."

Denis ran into the office, out of breath. "Where's Niko?"

"I brought Denis with me," Elissa said. "Niko was going to show him Oscar the raccoon."

"I think he's out back," I said, to which Denis ran off like a wild child.

"Aren't you worried about him getting bit?" Elissa asked.

"Oscar's been hanging around since he was just out of baby stage. We don't know what happened to his mother. We've even taken him to the vet to get vaccinations. He's very tame and likes to be petted. I doubt he'd ever bite unless someone got rough with him."

"Good to know."

I stood. "Would you like some coffee?"

"No, thanks. I won't keep you long, but some of this just wouldn't wait."

I walked over to the coffeemaker and picked up a mug. "That sounds like a coffee stop to me."

Elissa laughed. "Okay. Just black, please. And I'll start off with the hard part first. I've been planning an art auction at the Studios of Sequoia. So far we've attracted quite a few talented artists who are willing to donate their work for the Save Our Dunes group."

I handed Elissa her coffee as she continued. "I honestly didn't expect so many donations, but they've caught the attention of a few well-known art collectors."

"That's wonderful," I said.

"Well, word got out, and the response has been overwhelming. We're going to have a huge turnout. That's where you come in." Elissa sipped her coffee and let me wait for it. "I want you to landscape the mansion grounds. I'd like to turn the back patio into a luxurious space worthy of the wealthy art crowd."

"I'd be happy to," I told her.

"But I can't spend a lot of money," Elissa added. "We're on a really tight budget."

"You won't have to purchase a thing," I told her. "Spencer's can donate the landscaping and loan out some of our more expensive pieces of garden décor and really make it a special event."

Elissa placed her hands, warmed from the coffee, on mine. "I can't thank you enough, but there is one catch— the event is less than three weeks away."

"Then we'd better get planning."

As we had our coffee together, Elissa described her landscape needs, and I laid out a rough plan for her, drawing a sketch of what I envisioned for the back of the Studios. She thanked me again and moved on to the next topic.

"SOD is going to picket Harmon Oil Company this Friday, and I'm hoping you can join us and help spread the word," she said.

"I'd be happy to help, but why are you going to picket them?"

"It was announced in the newspaper today that Pete Harmon, the CEO of Harmon Oil, put in a bid to build on the former park property. His plans include a marina and a refueling station, a new office building and a parking lot. And Pearson just informed me last night that Harmon was behind the push to sell that tract of land. He's been hounding the council for months."

"That's outrageous," I said. "Just with the marina alone, he'd be taking up a huge chunk of the dunes all the way out into the lake."

"That's it exactly, but he's presenting it as his gift to the city. It's infuriating."

"What about the auction?" I asked. "What happens if you raise the money you need?"

She smiled, clearly hopeful at the thought, and began to enumerate. "It would guarantee the dunes renovation, stop Harmon in his tracks, and save the Studios. Basically, if we can raise the full amount before the deadline, we would win. And we are very close to making our goal."

"What happens if you don't raise enough money?"

Elissa sank back into the chair. "If we don't raise the money, the land goes up for sale, Harmon Oil would most likely win the bid, and all of this work will be for nothing. We're picketing to raise the public's awareness of what Harmon intends, and we're hoping you'll help us whenever you can spare the time on Friday."

"You're in luck," I said. "Friday is my day off this week. I'll try to rally some more people. In fact, there's a Greek Merchants' Association meeting here Wednesday night. Why don't you email me more details and I'll talk it up at the meeting? If you have any flyers for the auction, I'll put them out near the front door, on the base of the statue of Athena where they'll attract attention."

"Flyers," she said with a big smile. "That's a terrific idea. I'll print up some flyers and send them your way. Thank you so much."

"I'll do everything I can to help."

She studied me for a moment. "I can see why they call you the Goddess of Greene Street."

"I'm no goddess. Just someone who isn't afraid to stand up against injustice."

She was somber for a moment. "I guess that leads right into my next subject, but I'm hesitant to get you involved. You've already agreed to do so much."

"It's not a problem," I said, my curiosity piquing. "Go ahead."

"The detectives questioned Pearson, as you know, and let him go, but they told him not to leave town. It's making us both nervous. What do you make of it? Routine questioning or something else?"

"I don't want to scare you, Elissa, but I don't like it. Once the detectives set their sights on someone, it's hard to sway them. What did they want to know?"

"He didn't say exactly what they asked him. I think he's afraid to talk about it, even with me. He did say they wanted him to take a lie detector test."

"Not to alarm you, but I'd hire a lawyer and ask for advice. If nothing else, should the police ask to see your husband again, have the lawyer go with him."

"Thanks, Athena. I really appreciate the help." She got up and put her coffee cup on the console table. "I'd better get Denis and go home. I've got more people to call about Friday."

"I think the boys are out back," I said, walking with her.

We exited the rear door to see the boys trying to scoop up dirt to put in a clay pot that had big cracks down the sides, with dirt all over the ground in front of their shoes.

"Mom, it fell over and broke," Denis said, brushing off his hands. "We tried to put the dirt back in, but there's too much."

"Niko can sweep it up with a broom and dustpan," I said. "Niko, run and get it."

"Denis, did you do it?" Elissa asked, as Nicholas disappeared inside.

"Nope," he replied, shaking his head. "Niko did. But guess what? I got to feed Oscar."

"Good for you," Elissa said, tucking the sketch I'd made for her in her purse. "Thanks for your help, Athena. I appreciate it."

I walked them to the door and then returned to help my son clean up. "How did you tip it over?" I asked as I carried pieces of clay to the trash can.

"I didn't. Denis was chasing Oscar and ran into it. If I did it, Mom, I'd tell you."

"I know you would, sweetie. Thank you for cleaning up the soil."

I headed to my office to plan what I wanted to say at the GMA meeting. I couldn't help but think of Elissa's husband being questioned and feeling guilty because I'd mentioned that Hugo had made a point of talking to Pearson.

Delphi stuck her head in to say, "What did Elissa want?"

"She wants some landscaping done for the Studios of Sequoia. I'll need your help. It's going to be a big job."

"And that's all she wanted?"

"Yep."

"You're not lying to me?"

I gave her a scowl.

"Like you're lying about being Goddess Anon?"

"It's almost noon," I said. "Are you coming to the diner for lunch?"

"I shouldn't come, not after everyone laughed at me."

"No one laughed at you, Delph. You claim to have a seventy-five percent success rate with your predictions, right? Maybe your blogger theory is in the twenty-five percent range. Think about it. How in the world could anyone keep a secret in this family?"

"Tell me about it." Delphi looked downtrodden at the thought. I could tell she was keeping a few secrets of her own. One in particular came to mind.

"Is everything okay with you and Bob?"

"I don't want to talk about it."

I gave her a long look. She huffed and said, "Mama is driving me crazy. She's breathing down my neck about my love life. Ever since you managed to find a man, she's latched on to me with fully extracted claws and refuses to let go."

"*Managed* to find a man?" I asked.

"You *know* what I mean."

"No, I really don't."

"How did you deal with her?" Delphi plopped down into a chair, her lightweight, colorful skirt floating down around her. "And how could you go on blind dates with strange men? I can't handle it."

"It wasn't easy. Eventually I had to tell Mama that I had *managed* to find a man."

"You know what I mean."

"No, I still don't."

"You come crawling back from Chicago swearing off

men forever, and then two months later you're bringing Case home to Sunday dinner. And now he's just part of the family? He's not even Greek."

"He's part Greek, and I did not come *crawling* back. I just came back."

"Well, Bob isn't even remotely Greek, and Mama would flip if she found out."

I sat down next to Delphi, ignoring her increasingly rude remarks, and tried to talk some sense into her. "She just wants you to be happy."

"How does being Greek have anything to do with my happiness?" Delphi asked. "Besides, Dad isn't even Greek. Why is she so darn stubborn about nationality? I'm so sick of this town and this stupid family." She let out a groan of frustration.

If I hadn't known better, I would've thought Delphi was Goddess Anon, reliving my nightmare from when I moved back home. The only advice I could muster was to tell Mama the truth, kind of hypocritical coming from me.

I pulled Delphi's hands from her face. "I'm serious. Just tell her the truth. What's the worst that could happen?"

She closed her eyes and let her head slump backward. "Joey Patterson."

"Who?"

Delphi looked at me like I was crazy. "Joey Patterson. From my junior year? He asked me to the prom. He came over for pictures, and Mom grilled him so much that he wouldn't even stand next to me at the dance. It was humiliating."

"This isn't your junior year," I said. "You're a grown woman. And Bob is a very understanding man. Have you talked to him about it?"

"Not yet. I just want Mama to let it go."

"Mama is too Greek and too stubborn to let this go."

"*Greek* should be synonymous with the word *stubborn*," Delphi muttered.

"My advice is to talk to Bob. Let him know how you feel and see what he thinks about talking to Mama."

Delphi's initial expression said, *easier said than done*, but she did perk up a bit. "That's actually good advice," she said.

I smiled and reached over for a hug, but she stopped me. "Almost too good. Like I've heard it somewhere before—like, in a blog, Goddess Anon."

Had I written that in a blog? "You're not going to let this go, are you?"

"Not until you tell me the truth," Delphi said.

"The truth is, I'm hungry. Let's go have lunch."

It was tradition for all of us sisters to meet at the diner every Monday for lunch, so shortly before twelve, Delphi and I started the five-minute walk. It was so much easier now that my dad had Drew to help, although typically the noon hour was slow.

We sat in the last booth on the left side of the restaurant, a booth that my mom usually reserved for us. I scooted in first on the red vinyl seat, and Delphi sat beside me. Selene, my oldest sister, a hairstylist at Over the Top Hair Salon, was already there. We were waiting on Maia, a yoga instructor at Zen Garden Yoga Studio.

"Here you go, girls," my mom said, setting down a big bowl filled with hunks of ripe tomato, Feta cheese, and cucumbers, followed by a bread basket with a side dish of olive oil for dipping. The salad was a meal in itself, so I ate sparingly, saving my appetite for yummy *dolmades*, grape leaves stuffed with ground meat and rice, with a lemon sauce over the top. Selene, on the other hand, dove headfirst into the basket of bread.

"So, Delphi," Mom said, taking a seat opposite her youngest daughter, "tell me about the man in your life."

Delphi turned pale as she stared first at me and then at our mother. "What man?"

"I can tell when one of my girls is hiding something."

CHAPTER FOUR

"**M**ama, there's no man in my life," Delphi answered angrily.

I said nothing. If Delphi wanted Mama to know about Bob Maguire, she'd tell her. Mama wasn't going to hear it from me.

"Okay," Mama said, getting up when she saw Maia coming. "Keep your secret."

"How's everyone?" Maia asked, sliding into the booth opposite Delphi. "And why do you look like you're about to spit nails, Delph?"

"She isn't talking," Mama said.

"Athena, I heard you were at the festival when Hugo Lukan was murdered," Maia said, ladling tomato salad onto her plate. Maia was a vegetarian, something our family had a hard time wrapping their minds around. "Why didn't you tell us yesterday?"

"I didn't think discussing a murder was pleasant Sunday dinner conversation."

"But it's a perfect Monday lunch conversation," Maia replied. "Spill it."

I gave them a rundown, which didn't take long since I didn't know much.

"I heard that Hugo was divorced three times," Selene said as she dipped her bread into the oil. "Maybe one of his exes did him in."

"Hugo's ex-wife Carrie used to work at Zen Garden," Maia added. "She ranted about him all the time."

"Which wife was she?" I asked. "One, two, or three?"

"Three." Maia took a bite of her salad. "Hugo may have been a good photographer, but according to Carrie, he was a lousy husband. The last time I saw her, she told us she was still fighting him in court over their property settlement. It was a very bitter divorce."

"I wonder if she was at the art festival," I pondered aloud.

Delphi pushed her plate away. "I'm going back to Spencer's."

We watched her walk out the front door, and then Mama said, "Her secret is weighing heavily on her, Athena. What did you find out?"

I wasn't about to become the family snitch. "Sorry, Mama. I didn't have a chance to talk to her."

Mama eyed me suspiciously, then said, "Now two of my girls are keeping secrets."

With the mail that day came a large manila envelope addressed to Case in care of Spencer's Garden Center. I studied the envelope. The handwriting was scratchy, as if hastily written. The stamps were crooked, and the package itself was very lightweight. When I shook it, I could feel several items shifting back and forth. My fingers fairly tingled with the overwhelming urge to open the envelope, but my good sense stopped me. I sent Case a text message to let him know instead.

Case stopped by a little while later. "A package for me sent here?"

"Odd, isn't it?" I said.

"Very curious," he said. "I'm surprised you didn't open it."

"I wouldn't even consider doing that."

He met me around the desk, and I could smell his suntan lotion as he pulled me in for a kiss. His dark hair curled over his forehead, and his chin was dark with day-old stubble. Dressed casually in sandals, board shorts, and a white V-neck, he did not look like a man hard at work.

"You look pretty tan for a student hitting the books," I said.

He checked his tanned arm against mine. "That's the nice thing about living on the *Pamé*. I can sunbathe and study at the same time. You might want to join me one of these afternoons. You look pretty pale for a woman who works at an outdoor garden center."

I kissed him again to stop him from talking, then pushed the envelope his way.

Using a letter opener, he slit the top flap and looked inside. "Photos," he said, and removed them. A paper clip held the black-and-white eight-by-ten photographs together, and a note on top read, *I'll explain everything when we meet. Hugo.*

"Well, *that's* not going to happen," Case said with a

sigh, spreading the photos on the desk. He pointed to the first photo. "Two men sitting in a car."

"That's Pearson Reed in the passenger seat," I said. "It looks like he's taking an envelope from the man in the driver's seat."

Case turned the photo over, but nothing was written on the back. He flipped it back over and pointed to the driver. "Who's this guy?"

"I don't have a clue."

The man had thick, dark hair and a short, dark beard, and it looked as though he was wearing a light-colored suit jacket. His head was turned toward Pearson, making his identity harder to verify. His left hand was on the steering wheel, revealing a wide leather band with gunmetal studs. The photo being in black and white didn't lend itself to much more description.

"Same setup with the second photo," Case said, "but in this picture, the man in the passenger seat is counting money from the envelope. Do you know who this man is?"

I squinted at the grainy image. His long face stood out, as did his dark features and thick mustache. "He looks familiar." I studied the photo a moment longer, searching my memory. "Oh, wait. I remember now. We saw him working at the Sequoia Savings booth at the festival. He's the one who was having a heated discussion with Pearson."

"That's where I've seen him. This is getting interesting."

Case shifted to the third photo, in which a younger, light-haired man sat in the passenger seat looking inside the envelope.

"All of these photos seem to show people in a compromising situation," Case said. "This has to be about the conspiracy Hugo mentioned."

"If that's true, then Pearson is involved."

"That's what it looks like."

I hoped we were wrong. I could only imagine how the news would affect Elissa.

Case rubbed his chin, studying the black-and-whites. "What was Hugo up to?"

"The other two men could be on the city council, too."

"I'll go along with that, but this last photo doesn't fit," Case said.

The last photograph was not a professional black-and-white. It looked like it'd been snapped quickly from a cell phone, taken from behind a woman sitting in front of a laptop computer. The woman's dark hair was pulled back, revealing long, dangling earrings and a tattoo that ran down her neck onto her right arm.

We both stood at the desk studying the image. I couldn't see the woman's face, but I knew I'd seen the earrings and tattoo before. But where?

Case tipped the manila envelope upside down, and out fell an envelope addressed to Hugo with no return address. Inside was a piece of paper with a note typed on it.

Case read the note aloud. "'Play with fire and you get burned.' That sounds like a threat."

"Because of the photographs?"

"Possibly."

"Do you think he was using them for blackmail purposes?"

"I don't know, but I find it hard to believe Hugo would blackmail these people and then bring the photos to me for advice. That would take a lot of nerve."

"Knowing Hugo's reputation, Case, it wouldn't be out of the question."

He slid the note back inside the envelope. "Maybe Hugo wanted me to help him find out who among those pictured here was threatening him."

"It would explain why he seemed anxious on Saturday. And maybe the woman with the tattoo is the key." I snapped my fingers. "I just remembered where I've seen her. She was at the art fair selling jewelry at Jewel's Jewels. Remember the jewelry booth we stopped at? That's her. She's got a very eccentric look. I'd remember the tattoo and those big earrings anywhere."

I paused for a moment to think. "I have an idea." I sat down at the computer and opened Facebook. I typed in *Jewel's Jewels*, and a page came up for a Jewel Lizbeth Newsome. I clicked on it and showed Case. "That's one mystery solved. Let's see what else I can find."

I scrolled through her posts, but they were all about the jewelry she was selling. I pulled up her photo album, and lo and behold—"Look. She's got photos of Hugo and her together. Maybe she was his girlfriend."

"You could be right about her being the key, otherwise why would Hugo include a photograph of his girlfriend in the packet?"

"The much bigger question is, what was Hugo doing that got him killed? Was it because of these photos, a photo he'd taken Saturday, or not even remotely related to his photography?"

"I'll remind you again that those are not our mysteries to solve," Case said.

"Aren't you even the least bit curious?"

He slid his arm around my back and pulled me close to him. "You know I am, but we have more important issues to resolve, like the case of the missing P.I. license. Which reminds me, I have a big test coming up, and I'm still not prepared."

I turned him around and pointed him toward the door. "Then get to it, Mr. Donnelly."

"Are you trying to get rid of me?" He noticed me eyeing the photos that were spread across my desk and said, "What are you thinking, Athena?"

"Nothing."

"Right. I know you better than that. Just don't go digging around on your own, okay? Who knows what Hugo got himself mixed up in."

"Fine." I restacked the photos and notes and slid them back into the envelope. "Do you want me to keep them on file here, so you don't have to store them on the boat?"

"Do you promise to file them away and leave them alone?"

"Promise."

He gave me a quick kiss. "That'll have to do for now. I've got to get back and hit the books. Want to meet at the pizza truck for lunch tomorrow?"

"I'd love to. Good luck with your studies."

He paused at the door to say, "I'm this close to being able to apply," and held his fingers an inch apart.

In order to become a private investigator, Case had to meet Michigan's minimum licensing requirements before he could apply for licensure. He had to have a high school diploma or the equivalent; no felony convictions; no misdemeanor convictions for fraud, drugs, or illegal possession of a firearm; no more than two alcohol-related offenses; and no dishonorable discharge. That was the easy part.

In addition, there were education requirements that

he'd already met by having a computer science degree. He also had to be involved in investigative work for three years, which he had by working for his father in tracking down the statue of Athena. He was now taking an elective course in criminal justice that he felt would round out his degree. Once he had that under his belt, he could apply for his PI license, and then we'd be off and running.

"I almost forgot to tell you," Case said. "I found some office space for rent. I'll take you to see it tomorrow."

"That's great. I can't wait."

He left as I opened the file drawer. My fingers tingled once again as the manila envelope hovered over an empty file slot. Before temptation set in, I loosened my grip and filed the photographs away. Promise kept. For now.

"I don't know how you can call that pizza," Case said the next day as we pulled our slices from the order window. He had ordered a pepperoni and green pepper pizza, and I had ordered my usual spinach and Feta cheese pie.

Tuesday morning had started out slow, promising to be that kind of day at Spencer's, so I had no problem taking an extended lunch break. It was a gorgeous day for outside dining. The sun had just peeked out from behind a thick gathering of clouds, revealing a perfectly blue sky, and tourist season was in full swing, filling the sidewalks with happy shoppers, the parks with laughing children, and the plaza with hungry families.

Case passed by our usual table, messy with wrappers and empty soda cans, and opted instead for a bench near the street. I sat next to him and set my drink down by my feet.

"*This* is pizza," he said, taking a bite.

"Mine is healthy pizza," I argued. "Try it."

He made a face. "It's a salad on a crust. A pizza isn't a pizza without pepperoni."

"Whatever floats your gondola."

Case wiped his mouth and motioned for me to look across the street.

At first, I couldn't tell what he was looking at, but then I spotted a woman wearing large black sunglasses and clicking along the pavement in her high heels. She was talking on her phone so loudly we could hear her every word.

"Oh great," I said. "Hide your face."

Lila Talbot walked past the deli, did an about-face, and promptly entered the establishment, her phone conversation still audible through the open door. Now the wealthiest woman in Sequoia after her divorce, she was wearing a leopard-print top and a pair of black yoga pants with black high-heeled sandals and carrying a large straw purse. Her blond hair was tied up in a swingy ponytail.

When we'd first interviewed Lila during our Talbot murder investigation, she had come on to Case in a big way. Since then, she'd ingratiated herself into Case's life by offering to help financially when he first wanted to start a charter fishing boat operation. When that idea fell through, she'd decided to make herself indispensable by offering to finance the investigation business. I was still stewing about that.

"Good," I said. "She didn't see us."

Case finished another bite. "We can't keep hiding from her."

"We can try," I said under my breath. "I still can't believe she's a partner in your private investigation business. She doesn't have the first clue about investigating, and there's nothing private about her."

"It's *our* business, by the way. You're an equal partner in it. She's just the financial partner, a silent partner, so to speak. We don't have to worry about her investigative skills. But that's not what I wanted you to see. Take another look across the street."

I took inventory: a deli, a clothing shop, a law office, and plenty of tourists strolling along the wide sidewalk. "What am I looking at?"

"You can see the new office from here. See the door on the left side of the deli? That takes you to the second floor. Now look over the deli. See those two windows? That's it."

"Wow. Right downtown. Isn't that expensive? It's not like you need the foot traffic."

"But we need the advertising. Look at that location, right on the main thoroughfare. Imagine a big sign hanging beneath the windows, *Greene Street Detective Agency.* Plus, it's only several blocks from the garden center and within walking distance from my houseboat."

"And right near our favorite food truck," I added. "I'm sold. When do I get to take a look inside?"

He stuffed the last bite into his mouth, stood, and retrieved a key ring from his pocket. I finished my pizza, grabbed my drink, and followed Case across the street.

"It's a small space and needs a little work," he said as we walked, "but there are two offices and an outer office that would be a perfect reception area."

It needs a little work was an understatement. After leading me up an old stairwell, Case used his key to get inside, where the smell of must and grime greeted us.

"Here's where I'd have my desk," he said, showing me the first room past the reception area. I coughed at the cloud of dust we raised as we walked inside. "And here's where you'd have yours." He showed me the room adjacent to and identical to the first. "Both rooms have a window that looks out on Greene."

"It needs a thorough cleaning, but the space definitely has potential," I said. "I'd be happy to help you clean it."

"Hello?" I heard a woman call.

I turned as Lila Talbot walked in. "I just got out of my yoga class and was picking up a sandwich at the deli when I saw you two enter. And you know me. I just had to find out what you were up to." She paused and slid her large-framed sunglasses up onto her head. "Don't tell me this is the office I'm paying for."

"I know it doesn't look like much now," Case said, "but it's in the perfect location, right in the center of everything. It needs to be cleaned, but Athena volunteered to help."

"Sweetie," Lila said, strutting around the space, wiping dusty surfaces with her fingertip, "it would take forever to give this the professional cleaning it needs. What if I give you a welcome gift of a cleaning service?"

I glanced at Case, hoping he'd refuse it, but he didn't. "That would be very generous of you, Lila."

"Good," she said with a satisfied smile. "When are we moving in?"

We? I felt my eyes bulging and quickly blinked.

"As soon as possible," Case replied.

Lila peered out the front window. "I'll get the cleaning staff over here this week. But first, are you sure you want this office? It's rather small. Athena, why don't I take the smaller office and you can have this big open space?"

"This is the reception area," I said.

My phone rang before she could reply. I answered it to hear, "Athena, hi. It's Elissa. I'm sorry to bother you, but do you know a good defense attorney? The police just picked up my husband for the second time."

CHAPTER FIVE

I gave Elissa the name of my ex-boyfriend Kevin Coreopsis, a former New York City corporate lawyer who had since become a defense attorney in Sequoia. I asked her to keep me posted, then hung up and said to Case, "The police have pulled Pearson Reed in for a second interview, and Elissa is concerned. I hope Kevin can help him."

"He did a good job for that rat I was married to," Lila said. "Thank goodness my divorce came through. Now I need a way to take the tarnish off the Talbot name."

"Why don't you help the Save Our Dunes group?" Case suggested. "Athena is going to picket Harmon Oil Company with them on Friday."

I gave Case a discreet nudge, regretting that I'd told him about the picketing.

"Why Harmon Oil?" Lila asked.

"To make the point that an oil company would ruin the dunes," Case said.

"I don't know," I said. "Maybe we shouldn't go." I was being wishy-washy and hating myself for it. *Take a stand, Athena!* Where was Goddess Anon when I needed her?

Lila ignored me to ask, "Why does the name Harmon sound so familiar?"

"That's the company that's trying to buy the land behind the Studios of Sequoia," Case replied. "It was in the newspaper yesterday."

Behind Lila's back, I was signaling frantically for him to stop talking.

"I'd love to help," she said, turning to me with a big smile. "In fact, I'll drive us there in my new Tesla. What time do you want to go?"

"Tesla?" I asked. "What happened to the Lamborghini?"

"That pretentious old thing?" She studied her nails, stretching out her fingers to admire the bright gold polish. "That belonged to my ex-husband. It was time to divorce the car, too. Don't change the subject, Athena. What time are we going?"

I gave her the information, not sure whom I was most annoyed with. Now I was going to be stuck with Lila all Friday afternoon.

"I'm assuming you've heard about the photographer's murder," she said. "The news is all over town."

"We've heard," Case said. "In fact, we were there. We were on a dunes' hike at the festival when the body was found."

"Give me details," Lila said. "Was he holding anything in his hands? Were his clothes ripped? Any wounds?"

"We didn't get to see him," Case said. "Most of his body was hidden beneath a big bush, and then we were led away."

"And what about this Elissa?" she said to me. "You said her husband was taken to the police station? What's their story?"

She was already playing detective. I was grinding my teeth, growing more annoyed with her by the second. I took a deep breath, counted to three, and then said, "Elissa and Pearson are old friends of mine. The police seem to be targeting Pearson."

"Interesting," she said, tapping one highly polished fingernail on her chin. "But back to this office space, what kind of art will we hang on this big empty wall? A mural perhaps?"

On Wednesday morning Nicholas and I came into the store to find Delphi making a display out of a dozen or more clay pots. The pots were hand-painted with rings of different colors, all brightly hued.

"Remember that large colored planter I brought in?" she asked. "There was so much interest in it, I decided to make smaller copies."

"Can I paint some, too?" Nicholas asked her.

"Let's see how these go over first," I said, ruffling his hair.

"They'll go over," Delphi said confidently. "Niko, I stacked more right over there. Help me arrange them."

I left them working and went back to the office. Shortly after the store opened, Elissa came to see me again, waving a thick stack of papers. "I brought flyers for you."

"Come in," I called.

She laid them on the desk. "I'm also here on behalf of my husband. Kevin Coreopsis suggested I talk to you. Do you have time now?"

"Yes, I do. Have a seat."

She took the chair across the desk from me. "The police are definitely considering Pearson a person of interest in the Hugo Lukan case."

I bit my tongue. My first instinct was to apologize for pointing the police directly at Pearson Reed, but she didn't have to know that, especially now that he was being seriously considered a suspect. "I'm sorry to hear that."

"Kevin thinks the detectives are building a case against him."

"Based on what?"

Elissa paused and looked over her shoulder at the open office door behind her. She looked back to me and said in a soft voice, "The day of the murder, I found my husband coming up the path from the dunes with scratches on his hands and arms that were bleeding. When the police interviewed him, he told them he'd tripped and fallen into a thornbush, but they didn't seem to believe him."

"Do you believe him?"

"Absolutely," she said emphatically. "The trouble is, he can't prove where he was around the time of the murder because he was all over the festival grounds. With the cuts and scratches, and the fact that he was seen talking to Hugo that morning, it doesn't look good." She took a deep breath. "That's why I want you and Case to investigate."

I paused to think of what to say. "You have to understand something first, Elissa. Case doesn't have a private investigator's license yet. He's very close to getting it, but officially he's not allowed to take cases."

"Kevin explained that, and truthfully, I don't care. I read in the newspaper about how you and Case unofficially solved two murder cases, and that's good enough for me."

"How does your husband feel about this?"

"To be honest, he's not in favor of it. He thinks we're making a big deal out of nothing. He's sure the police will realize they're on the wrong track."

I'd heard that before. I tapped my pen on the desktop. "We'll need to interview him. How will he take that?"

"Don't worry about Pearson. I'll make sure to prepare him. How soon can you start?"

"I'll need to check with Case first, but I'm going to suggest tomorrow evening."

"Perfect. I'll take Denis out at seven so you can talk to Pearson alone." She heaved a big sigh as she got to her feet. "I feel so much better. I can't thank you enough. I'd also like to talk to Delphi. Maybe she can tell me more with another reading."

This time it was me who paused and looked over her shoulder at the open door. Delphi was nowhere to be seen, so I leveled with Elissa. "Delphi's busy at the moment, but if you do talk to her, just take what she says with a grain of salt. Do you understand what I'm saying?"

"I think so." Elissa blushed. "I've never really believed any of that psychic stuff. I did it for fun, because I like Delphi, but her reading was correct. She saw a black knight, Hugo was murdered, and now my husband is being questioned by the police. That can't be a coincidence."

"But it can be," I replied. "Let us look into it before

you tap my sister for any more guidance. I promise I'll produce more reliable results."

Elissa smiled and looked out toward the showroom. By her demeanor I could tell that her quest for other-worldly advice was not over. Before she left, she added, "And by the way, whatever you charge for your services, I'll be happy to pay it."

I hadn't even considered that aspect of our investigations. What would we charge? I was surprised that Elissa had offered up any amount as a reasonable fee. Surely, she wasn't that desperate for answers just yet. "I'll check with Case and let you know."

"We are officially hired as unofficial private investigators," I told Case over the phone.

"Athena, I can't take on an investigation. If I'm not careful, I'll get into trouble."

"Then we'll be careful."

There was a long moment of silence. I could almost picture Case shaking his head. "You're going to do this even if I say no, aren't you?"

"Yes, I am, so don't say no because I need your help. If you're still worried, we don't have to take payment for our services. It could be a favor for a friend. Completely unofficial."

He was silent for a moment longer, then finally heaved a sigh. "Okay, I'll help you, but it has to be as a favor."

"Although she did say that she'd pay whatever we charged. Have you researched private eye fees?"

"There's a standard pricing model," Case said. "I've looked into all of that. But there's no one in town who does professional investigations, so we might be able to adjust our prices depending on the client's case."

"And the danger level," I added.

"You leave the danger to me, Goddess. But for this *favor*, no charge."

"Let's go see Pearson tomorrow evening at seven o'clock to get the ball rolling."

"You sound excited."

"I am excited. I love helping people."

"You love meddling."

"Meddling in the name of justice."

"A rose by any other name . . . Why don't you come over tonight, and we can work up a list of questions?"

"Now *you* sound excited."

He lowered his voice. "Excited for what happens after we're done working."

I felt a happy fluttering in my stomach, then immediately squeezed the phone in frustration. "I can't tonight. GMA meeting at Spencer's."

"Okay. I understand. I'll work up a list of questions all by my lonesome. Let's meet at the boat tomorrow at six thirty to review. Or earlier, if you can."

"I'll see what I can do. Don't get too lonely without me."

"*Kalinýchta*, Thenie."

"Good night, Case."

That evening, as soon as the general meeting was concluded, I stood before the members of the Greek Merchants Association and explained the mission of Save Our Dunes. I hit the highlights of what Elissa had told us about the proposed land development, and I could see people nodding along with me as I explained how we should be opposed to an oil company, or any business for that matter, spoiling the lakefront.

"But isn't it true that a new building and marina would generate a lot of tax revenue for the city?" one of the members asked. "According to the article in the newspaper, Pete Harmon said some of the money would go to the schools, and we know the high school could use new computers."

"It's true a new business would generate some tax money," I said, "but wouldn't we rather be able to enjoy the dunes and forest as a beautiful park for our families instead of just a marina for boat owners?"

"I'll go along with that," my friend Barb said, and got a round of applause.

At the end of my presentation, I asked interested members to take flyers to leave out at their businesses, and within minutes all of them were gone. I didn't have as much luck with the plan to picket Harmon Oil. Most members were busy running their businesses and couldn't take time off. But a majority were in agreement that the duneland should be saved.

"I'll meet you there," my sister Maia said. "I can find someone to cover my yoga class. I'll hand out flyers, too. I know several people who can pass the info along."

"I'll see how my schedule is," Selene said, holding a stack of flyers. "Maybe I can rearrange some things and come down for a while."

"I'll come, too," Mama said. "I can take off for an hour or so. We'll have fun."

Maia, Selene, Mama, and Lila, all afternoon. *Fun* was not the first word that came to mind.

CHAPTER SIX

I was so eager to get started on our investigation that Thursday went painfully slow. My dad was busy reorganizing shelves to accommodate a shipment of new garden tools. Nicholas spent the day wiping down all the outside furniture and playing with Oscar. Drew was in his element behind the register, and Delphi, who had been preoccupied with her painted pots all afternoon, was still undecided on whether or not to tell Maguire about her mother dilemma.

Spencer's was too busy for me to leave early. Not only was I working up a more detailed plan for the Studios of Sequoia and filling in on the sales floor when needed, but I was also tasked with watering the new saplings in the outdoor area. It was normally Delphi's responsibility, but she seemed so laser-focused on her painted pot project that I did it as a favor. I texted Case to give him the bad news. Again, he was frustrated, but understood.

It wasn't until six fifteen that evening that the store cleared out.

I found my dad taking a break in the office. "Hey, Dad. I need to leave soon. Have you seen Delphi?"

"The last time I saw her, she was out back."

I thanked him and did a quick walk through of the outdoor area, but found only Drew munching on a bag of peanuts. "Are those Oscar's peanuts?"

"Sorry, Athena. I'm starving. I haven't had a break since lunch."

"Don't let Niko catch you—or Oscar, for that matter. Have you seen Delphi?"

"She's out front with Niko."

I finally caught up with her by the front door, where she flounced inside covered in flecks of paint. Nicholas walked in after her, also splattered.

"All of the pots are now front and center," Delphi reported. "When people walk by, they can't help but see them. Right, Niko?"

"I have to leave, Delph," I said. "Will you be okay taking Nicholas home?"

"It's Niko, Mom," my son said, rolling his eyes. "And Theia Delphi said we could stop for ice cream on the way home since I helped her today."

I gave Nicholas a big hug. "That's fine with me. But just a single dip. You haven't had dinner yet."

I left the garden center and walked south on Greene Street for four blocks, then crossed the street and headed to the marina along the lake. The streets weren't as busy at that time of day, most people being at dinner. At the marina, some boats were leaving their dock for sunset cruises while others were coming in from a day out on the lake.

The *Pamé*, my pappoús's boat, was docked at the southern end of the harbor on the last of three piers along the wide, wooden dock, directly across from Little Greece. Pappoús's arthritis had gotten so bad he'd given up taking the boat out, making it the perfect place for Case to live. In fact, Case liked it so much he was in the process of buying the *Pamé* from my grandfather.

I walked along the dock to the very last pier and then down to slip twenty-six, where the *Pamé*—which was Greek for *Let's go!*—was berthed. I stepped onto the boat and climbed down into the stern, memories of many family outings flooding back.

The flat-backed stern had a blue vinyl *U*-shaped seating area surrounding a plastic table for outside dining. Up a step and toward the cockpit were the swivel seats for fishermen, and beyond that the helm. A deck on either side of the boat led to the bow, where a sundeck could be used for tanning or cooling off after a swim.

"I'm here," I said, knocking on the door that led below.

"Come in," I heard.

I opened the door and went down into the living area. To my right was a blue vinyl built-in sofa across from the galley kitchen on my left, with two plastic chairs and a small, square white Formica table in the middle that was bolted to the floor. Beyond the kitchen was a small bathroom, followed by a cozy bedroom tucked into the front of the boat. It was the perfect bachelor pad.

"Here are the questions I worked up," Case said, handing me his iPad. He had just come out of the shower—his hair was still wet—and he looked so yummy in a blue

T-shirt that showed off his torso and slim-fitting jeans that I had to force my mind back to the subject at hand.

I sat down at the kitchen table, read through his questions, and closed the iPad. "Looks good. Let's go. Elissa is going to be leaving their house about now."

We took Case's new Jeep Wrangler and headed east across town to an area of older, craftsman-style homes. We pulled up in front of their house and walked up the sidewalk to the covered front porch. I rang the doorbell, and within a minute Pearson opened the door.

He was an average-sized man with reddish-brown hair, freckles, and a slender build. He was wearing a white golf shirt, tan pants, and brown loafers. His hair was neatly combed back, exposing a very tan face. I also noticed the deep cuts on his arms and hands that Elissa had mentioned and made a mental note to ask him about them.

He smiled when he saw me and wrapped me in a friendly hug. "Athena, it's good to see you again." He welcomed us inside and, offering his hand, said, "You must be Case."

"Case Donnelly." They shook hands.

Pearson took us into the living room. As he muted the TV, we sat on a navy-blue sofa, and he sat on one of two tan armchairs adjacent to the sofa. I took out the iPad and opened the file to take down his answers.

"Let's get right down to business," Pearson said. "What do you need to know?"

"I know you talked to Hugo on Saturday, and I thought maybe you'd have some insights into his frame of mind," Case said.

Pearson scratched his eyebrow. "His frame of mind?"

"For instance," Case said, "did he seem preoccupied when you spoke with him?"

"As I recall, he seemed a bit on edge."

That matched with what we'd seen. "How long have you known Hugo?" Case asked.

"I've seen him at various functions, always in the role of photographer, but I'd never personally met him before Saturday."

I typed it in. "When we spoke with Hugo, he indicated that he had some business to discuss with you. Would you share that with us?"

"Hugo said he wanted to help me," he replied.

"Help you with what?" I asked.

"He said he could help me save the dunes. I didn't let him go beyond that. I didn't completely trust Hugo, and I didn't want to be seen with him. You know his reputation."

"What was his reaction?" Case asked.

"He seemed frustrated."

"What time was this?" Case asked.

"I didn't look at my watch. Sometime midmorning."

Case waited for me to finish typing, then said, "Did you see Hugo talking to anyone else?"

"I was busy helping my wife. I wasn't paying any attention to what he was doing."

Case watched me type in the answer, then asked, "Did Hugo mention who else he wanted to talk to?"

"He didn't tell me." Pearson rubbed his arm, almost as a subconscious flashback to Saturday's events.

"I'm sorry if I seem to be prying," I said, "but I couldn't help noticing the cuts on your hands and arms. They look painful."

"They were at the time. I tripped and fell into a thorn-bush while I was looking for my son."

"You were looking for Denis?" I asked. "Where was he?"

"Out in the woods. He's been told not to go in there, but you know how boys are."

"What time was that?" I asked.

He stopped to think. "Around eleven, maybe a little before."

"Do you have any evidence to prove you fell?" I asked.

"Just the cuts and a torn golf shirt."

"Did you share all of this with the police?" Case asked.

"Yes, the police already have this information, as well as the shirt."

I glanced at Case, and Pearson caught it. "Is that bad? I thought it would help me."

"It might help," Case said. "It might also show you were on the trail where Hugo was killed. Circumstantial evidence. Did anyone see you trip and fall?"

"No one that I noticed." He glanced from Case to me. "That's bad, too, isn't it?"

"A witness would be helpful," I said.

Pearson looked up as though searching his memory. "There were people everywhere. I'm sure someone could verify it." He rubbed his brow as I finished typing. "There has to be a witness or some kind of evidence that proves I'm telling the truth. Or are the police really going to hang this on me?"

I didn't know what to say, and Case was staying silent, so I tried my best to ease his growing fears. "Not if we can stop them."

Unfortunately, that didn't seem to ease anything. Pearson's worried expression only deepened as Case continued.

"We have some photos for you to look at." He shook the three black-and-white photos out of the manila envelope onto the coffee table in front of us. He put Pearson's photo on top, and we watched Pearson's expression go from worry to shock.

"Who gave this to you?" Pearson asked.

"Hugo mailed it to me before he died," Case said. "Unfortunately, he didn't send any explanation with it, so we're hoping you can fill us in."

Pearson stared at the picture. "Clearly this puts me in a bad light."

Case pointed to the bearded man sitting in the driver's seat. "Who is this man?"

"That's Pete Harmon, president of Harmon Oil."

I glanced at Case in surprise. "Pete Harmon?" Now the conspiracy idea was starting to make sense.

"What's he handing you?" Case asked.

"Nothing. That is, he tried to hand me money, but I refused it."

"What did he want in return?" I asked.

"He wanted my vote." Pearson studied the photo and shook his head slowly, as if he couldn't believe it.

"Tell us the whole story," Case said. "How did you get into this position?"

Pearson exhaled as he stood, as though reluctant to tell us anything. He walked over to a dry bar and opened a bottle of whiskey. "Can I offer you anything?"

After our polite refusal, he poured himself a drink and sat back down. "Pete Harmon called me and asked me to meet him in the Harmon Oil Company parking lot. He said he had something important to show me regarding

the lakefront property. When I arrived, he asked me to get
into his car and then he tried to offer me money to vote
against the park restoration project. I told him I couldn't
do that and got out. The end."

"Do you know if he offered money to other councilmen?"

Pearson swirled the golden liquid in the glass before
taking a sip. "I don't know, but if he offered it to me, he
probably did to the others, too."

His expression was so genuine that I wanted to believe
him. My gut was telling me that he wouldn't betray SOD.
It was also saying that he didn't kill Hugo Lukan.

Case seemed less empathetic. "Why didn't you report
Pete?" he asked.

"First of all, report him to whom? The police? Pete
would deny it. He told me so. And it would've made me
look bad for agreeing to meet him." He shook his head. "I
can't believe Hugo was able to catch that on camera. He
must have been stalking me."

"He wasn't stalking you," I said. "He was stalking
Pete Harmon."

Case put Pearson's photo on the bottom of the pile and
showed him the next one, of Pete Harmon and a man with
a long face and dark mustache. "This is obviously also
Pete," Case said. "Do you know the other man?"

Pearson leaned forward. "That's Tom Silvester, from
Sequoia Savings and Loan. He's on the city council, too."
He sat back. "It looks like he took the money."

"The fact that he's counting it makes me suspect
you're right." Case turned over the third photo. "And this
man?"

"Wow." Pearson tapped the photo of a younger man

with light brown hair. "That's Beau Clifford, also on the city council. As of last month's meeting, Tom and Beau hadn't decided which way they were going to vote. Obviously, Pete's trying to sway them."

"And obviously," Case said, "he thought he could change your vote, too."

"Maybe Pete doesn't know your connection to Save Our Dunes," I said to Pearson.

"Not true," he said. "When the council voted to sell the land, I added a clause stating that SOD would have a chance to halt any sale by giving the city a down payment that would start the park's renovation. Pete knew that."

"Was the land for sale?" I asked.

Pearson took a long sip of whiskey and set his glass down. "No, but Pete's been pushing the city to do something with that property. He forced the council's hand. And I'm telling you now, he will stop at nothing to get that land."

"Why does he need your votes?" I asked.

"The land is city property," Pearson said. "When a matter like this comes up, we have to decide what's best for the community and put it to a vote."

"How much money was in the envelope?" Case asked.

"I don't know for sure—I didn't open it—but his stated offer was for twenty-five thousand dollars. I'm guessing he offered the same deal to Beau and Tom. If they vote yes, all it'll take is one more vote and we'll lose the land to Harmon Oil."

"Not if you raise the money with SOD," I said.

"We have less than three weeks to make our goal," Pearson countered. "We're close, but I'm afraid it won't be enough time."

"If you've declined Pete's proposition, then he won't have the votes to buy the land. Isn't that correct?" Case asked.

Pearson sighed heavily. "There are two other members of the city council. If one of them flips, we'll lose the land three to two. But since Pete came to me, that means he's desperate. So maybe that's a good sign."

Case pointed to the photographs on the coffee table. "Do you know if any of these men were at the festival?"

"I know Tom was," Pearson replied. "I don't know about Beau Clifford or Pete Harmon, but I doubt Pete would've been there since it was a benefit to help SOD."

"We saw you talking with Tom after Hugo's body was discovered," Case said. "It looked like an argument. Can you tell us what that was about?"

Pearson paused as he raised his glass for a drink. The question had clearly caught him off guard. "Tom and I used to be friends, but we don't get along anymore. We've been on the council together for years, and lately it doesn't take much to start an argument. I don't remember what that specific argument was about."

"Would you give us the names of the two missing city council members?" Case asked.

As I typed the names into my iPad, Pearson finished his whiskey and set the glass down with a bang. "This is all my fault."

"What do you mean?" I asked.

"Hugo," Pearson said. "He really was trying to help." He shook his head, his expression somber. "I should've heard him out."

"It's not your fault," I said, "but if you feel that way, you can make up for it by helping us find his killer."

"I'll do whatever I can."

"Thanks," Case said, handing him his business card. "That's all we have for now."

"What's next?" Pearson asked.

"We're going to look for a way to clear your name," I said. What I didn't add was, *before the police come calling again.*

We rose, and Case shook Pearson's hand. "Thanks for taking the time to talk to us."

I shook his hand, too, and noticed that it was very damp. "Thanks, Pearson. Give Elissa my best."

The summer breeze was warm as we walked away from the house. Case had put the doors back on his Jeep, so I rolled down the window to let the heat out. "What do you think?"

With one hand on the steering wheel, Case reached out to put his other hand on the back of my neck. It was casual, yet it brought an odd thumping to my heart. "Pearson was sweating," he said, "so my guess is that he's realizing he's in more trouble than he thought."

"Then he's finally getting the picture."

"But are we?" Case glanced at me. "He says he refused the money, but all we have is his word on it."

"Why would he lie?"

"So his wife doesn't find out."

I shook my head. "I still don't believe he would've accepted the bribe. He's a better man than that."

"People will always surprise you, Athena. Never forget that."

"Let's reserve judgment until we interview all the members of the city council."

"Why don't you talk to Bob Maguire?" Case asked. "I'd like to know what the detectives have on Pearson."

"I'll text him. In the meantime, why don't we swing by

the Studios of Sequoia to see if we can find any evidence the police might have missed?"

"Now?"

"It's supposed to rain tomorrow on and off."

"It's getting late."

"And?"

"And . . . is there anything I can do to convince you otherwise?"

We exchanged a look, and he knew the answer. "Turn left in four blocks," I said.

As we drove toward the Studios, I pulled out my phone and texted Maguire: *Call me when you get a chance. I have a question for you.*

"So," Case said, "who do you think we should interview next?"

"Tom Silvester."

"With so little to go on, that won't be easy."

"Beau Clifford?"

"Won't be easy, either," Case said. "How about Jewel? If she and Hugo were dating, we might get some good information from her first."

"Why do you even ask my opinion?"

He smiled and rubbed my shoulder. "To see if we're on the same page."

"Maybe you're on the wrong page," I teased, "because you just missed the turn."

Case put his blinker on and looked for a place to turn around.

My phone rang, and before I could say hello, I heard, "I wondered how long until I got a call from you." Maguire chuckled at his joke. "What can I do for you today?"

"Would you find out what the detectives have on

Councilman Pearson Reed? They seem to be targeting him in this murder case, and we're wondering why."

"You're merely *wondering*?"

"Okay, off the record, Maguire, we're hoping to prevent the detectives from drawing a big bull's-eye on Pearson's forehead."

"*Off the record*, Athena, I have to be very careful with what I tell you. As you know, I can get into big trouble if I divulge sensitive information."

"Nothing sensitive, then. Just what makes them think Pearson could've killed Hugo."

He laughed. "Nothing sensitive."

"May I gently remind you that we helped you out in the last investigation?"

"And I'll help you now as much as I can. I'm not privy to everything the detectives know, but I should be able to get some information for you."

"That's all I ask. And please take Delphi out to dinner. She's so down lately. Maybe you can cheer her up."

"I'll do my best."

Ten minutes later, we arrived at the rambling Victorian mansion, pulled into the gravel parking lot on one side of the house, and got out of the Jeep. At least a dozen cars were in the lot, no doubt belonging to the artists who rented space at the Studios.

We walked across the wide lawn behind the house to get to the dunes. The sun was settling lower in the sky, casting long shadows across the sand as we came to the path that led into the woodland. We spotted the thorny barberry bushes just after we entered the forested trail. Sure enough, there was a large dent splitting one of the bushes in two.

I pulled out my cell phone and turned on the flashlight,

aiming it at the damaged bush. "Look how deep this goes. It looks like Pearson fell right into the middle of it."

Case looked back toward the dunes, rubbing the short, scruffy beard around his chin. "Think about it from Hugo's perspective. This is the perfect spot to meet someone for a private talk. It's just beyond the peak of that dune, where no one would've seen them."

"But it's not where the murder happened. Somehow Hugo made it farther back into the woods before he was killed. Is it possible he was running away from the killer?"

"It's possible. But why run deeper into the woods?"

"Maybe the killer was blocking the path out." I shined my flashlight into the bush and noticed several green threads caught on some thorns. "Look, Case." I carefully removed one of the threads and showed him.

"It looks like Pearson was telling the truth about his golf shirt." Case studied the broken branches. "I hope he was telling the truth about everything else."

We trekked farther into the woods until we came to the distinctive black cherry tree. Case stopped and glanced around. "This is the spot."

"What are we looking for?"

He crouched down next to the tree. "Hugo was carrying a camera." He stood up and joined me. "So look for a strap or a cord, or broken pieces of camera."

"Or the camera itself?"

Case gave me a sideways glance. "I think the police would've spotted that."

"Maybe the killer took the camera," I said, "to destroy the evidence."

For the next half hour, we searched beneath and all around the bush where Hugo's body had lain, but we found nothing. If there had been some evidence, the police had done a thorough job of finding it.

"Let's go see Jewel tomorrow," I said. "Maybe she can shed light on those photos."

As we walked out, Case put his arm around me and gave me a gentle squeeze. "How about for now we put all this aside, open a bottle of wine, and watch the sunset from the boat?"

My stomach fluttered in anticipation. "Sounds like a perfect night."

"And don't forget, Lila is picking you up tomorrow afternoon."

Perfect night ruined.

The skies were cloudy, and the air was heavy with the threat of rain when Lila and I pulled into the visitors' parking lot in front of Harmon Oil Company Friday afternoon. It hadn't stopped the picketers, however. Some were standing by a folding table handing out signs, and others were walking in a large oval near the main gates. The building was set back from the road, beyond the large, well-maintained front lawn and employee parking lot. A sturdy hurricane fence encircled the property, and the front gates were being guarded by two men from the oil company.

It was quite a spectacle. Many more people than I'd expected had shown up, including a local news van with a satellite extending above the growing crowd. We got out of the Tesla and headed for a folding table someone had set up to hold extra picket signs.

"Isn't this fun?" Lila asked, testing out her sign. "I've

never been in a protest march before." She was wearing white canvas sneakers, skintight white jeans, and a shiny silver-and-white-striped top, sure to get lots of attention. Her blond hair was fashioned into lots of ringlets, a playful, bouncy look that also said, *Look at me*.

The *Sequoian Press* had sent Charlie Bolt, the newspaper reporter who'd interviewed me after we'd solved the Talbot murders, and a photographer who'd arrived about the same time we did. Seeing us, Charlie strode over, his mini recorder in hand and the photographer on his heels.

"Athena Spencer, have you come to join the picketers?" he asked.

"I have."

"And what have you to say about the proposed building project at the dunes?"

"You'll have to ask Elissa Reed, Charlie. She's heading up the Save Our Dunes initiative."

"But you're the Goddess of Greene Street. The champion of the people. How will you be contributing to the initiative?"

"Picketing is a great opportunity to let the head honcho of Harmon Oil know how people feel about his proposed land development. And you can quote me on that."

"And how *do* the people feel?"

I gestured to the demonstrators. "Take a look for yourself."

The men and women were chanting in unison as they waved and jabbed their picket signs in the air. *Save the Soil from Harmon Oil* and *Harmin' the Environment* were just a few of the picket phrases being hoisted in front of the television cameras.

"Hi, I'm Lila Talbot," Lila said with a flirtatious smile. "I'm here to protest Harmon Oil Company, too."

"Lila Talbot?" Charlie exclaimed. "Grayson Talbot's wife?"

"Ex-wife," she said proudly. "And for your edification, not all of the Talbots are bad news."

Charlie looked at her oddly. "Uh-huh."

I spotted Elissa standing by the table with a clipboard in hand, but before I could make my way to her, my mother came hurrying toward us.

"This is my daughter, the Goddess of Greene Street," my mother announced to Charlie, slightly out of breath as she stroked my hair. She completely ignored Lila.

"Yes, Mama, he knows that," I said with a hot blush.

"Does this kind reporter also know how proud we are of you for taking a stand against Harmon Oil?" she asked, looking directly at Charlie. "Does he also know that you've rallied the Greek Merchants Association to help?"

"I'll put that in the article," Charlie said, jotting it down in a small notebook.

"Please don't make the article about me," I said. "This is too important."

"Let me introduce my other daughters," Mama said, rounding up my sisters, "also named after goddesses."

"Mama," I said, taking her arm and leading her away, "let's let Charlie get on with his business. He's here to report on the picket, not the Spencers."

My mother wasn't too happy, but she conceded that I had a point. After posing all of us for a photo, Charlie and the photographer went their own way. I introduced Lila to my family and picked up picket signs for the three newcomers.

"Athena," I heard, and turned to see Elissa Reed coming toward me. "Thank you so much for joining us. Isn't this a great turnout?"

"It is. Obviously, Harmon Oil buying the land is a hot-button topic."

She motioned for me to join her away from the protesters. "How did your talk with Pearson go?"

"It was brief, but so far his story checks out."

She smiled in relief.

I introduced Elissa to Lila and my family, and then we joined the marchers for almost an hour before the rain began, at which point everyone scattered for their cars. We waited about fifteen minutes, and when it didn't look as though it would let up, my mom and sisters left. Lila and I waited another long thirty minutes in her new electric car, and then we, too, gave up and headed back.

"That was fun," Lila said, "but when are we going to start investigating the murder?"

CHAPTER SEVEN

After successfully ditching Lila, the rest of my day off was spent peacefully at home, writing up a list of interview questions for Jewel. As we had done the previous evening, I met Case at the boat at six thirty to go over my list. I was excited to continue the investigation, but even more excited to see Case. I found him in the boat's stern, stretched out along one of the cushions built into the side. He was reading a study guide with his shirt off when he noticed me.

"Welcome aboard," he said casually. "Ready to get to work?"

The last thing on my mind at that moment was work. "Not if you're dressed like that."

He grinned. "I'll put a shirt on so you can concentrate."

After reviewing my questions, Case added a few of his

own, and then we left for Jewel's house. He'd found her address online. She lived in a small, shotgun-style cottage on the southeast side of Sequoia, where the pocket-sized lawns were well tended. We knocked on her front door and rang the doorbell, but although there was a compact car in the gravel driveway that ran alongside the house, no one answered. We finally followed the driveway to the detached garage behind the house, where we could see a light on. We looked in a small window and saw her sitting at a table bent over something in her hand.

We tapped on the door, and in a minute, it was thrown open by a thirty-something woman wearing black sneakers, jeans with holes in the knees, and a bright pink tank top. A pair of jeweler's magnifying glasses were perched on her forehead, and her black hair was pulled back in a messy ponytail. "Yes?" she answered impatiently.

"I doubt whether you remember us from Saturday," I said, "but we met you at the festival. I'm Athena Spencer, and this is Case Donnelly. We're conducting a private investigation into Hugo Lukan's death and thought you might be able to help us."

She stepped fully into the doorway and looked down her nose at me. Standing on tiptoe, I barely reached her shoulder. She was as tall as Case if not a tiny bit taller. "I don't remember you from the festival," she said. "Who are you again?"

"My name is Athena Spencer, and this is Case—"

"Oh, right," she said, giving Case a smile. "Donnelly. I've heard a lot about you."

"From Hugo?" I asked.

She looked at me as though she couldn't decide whether to trust me, then blew a strand of hair from her face. "Maybe."

"Judging by what you posted online, you and Hugo were friends," Case said.

"Snooping around on social media won't gain *you* a lot of friends, Donnelly. What are you getting at?"

"We're wondering whether you'd answer a few questions," Case said.

"I don't know anything about Hugo's death," she said bluntly, one hand on the door. "Sorry."

She certainly didn't act like a grieving girlfriend.

Before she could shut the door, I said, "We just need a few minutes of your time, then maybe we can start piecing together what happened. Our client would really appreciate it."

She stared at us for a long moment, as though trying to decide. "Who's this client?"

"We're not at liberty to say," Case answered.

"We thought you might want to help, for Hugo's sake," I added.

She studied us a moment longer and finally gave the door a shove. It hit the wall with a bang. "I don't know much."

"You may know more than you realize," Case said.

With a sigh intended to show us how put out she was, she said, "Come in, then." As she led us through the converted garage back to her worktable, she added, "I'm right in the middle of a project, so I can't give you much time."

Her workspace had a cement floor and walls lined with shelves full of plastic bins, each containing different components of her jewelry. On a worktable under a fluorescent light were a magnifying lamp, a pair of wire clippers, a plastic bin with small blue beads in it, and another filled with coils of wire. The room smelled faintly of motor oil and glue.

She leaned one hip against the table and crossed her arms like a recalcitrant teenager, not offering us any place to sit, although there were two white plastic chairs against a wall. "Hugo and I have been friends for a long time. Anyone can tell you that, so I'm wondering what all this has to do with me."

I pulled out the iPad and opened the file marked *Jewel*. "Did you talk to Hugo on Saturday?"

Jewel reached across the table for a cardboard box stuffed full of small, plastic-wrapped items. She pulled one out and studied it. "Briefly. I was trying to sell my jewelry, so there wasn't much time to talk."

"What did you talk about?"

"You know, this item right here is my biggest seller." She held up a silver bracelet lined with colorful round stones. "What do you think?"

She handed me the bracelet. "It's beautiful," I said politely.

"Yeah?" She seemed to be waiting for me to say more, and when I didn't, she rummaged through the box until she found a leather strap adorned with gunmetal studs. The strap immediately caught my eye.

"This," she said to Case, "is one of my most popular items. I sold a ton of them at the Art in the Park festival. Don't you think it would look good on you?"

Pete Harmon had been wearing the identical strap in the photos. Had he attended the festival after all?

Case caught the item midair after Jewel tossed it at him. "How much?"

"Now, there's a question I can answer," Jewel said, finally giving us a smile. "That right there is a mere twenty-five dollars. So, how about for every question I answer, I pull a new item out of this box?"

Blackmail? Bribery? I was so flummoxed I couldn't even think of the right word. Did she expect us to pay her for cooperating? I slammed my iPad closed and crammed it down into my tote bag just as Case clamped the leather strap around his wrist. "It's a deal."

I stared at him with an open mouth.

"I remember it all so clearly now," she said. "Hugo and I were talking about the festival, the weather, small talk like that."

"Did he seem preoccupied? Nervous?" Case asked.

She pulled another item from her box. "No. He was in a good mood."

At least she seemed to offer up useful information in return for her extortion. Aha! *Extortion*. That was the word.

"Did he mention wanting to talk to Pearson Reed?" Case asked.

He'd barely uttered the name before she said, "I don't know who that is."

She pulled out another item, but Case rebuffed her. "I'm only paying for answers. 'I don't know' doesn't count."

"He didn't mention anyone to me," she said, rummaging through her box.

"What time did you talk to him?"

"Like I said, I was busy with customers. I couldn't tell you a specific time."

Case pulled out his wallet. "Are you sure about that?"

"It was sometime before noon. Way before the police arrived. That's all I know."

I glanced at Case, and he gave a nod. Time to show her the photos.

"We'd like you to look at some pictures," Case said, as I laid one on her desk.

She bent over for a look, and I could see her visibly pale, as though she recognized something in it. Making an attempt to sound casual, she asked, "Where did you get this?"

"Hugo sent it to me," Case said.

She pressed her lips together in a hard line, the same face I made when I was angry. "What do you want me to say?"

"Can you identify the men in the photo?" Case asked.

"Just one." She tapped on the bearded man's face. "My boss, Pete Harmon, from Harmon Oil."

"You work at Harmon Oil?"

For the first time she stumbled a bit before answering, "Yeah."

"What do you do?" Case asked.

"I'm Pete Harmon's administrative assistant."

"Is that your leather strap on his wrist?" I asked.

She nodded.

"Did he buy it at the art festival?"

"No, I gave it to him as a gift."

That cleared up one question. "Do you know the other man?" I asked.

She shook her head. I took out another photo and laid it beside the first. "This must also be Pete Harmon, then," I said. "How about the man in the passenger seat?"

"I don't know him." She said it with an embarrassed blush that told me she was lying. I made a mental note. The man pictured was Pearson Reed.

"What's your impression about what's going on in the photos?" Case asked.

She put the cardboard box down and stuck her hands

in her jeans pockets. "No clue. I'm just Pete's administrative assistant. I don't set up appointments in cars."

I laid out the photo of Beau Clifford. "Do you know who this man is?"

"Nope."

"Why do you think Hugo sent me these photos?" Case asked.

She eyed him warily, as though it was a trick question. "I don't know. He must've trusted you."

"He barely knew me."

"Well, obviously he didn't trust me with any of this."

"Any of this what?" I asked.

She sighed, as if talking to us was boring her. "He wouldn't tell me what he was up to. He just kept asking me for information. He wanted to know Pete's schedule, who he talked to. I swear the reason he got close to me was to get close to Pete Harmon."

"Did you share any information about Pete with Hugo?"

"No way," Jewel answered. "But that didn't stop him. Hugo was a snoop. I would catch him going through my stuff all the time. Finally, I told him to get lost, and we didn't really speak much after that."

"But you said you saw him at the art festival," I said.

"He might've said hi," Jewel responded defensively.

"Which was it?" Case asked. "Did he just say hi, or did you make small talk?"

She lifted one shoulder as if it didn't matter. "We just said hi."

I noted it.

"Do you think your boss could be responsible for Hugo's death?" Case asked.

Jewel's eyes narrowed as she studied the photos again.

"I hope not." She paused, then added, "But I really don't know."

"Do you think you could set up a meeting for us with your boss?"

Again, she stumbled before answering. "Um, no. That's not possible. He wouldn't like that."

Case and I glanced at each other.

"Are we done yet?" she asked.

"I guess that's all for now." Case lifted a few bills from his wallet and laid them out on her worktable. "Can we count on you for future questions?"

"I appreciate the offer," she said, pushing the money back, "but I don't think I should get involved. Pete Harmon isn't a man to mess with. I don't want any part of it."

Case slipped out a twenty-dollar bill and wrapped his business card in it. "Just in case you change your mind," he said.

We thanked her, left her studio, and headed back to the Jeep.

"What did you think?" Case asked as we pulled away.

I sat in the passenger seat with a sack full of cheap jewelry. "That you got ripped off."

"Consider it an investment." He held up his wrist. "You don't like the bracelet?"

"We know Pete Harmon did," I answered, trying to be tactful. "I was hoping he'd purchased it at the festival, but that didn't pan out."

"I could tell by Jewel's reaction she knew who Pearson was," Case said, "and probably the other men, too. The question is, why didn't she want to admit it?"

"She claimed she was afraid to get involved, but she

certainly wasn't afraid to tell us who her boss was." I sighed. "I'm having doubts about her being the key to the photos."

"She *is* Pete's administrative assistant. Who else would know more about his business dealings than her? She has to be the key. Why else would Hugo include her?"

"Maybe we should've confronted her with her own photo."

"We might have to do that," Case said. "But not yet. Let's dig up some more info before we circle back around to Jewel."

My phone rang, and Bob Maguire's name popped up on the screen.

"It's Maguire," I said to Case. "Hi, Bob," I spoke into the phone.

"Athena, I've got some information for you. It looks like Pearson has some ties to Hugo Lukan."

"Really? What do you have?"

"The detectives went through Hugo's laptop computer and found two letters he wrote to Pearson. I'll read the second one to you. It says, '*Pearson, this is your last warning. I have a photo proving what you did. If you think I won't publish it on the internet, think again. It's time to pay the piper, pal.*'"

"That sounds like blackmail," I said.

"Yes, it does," Maguire replied. "Now we need to find the photo he's talking about."

"Actually," I said carefully, "I was just about to tell you about some photographs we received from Hugo after his death."

"You were just *about* to tell me?"

His tone was teasing, but I sensed the seriousness behind his question. "Honestly, Bob, I didn't know if there was anything to these photos until now. Why don't you come by the garden center and take a look?"

"Okay, I'll do that. It won't be today, but I will stop by soon."

"Great."

"Are there any other secrets you're keeping from me?" Maguire asked.

"No, I promise."

"Good. See you soon."

I hung up and said to Case, "Pearson might be in trouble."

"What did Maguire say?"

I gave Case a rundown on the letters.

"So our friend Hugo *was* involved in a blackmail scheme," Case said. "It still baffles me why he would want to involve me in it." Case turned the corner onto Greene Street. "It also means that Pearson was withholding information from us, and that's not good."

"I'm not giving up on him yet, Case. I think we're going to have to pay him another visit to tell him what we know and see what he says."

"I just want you to promise that you'll keep an open mind. Don't assume that because Elissa is your friend, Pearson is innocent."

Although I knew Case was right, I couldn't bring myself to admit it. I also knew I was going to have to share the information with Elissa at some point, and I wasn't looking forward to that. Plus, I couldn't help but remember Delphi's prophecy about the black knight. Maybe she'd gotten it right after all.

"Let's go talk to Pearson again before we interview anyone else," I said. "What time can you get away on Monday?"

"Whatever time you're free. And not to change the subject, but how about joining me for dinner tomorrow evening? I wouldn't mind trying the new Italian restaurant on Elm."

"It's a date," I said. And it actually was a real date and not something set up by my mother. Wow.

"She wants to set me up on a date, Athena."

Delphi had come into my bedroom that evening and plopped down on my bed with a heavy sigh. "What am I going to do?"

I shut my laptop and got up from my desk to turn my chair around. Delphi was wearing a pink-and-white-swirl T-shirt with gray, wide-bottom lounge pants. Her bare feet had toenails painted a bright pink. Her black curls hung in soft ringlets on her shoulders.

"Tell her about Bob," I said.

"I can't do that."

"Then go out on a blind date and tell her it didn't work out."

"That's horrible. What would Bobby say?"

Bobby? I had to hold in a laugh. I hadn't heard Bob Maguire referred to as "Bobby" since someone had made fun of him in high school. "Just go on one date so Mama will get off your back. You don't even have to tell Bob about it."

"I don't know," she responded. "It doesn't feel right."

"Then tell Mama that."

She ran her hand over my teal bedspread. "No way."

"Is this a sister meeting, or can anyone come in?" my mother asked from the doorway.

"We're just chatting about work," I said quickly. "Delphi is painting some very pretty pots to sell at the garden center."

Mama came in and sat next to Delphi. "*Glykiá mou*," she said. *Sweetie.* "It's just one date. I'm doing this for your own good. Tell her, Athena."

"Why don't you find Selene a date?" Delphi asked. "She's the oldest."

"She says she is still recovering from her divorce. I don't want to rush her."

"Or Maia, then."

"Maia." Mama sighed. "She has her circle of friends from the yoga center." She stroked Delphi's thick black curls. "But you're always alone, my *kori*." *My daughter.* "Just try meeting Steve one time. For dinner tomorrow. Maybe that new Italian place on Elm."

"No," burst out of my mouth.

My mother stared at me in surprise. "Why not?"

"Well," I said, thinking fast, "I've heard that the service is so slow you can grow roots. New waitstaff. Still working out the bugs. Not a good place for a first date."

Delphi gave me a pained look, and I wanted to cut out my tongue. Not *first* date, Athena, her look said. The *only* date!

Mama rose. "I'll set something up. You'll like Steve, Delphi. He's Maria's son. Never been married, no children, a good job in management . . . what more can I say?"

Delphi sighed morosely, looking resigned. After Mama left, she got up with another sigh. "Why did I have to be born Greek?" And with that she left.

She had given me the perfect topic for my blog. I opened my laptop and began.

CHAPTER EIGHT

IT'S ALL GREEK TO ME
Blog by Goddess Anon

MEDDLING MOTHERS
"One who wins the world does so by not meddling with it." —Tao Te Ching

Do all mothers meddle, or is that unique to the Greek community? All I know is that my mother is the supreme meddler. She thinks she has to oversee what I eat, what I wear, what I do in my spare time, and even who I see— and I'm an adult! Is it a lack of confidence in me? Is it too much time on her hands? Is it a big ego boost?

Whatever it is, it has got to stop. But what's the best way to stop it? I can't just cut her out of my life. I don't want to hurt her feelings. She's still, after all, my mother.

Any suggestions would be appreciated.
Adio Sas,
Frustrated Goddess Anon

Saturday morning, Nicholas and I made our usual stop at the diner. Nicholas had waited to eat until we got there, once again preferring a plate of his grandfather's scrambled eggs to my instant oatmeal. When we arrived, Mama, Maia, and Selene were gathered around Maia's laptop, chortling. Delphi was suspiciously absent.

"Let me guess. You're reading the goddess's blog again," I said.

"It's about meddling mothers," Selene said. She made sure Mama wasn't looking, then rolled her eyes at me.

"Isn't it a good thing I don't meddle?" Mama asked. "Now, *my* mother, your yiayiá, *she* was a meddler."

"Did she fix you up on dates?" I asked.

"Oh boy, did she," Mom replied. "And guess what? She struck gold with your father."

"She actually fixed you up with Pops?" I asked. "He's not Greek."

"She ran out of Greek men." Mama laughed. "Ask your dad about our first date. It was a disaster. I'm still amazed there was a second."

Interesting. So there *was* hope for Delphi and Bob. Unfortunately, if Delphi didn't come clean about him, Mama would have to run out of Greek men first.

After breakfast at the diner, I'd just arrived at Spencer's and was settling into my morning routine when my dad appeared at the door.

"Athena, have you seen the newspaper this morning?" He handed me the paper.

PROTEST MARCH RALLIES HUNDREDS, the banner head-line read. And beneath it was a photo of me holding a sign, with a big circle of protesters in the background. A caption under the photo read THE GODDESS OF GREENE ST. JOINS PROTEST AGAINST HARMON OIL.

I groaned. "I asked him not to make the article about me."

"It's a good article, though," my dad said. "It really lays out the case for SOD."

I read through it quickly. "It certainly leaves no doubt as to whose side I'm on."

I hoped there were no repercussions. As the day wore on, however, the customers I worked with who'd seen the news article congratulated me for taking a stand.

Shortly after eleven, my dad came back into the office to grab a cup of coffee. "What a morning," he said. "Bus-ier than ever."

"Hey, Pops." I went to the filing cabinet and took out the photos. "Would you take a minute to look at these?"

My dad's eyebrows rose as he looked through the photos. "Where did you get them?"

"Hugo Lukan sent them. He wanted to meet with Case, but that didn't happen before he was killed." I pushed the one of Pearson forward. "We know who these two men are. This is Pearson Reed, and this is Pete Har-mon, the owner of Harmon Oil."

"I recognize Mr. Reed. I've attended my share of city council meetings on behalf of the GMA. But frankly, I'm shocked to see him in this situation."

"He says Pete Harmon tried to give him money to vote for Harmon's lakefront land proposal, but he refused."

"Good. I've always liked Pearson." He studied the second photo for a moment. "This man is Tom Silvester, also on the city council. He's the senior vice president of lending at Sequoia Savings Bank. A real piece of work, that man. This photo doesn't surprise me."

"Why do you say that?"

"He turned your grandfather down for a loan to renovate the diner because your pappoús wouldn't give him money under the table to expedite the loan approval."

"Did Pappoús report Silvester?"

"Not your pappoús. He just stormed out and took his business elsewhere."

My dad was right. Tom Silvester was a piece of work.

"This man is also on the city council," Dad said of the third picture. "Last name is Clifford, I believe. He's the store manager at JumboMart." He looked at all three photos again and said, "It appears that Pete Harmon is working hard to get these men on his side. I hope they didn't take the bait."

"We do, too, Pops."

"I don't know who the woman in the last photo is."

"That's Jewel Newsome, a friend of Hugo's. We don't know why her photo was included."

"Have you shared these with the police?" Dad asked, taking a sip of coffee.

"Not yet. Maguire said he would come take a look."

"I think that's a good idea. They could be important."

I worked in the office until eleven thirty, then came out to the main floor to help with sales, only to find people lined up in front of Delphi's colorful pot display, while she sat on a stool putting her autograph on the bottoms with a felt-tip pen.

"Can you believe it?" Drew asked me as I looked on. "She took my advice. I had her post a few of her painted pots to Instagram, and now they're a hit."

"I'd say so," I said. "People are actually asking her to autograph them?"

Drew leaned close. "I don't think anyone actually *asked* her to sign them."

"Excuse me," a woman stopped me to say. "I'm looking for a wrought-iron patio table set and didn't see any in the store."

"Let me show you our outside display," I said, and took her through the store, out the back door, and right to the furniture area.

"Thank you," she said, and headed straight for the tables.

I caught sight of Nicholas and Denis in the shrub area and went to see what they were doing.

"We're playing hide-and-seek with Oscar," Nicholas said. "We hide this shiny star ornament, and he finds it."

"He's so much fun," Denis said, smiling at our little black and gray bandit, whose watchful eye was on my son. "You're lucky, Niko. I wish I had him for a pet."

"He's not the kind of pet you can keep inside," I said. "He's still a wild animal."

"But look how tame he is, Ms. Spencer," Denis said, holding out a handful of peanuts. "I'm going to ask my mom to get me a baby raccoon."

"Excuse me?" the woman called. "I think I've found the table I want."

"I'll be right with you." To Nicholas, I said, "Don't overfeed Oscar," and then I left.

The Saturday rush tapered off around five o'clock. Nicholas wanted to stay until closing, so he promised to behave and wished me luck on my date. I drove home and changed quickly because the only reservation Case could get was a little on the early side. I was just happy he'd remembered to make one at all.

By six o'clock, I was ready to go. Case met me on the front porch, and we were off on our first real date to *Piatto,* the new Italian restaurant on Elm Street. Case wore a blue shirt and a blue-and-gray-striped tie with gray pants, his dark hair providing a sexy contrast with his clothing. I had on a long, cream- and mango-colored cardigan over a cream tank top with cream pants. I left my long hair loose but tucked one side behind my ear.

Our table was nestled into a cozy corner along the back wall. Case pulled out my chair, and I sat down facing the long, narrow dining area. We were lucky to have a reservation because the restaurant was filled. All of the tables were dressed in white tablecloths with dark blue candles in the center. Waiters and waitresses wove through the crowded room wearing white shirts and navy pants. The windows were draped with dark blue curtains, and the art on the walls were paintings of Italy. It was a beautiful place.

We had just ordered a bottle of cabernet when I heard, "Case, Athena, how about that?"

I looked around and saw Lila coming toward our table. With a muttered, "Unbelievable," I glanced at Case, but he ignored me and gave her a smile instead.

She was wearing a very short, very tight, sleeveless black dress with high, thin-strapped black heels. Her blond hair was a mass of curls pulled back off her face.

She looked stunning, the contrast between us making me feel like a dowdy hen.

She pulled out a chair and sat down. "I'm not going to stay. I'm here with friends." In a voice that could clearly carry to nearby tables, she said, "Are we investigating Hugo Lukan's murder or not? You haven't told me a thing about what's going on."

I was so shocked that she would bring it up in a public place that I couldn't answer. Apparently, Case was having the same reaction because he only stared at her. I finally leaned toward her to say quietly, "We can't officially investigate his murder, Lila."

"As I mentioned before," Case said in a low voice, "I don't have my PI license yet. We're just looking into Hugo's death as a favor for Elissa Reed. I could get into trouble if I opened an official investigation."

"Favor or not," Lila said, still talking loudly, "you've got to keep me in the loop."

"Number one," I said, "lower your voice. Number two, how did you find out?"

"I have my sources," she said with a sly smile. At least she was talking quietly now. "So, where are we on this *favor*?" She made quote marks around the word.

"We've talked to Pearson Reed," I said, "and a woman with a booth at the festival."

"So, do you think this Pearson's the killer?"

I glanced around to see if anyone was listening. I was about to shake my head when Case said quietly, "We haven't ruled anyone out."

"Seriously, Lila," I said, "who are your sources?"

"I," she answered with an upward tilt of her chin, "am a well-connected woman. I have sources all over town, and I can be a vital part of this investigation if you'll just keep me in the loop. Do you have any notes I can look over?"

"They're on the boat," Case said. "It'll be easier when I get moved into the office."

Lila rubbed her hands together. "Then let's get you moved in. Do you have desks? No? Okay, I'll go desk shopping tomorrow and have them delivered Monday. What else? A few nice chairs for the waiting room? Oh. Desk chairs, too. Let's see. We'll need a coffee machine, cups, napkins . . ." She made small clapping motions with her hands. "This is so much fun. And what about this murder case? What's our next move?"

"Lila, you've got to keep it down," Case said. "And remember, I still have to pass my exam before I can apply for my license."

"Okay," she whispered, "you work on that, and I'll have the office ready to go by Monday. Is there anything else I can help you with?"

"Not right now," Case said. "And we promise to keep you in the loop."

She smiled graciously through several layers of make-up. "That's all I ask."

Our waiter came to our table with a bottle of wine and two glasses. "Shall I bring a third glass, Mrs. Talbot?"

She rose from her chair. "No, thank you, Henry. I'll let these two lovebirds get back to their date. Oh, and add an order of the fried calamari appetizer. Put it on my tab. It's *delicioso*," she said to us. "*Ciao*." Then, with a smile, she turned and sashayed away.

"Don't bother with the calamari," Case said to the waiter as he poured our drinks.

"Thank you," I said. He knew nothing born with suckers would ever touch my lips.

After we'd ordered, I said to Case, "For a woman who wants to be known for more than her money, Lila sure throws it around easily. Free cleaning service, free furniture, free calamari. But there's a price to pay for keeping her in the loop. She likes to talk. Loudly."

Case smiled at my statement. "Nothing in life is free, but Lila *is* well-connected. I'd bet she knows just about everyone of importance in this town. Not a bad person to have on our side."

I couldn't argue with that. And honestly, Case was correct. As much as Lila got under my skin, she did know practically everyone in town, and her intentions seemed sincere. I just wasn't convinced that our silent partner would be able to keep her mouth shut.

"Now," Case said as he held out his wineglass, "where were we?"

I held mine out in anticipation.

"Here's to our first night out as an official couple," he said. "No secrets, no parents, no warrants, no problems." He clinked his glass against mine. "Just you and me."

But before I could take a sip, my eyes were drawn to the young woman being seated near the front windows, and I let out a groan. "And Delphi makes three."

CHAPTER NINE

"Delphi?" Case turned in his seat to see. When a handsome older man sat down across from my sister, he said, "Make that four."

The man was clean-shaven with wisps of gray blended into the temples of his thick brown hair. His suit was sharp, and his smile was vibrant. Delphi, on the other hand, did not look excited to be there.

"Who is she with?" Case asked.

"A man named Steve. Remember the blind dates my mother set up for me? It's Delphi's turn now."

"Then your mom doesn't know about Bob Maguire?"

"Delphi's afraid to tell her, so she's having to go through what I went through."

"Maybe Bob should talk to your parents."

"Easier said than done."

"Poor Delphi," Case said. "She doesn't look happy."

I watched as Delphi snuck her phone out from her purse and checked it while the man across from her chatted away, smiling and looking through his menu.

"This is excruciating," I said. "I'm the one who convinced her to go on the date to get Mama off her back."

"Let's try to focus on something else, then," Case said as the waiter came with our food. He set his napkin across his lap and looked at me with a playful grin. "Like what we're having for dessert back at my place."

After Case had paid for our meals, we did our best to avoid Delphi and her date on our way out of the restaurant. We'd successfully exited when I heard my name.

"Athena?"

I swung around to see Bob Maguire walking up the street toward us. He was out of uniform, obviously off duty and coming dangerously near the restaurant. "Bob!" I blurted in a surprisingly high-pitched tone. "What are you doing here?"

"In Sequoia? I live here. Hello, Case," he said with a laugh.

"Bob," Case said, extending his hand. We had stopped directly in front of the restaurant's windows. I broke out into a sweat as the wheels in my head began to turn furiously. How could I get him to move along?

"I know you live here," I said, standing so that I hid my sister from view. Unfortunately, in that position it would take only a slight turn of Delphi's head to notice the three of us on the other side of the glass. I inched away from the window, hoping the men would follow. "I'm just not used to seeing you out of uniform. What are you up to?"

"Actually," Maguire said, "I'm glad I ran into you. I've been trying to reach Delphi all evening, but she's not answering her texts. Do you know where she is?"

The wheels in my head ground to a halt, and my throat froze. I had no idea what to say.

Case must have noticed my shock because he jumped in. "Maybe she turned her phone off. Did you two have plans tonight?"

"I asked if she had plans, and that's when she stopped texting back." Maguire shrugged. "Maybe you can talk to her? See what's wrong?"

My throat thawed enough to say, "Sure, Bob. I'll talk to her. But I wouldn't worry about Delphi. You know how she is, probably forgot to charge her phone. Or forgot to bring it. Or . . ." I was rattling on and knew I had to stop. "Why don't we move away from the window? I'm sure the diners don't want us blocking their view."

And right on cue, Maguire turned his head toward the window and caught sight of Delphi with her date. As we stepped away from the window, he gazed at me with knowing eyes. "I get it now. It's okay, Athena. No need to make up excuses. Delphi can see whoever she wants."

"It's not like that, Bob, believe me."

Case put his hand on Maguire's shoulder. "Why don't we go up the street and have a beer together at the bar. Then I can explain how this crazy Greek family works."

As if matters couldn't get any worse, I heard Delphi call, "Athena, what are you doing out here? Bob?"

"Delphi," Maguire said, a smile lighting up his face. "Hi."

Before Delphi could respond, her date joined us outside, too, clearly confused. "What's going on, Delphi?"

The four of us stared at Steve in shocked silence. I

turned to see Maguire's cheerful expression crumple in painful, slow motion. Hoping to end the awkward encounter as quickly as possible, I stuck out my hand. "Hi, I'm Athena. I'm Delphi's sister. This is Case Donnelly and Bob Maguire. We were just standing here talking. Nothing to worry about, Delphi. I'll tell you about it later."

Maguire understood the situation immediately and looked at Delphi and her date with a fake smile. "I'll be shoving off now. Good to see you folks. Nice to meet you, Steve."

My sister watched him with sad eyes.

"Shall we go?" Steve asked Delphi.

As he strode away, Delphi turned to me and pointed her finger. "This is all your fault," she said in a low voice. "I told you I had a bad feeling." She walked off in a huff, following Steve.

Case put his arm around me. "Well, shall we go have that dessert, or does another glass of wine sound good?"

"Wine. Definitely wine."

I couldn't get Maguire's stricken look out of my head, and so my first date with Case ended with a whimper, not a bang. When I got home, Delphi was already there, and all she would say was that Mama had quizzed her about her date and Delphi had made it clear there wouldn't be a second one. Unfortunately, that only gave my mother new impetus to find her another "good Greek boy."

On Sunday afternoon, Case came over for a dip in the pool with Nicholas while my sisters and I helped Yiayiá and Mama prepare for dinner. After having been interrogated by every member of our family on his last visit, I was surprised that Case was still willing to join us. We'd managed to squeeze in an extra chair across from me, which had him seated right next to Delphi.

Fortunately, the dinner passed uneventfully, with everyone offering an opinion on the newspaper article about Harmon Oil wanting to purchase the lakefront property. From the comments left online by readers, Uncle Giannis reported, the public was fairly evenly split, some wanting the park brought back and some preferring to see the land go to Harmon to bring in more tax revenue. The SOD members had their work cut out for them.

Monday was a slow day. I did my usual morning work on the computer, then worked on Elissa's landscaping project until my dad came into the office.

"Athena, we have a customer who wants a custom landscape job done on her house. She's coming in at eleven. Do you want to handle it?"

"I'd love to. And I'll be out this afternoon for a while. We have to go see Pearson Reed." I glanced around. "Where's Niko?"

"He's helping Delphi. She's got another project underway. Have you called Bob about the photos yet?"

"He was supposed to stop by. I'll send him a reminder."

As Dad refilled his coffee cup, I texted Maguire: *Don't forget I have those photos Hugo Lukan sent to Case. Can you stop by sometime this morning?*

Ten minutes later, I heard a knock on the door.

"Hey, Bob," I said, as I walked to the file cabinet to re-trieve the packet of photos. "Thanks for stopping by."

"Oh, so now you recognize me," he said playfully.

He was wearing his dark blue police uniform. And even with his polished brass badge, a radio attached to his shoulder, and a chunky belt with his holstered weapon, he still reminded me of the goofy stringbean kid I joked around with at the back of the class.

"And I recognized you last night, too," I said. "I was just caught off guard. I'm sorry."

"You and me both, but you don't have to apologize."

"Have you talked to Delphi yet?" I asked him.

"No, is she around?"

"I'll find her, but first take a look at these photos. Hugo wanted to arrange a meeting with Case to discuss them, but he never got the chance."

Maguire studied the photos for several moments. "Now it's starting to make sense." He singled out the photo of Pearson. "This must be the photo Hugo was re-ferring to in the threats he sent to Pearson Reed. But if you're trying to clear your friend, Athena, this photo doesn't help. It gives him a motive."

"Trust me. I wasn't sure if I should show it to you for that very reason."

"I'm glad you did. If it were to turn out that Pearson is guilty and you withheld evidence, let's just say it wouldn't be a good look for the Goddess of Greene Street. You'd be facing jail time."

"I get that, Bob. But as these photos show, Pearson isn't the only one with a motive. Obviously, Hugo found out that there was something going on with these other men, too. And I know for certain that this man"—I tapped a photo—"Tom Silvester, was at the festival. That gives the detectives another suspect to investigate."

Maguire looked at the photos again. "I recognize Pearson and the other two city councilmen, but who is the man handing them the envelopes?"

"Pete Harmon," I said, "owner of Harmon Oil, the company that wants to buy the lakefront property."

"And who is this woman?"

"This is a friend of Hugo's. We haven't figured out why her photo was included."

I shook the envelope to remove the folded note inside. Maguire leaned over the desk to read it. "'Play with fire and you get burned.' That sounds like a threat."

He took out his cell phone and snapped pictures of everything. "I'm going to make copies to show to the detectives."

"You see what's going on here in the photos, don't you?" I asked. "Harmon wants that lakefront land, and he's trying to buy the councilmen's votes."

"I see that. The only problem is that the detectives are working on the murder case, not the land deal."

"But there's a direct correlation between the two. Hugo was on to Pete Harmon's little scheme. Someone threatened him, and now he's dead."

"You may be right, but if you want to clear Pearson's name, you're going to have to dig up more than just these photos."

And that was exactly what I intended to do, because I *was* going to clear Pearson. "Do you know whether the detectives found Hugo's camera?"

Maguire folded his arms across his chest. "You know

I'm not supposed to talk about an active investigation. I took heat for it last time."

"Then blink once for yes and twice for no."

He pointed his finger at me. "You know what'll happen if Detective Walters finds out I'm giving you all this information. I'll be written up."

"I understand. But you've already told me that the detectives found ligature marks around Hugo's neck, so I'm assuming the camera strap was most likely used to kill Hugo. I just need to know one more *tiny* detail."

Maguire sighed. "They didn't find the camera, if that's what you want to know. But you're barking up the wrong tree."

"How? Tell me. I promise not to reveal my source."

"I saw the autopsy report," Maguire said. "The official cause of death is blunt-force trauma to the head, not strangulation."

I sat back in surprise. "What about the ligature marks?"

"There was definitely a struggle of some kind, but that wasn't what killed him."

"Then the logical question would be, can a camera cause blunt-force trauma?"

"It wouldn't be my weapon of choice," Maguire replied. "And if the camera was the murder weapon, I would have expected to have seen pieces of it on the ground, but there weren't any."

"Athena, the landscape customer is here," Delphi called, then immediately blushed. "Hi, Bob. I didn't know you were here."

"I was hoping I'd see you," Maguire said.

I pointed to the doorway. "I'm just going to step out and shut the door so you two can talk."

When I got outside, I dialed Case's number and found out he was studying. "I won't keep you then," I said, "but let's go see Pearson this afternoon, and on the way over I'll fill you in on my conversation with Maguire."

Noon found Delphi and me headed down to the diner for lunch. Delphi was smiling again, so I took that as a good sign.

"Don't mention Bobby stopping by," she cautioned.

"I'll keep your secret as long as you fill in for me this afternoon. I have unofficial business to take care of."

"I know," Delphi said. "Bobby told me about it. And by the way, I'm not the only one with secrets."

I had almost completely forgotten about Delphi's quest to uncover my secret identity. I ignored her and switched the subject. "I take it you two worked out what happened?"

"Sort of. Bobby still doesn't understand why I don't just tell Mama I'm seeing someone."

"He doesn't know our mother. You have to lay the groundwork first."

"If I only knew how."

"If I only knew what to tell you."

At two o'clock, Case picked me up, and we headed to Pearson's printing company, Quick As an Ink. On the way, I filled him in on my conversation with Maguire.

"Blunt-force trauma," Case mused. "And the camera was never recovered."

"It's not definite that the camera was the murder weapon."

"Yet it did disappear."

Case turned in at a strip mall on White Street where Pearson's print shop was located. We asked a woman at the counter if we could see him. She left through a doorway behind her and came out a minute later to say, "Have a seat. He'll be with you shortly."

Ten minutes later, we were shown into his office and found Pearson seated behind a black industrial-style desk, wearing a blue button-down shirt and black pants. He rose and came around the desk. "I'm hoping you have good news for me."

Case and I glanced at each other. "May we sit down?"

"Let's walk and talk." Pearson led the way out of the office and down a long hallway.

We followed him into the main printing room, where large, heavy-duty printers were lined up along the wall, the smell of ink and newsprint heavy in the air. But as we walked, I noticed that most of the machines were turned off, and only a handful of employees were working.

"So, what's the good news?" he asked, as he stopped to check a printer.

Case and I glanced at each other.

"Okay," Pearson said slowly, "so it's not good news."

"When we talked to you before," Case said, "you didn't mention that Hugo had tried to blackmail you."

Pearson looked stunned.

"We know he sent you two threatening letters," Case said. "Why didn't you tell us about them?"

Pearson ran his hand through his hair. "I didn't know who sent them."

Case leaned in, lowering his voice. I could tell by his expression that he was not happy with Pearson's answer.

"You must have made the connection when we showed you the photos Hugo took. Why didn't you tell us then?"

"What could you do about it after the fact? It only stands to make me look guilty."

Case folded his arms across his chest. "Yes, it does."

"Tell us about the blackmail threats," I said.

He hesitated as one of his employees walked past. "Let's go back to my office."

As we sat down in chairs facing his desk, Pearson settled into his swivel chair. "I received an anonymous letter in my email with a vague threat in it and dismissed it as nonsense. But then I received a second letter threatening to publish a photo that showed me accepting an envelope from Pete Harmon. It was so specific that I got cold feet and paid the amount requested. I didn't need that kind of publicity."

As Case and I sat there pondering his response, Pearson leaned forward in his chair, his hands clasped together on the desktop. "I'm sorry I didn't tell you."

"How did you pay?" Case asked.

"I had to send cash to a post office box."

"Why didn't you tell the police about the threats?" Case asked.

"I know it sounds foolish, but I didn't want to get the police involved."

"It doesn't just sound foolish," Case said. "It also sounds like you took the bribe money."

"You're right. I should have contacted the police."

"How do we know you didn't accept the twenty-five thousand?" Case asked.

"That's the problem. There's no way I can prove it."

"What about a bank statement?" Case asked. "Wouldn't it show a big deposit?"

"That's not how Pete set it up. He was going to have someone hand-deliver smaller cash installments every week. He had it all figured out."

"Pearson," I said, "do you see how this is going to make you look to the police? You have no alibi, you were found with cuts on your body after being on the trail where Hugo was murdered, and now there are blackmail threats and a photo that give you a motive."

Pearson just sat there staring at us. In a tight voice, he asked, "What can I do?"

"Be prepared," Case said, "because the police have a copy of that photo. Have you taken the polygraph test yet?"

Pearson shook his head again.

"If they want you to go down to the station again," I said, "be sure to have your attorney with you. Don't do or say anything unless he gives you the okay. And you'd better give your lawyer the full story so that he knows what happened."

Pearson jumped when his phone rang. His hands were visibly shaking as he picked it up and listened. "I have to take this call," he said quietly. "Is there anything else?"

"No," Case said as we stood. "Just be careful."

As we got into Case's Jeep, I said, "He seemed completely up-front with his information. I really want to believe him."

"I don't know, Athena. He didn't give us the full story the first time. How do we trust that he did now?"

"I hope he did. The police are going to be breathing down his neck now, and we've got to help him."

"Hope isn't going to cut it. What we need to do is verify motives for the other suspects." Case pulled out of the parking space and turned onto White Street. "Let's find a way to interview the other men Hugo photographed."

"I'll set up an appointment with Tom at the bank. I won't state a reason, and he'll think it's just someone coming in to apply for a loan. We can take him by surprise."

"Good thinking."

"That reminds me, I forgot to tell you about my pappoús. When he applied for a loan to improve the diner, Tom wanted money under the table to get it on the fast track for approval. Pappoús refused, but he didn't report him. He just went elsewhere for the loan. So, Mr. Silvester may be involved in some shady dealings in the loan department."

Case turned onto Greene Street, heading toward the marina. "That doesn't give Tom a motive for murder."

"But it gives you a good idea of his character. I'd be willing to bet he took that bribe money from Pete Harmon."

"I'd take that bet."

We sat in silence for a while, which gave me time to think. What other motive could these men have besides fearing the release of the photographs? We'd have to interview Tom and Beau to find out if they'd received blackmail letters from Hugo.

Apparently, Case was thinking the same thing.

"When Maguire told you about finding those threatening letters to Pearson on Hugo's laptop," he said, "did he mention anyone else receiving letters?"

"He didn't," I said. "I'm sure Maguire would've told me if more letters were found, especially after he saw the photos of the other councilmen."

"Then the question is," Case said, "why was Hugo blackmailing Pearson and no one else?"

I had no answer.

"I know you really want Pearson to be innocent, Athena, but if Tom and Beau didn't get threats like Pearson did, then they may not know about the photos. And if they don't know about the photos, they don't have motives for murder."

"Then someone else does, Case. Pearson is innocent. My gut is telling me so."

"Maybe you're just hungry. Let's grab some lunch."

CHAPTER TEN

As Case parked the Jeep in the marina's parking lot, he said, "Hey, our office furniture was supposed to arrive today. Let's grab some sandwiches at the deli and go check out Lila's handiwork."

We walked the few short blocks to 535 Greene Street, bought turkey and Swiss cheese sandwiches, and took the inside staircase to the second floor. Case opened the door to the office, and the first thing that greeted us was the smell of a freshly cleaned space.

"Look at this," Case said, opening the door of his office. "I have a desk, a bookcase, and a credenza."

I followed him into the room and took in the beautiful walnut desk with a matching credenza that sat beneath the window. A bookcase, also in walnut, stood against the opposite wall. Lila, it seemed, had spared no expense.

We checked out my office next and saw the same setup

but in a light oak. At least I was supposing it was my office.

"Of course, it's your office," Case said. "Lila was joking about having a desk here."

"I don't think she was joking." I sat down in the chair and swiveled around to glance at the view out the window. Across the street was the plaza with the food trucks, and beyond that the bright blue waters of Lake Michigan. "You were right. This is the perfect place for our office."

"I'll get a sign ordered," Case said. "By the time it arrives, I may have my license."

"The Greene Street Detective Agency," I said. "I like the sound of that."

"I'll give Lila a call and update her on our investigation so she's in the loop. It's the least I can do."

"Meanwhile, let's celebrate having furnished offices," I said. "How about dinner out tonight, this time without any interruptions? It's on me."

"Or," Case said, "a dinner out on the lake, miles away from everyone."

I leaned back in the chair and smiled. "Even better, Mr. Donnelly."

Tuesday morning, after my work in the garden center office was finished, I called Sequoia Savings and Loan and made an appointment to see Tom Silvester. Shortly before three o'clock that afternoon, Case and I entered the stately, three-story, gray-stone bank building on Oak Street, rode the elevator to the second floor and took seats in the waiting area outside the loan department offices. In a few minutes I heard, "Mr. and Mrs. Donnelly?"

Seeing the tall, mustached Tom Silvester come toward

us, Case and I stood up. "Case Donnelly," Case said, shaking his hand. "This is my partner, Athena Spencer."

"I'm sorry. I assumed you were married." His face was long and pockmarked, and he smelled of sweet cologne and cigarettes. "It's nice to meet you. Come on in." He led the way into his office, furnished in dark, modern office furniture, and indicated the chairs facing his desk. "Have a seat. I understand you're here about a bank loan."

"Actually, we're here to pick your brain," Case said, as I took out the iPad and opened the file marked *Tom Silvester*. "We're looking into Hugo Lukan's death, and we would like to ask you a few questions."

For a brief instant, Tom looked surprised, which morphed into anger, and then he seemed to pull it back and paste on a bland expression. Speaking carefully, he said, "I was told this meeting was about a loan. I haven't agreed to answer any questions."

"Don't worry, Mr. Silvester," Case insisted. "We have just a few questions, and then we'll let you get back to work. Were you at the art fair on Saturday?"

Tom twirled a gold-colored pen between his fingers. He looked back and forth between the two of us, his thick mustache twitching impatiently. "I was there."

Case began the questioning. "Were you acquainted with Hugo Lukan?"

"I knew of him, but that's all."

"Did you meet with Hugo Lukan during the festival?"

"Of course not."

"Did you speak to Pearson Reed at the festival?" I asked.

"No, I was busy at my booth all morning"—he glanced over at Case—"but I do recall seeing Hugo talking to Pearson Reed."

I stopped typing and looked up at Tom, trying to catch any more twitches or tells that could indicate he was lying, but his expression gave nothing away. The gold pen continued to bounce between his fingers.

"Where did their conversation take place?" Case asked.

"Pearson and Hugo were heading down toward the dunes."

That wasn't an answer I wanted to hear, but I typed it into my notes anyway.

Case continued. "Were you aware that Hugo had photographic evidence of you and Pete Harmon exchanging money?"

That piece of news should've surprised Tom. So I was suspicious when he answered casually, "He never mentioned anything about photographs to me."

Case must've been suspicious, as well. "You just told us that you didn't speak to Hugo."

The pen in Tom's hand stopped twirling. "Look," he said irritably, "I spoke with Hugo briefly. He took some photos of the Sequoia Bank's booth, and that was it." Tom checked his watch. "I have another appointment, so, if you don't mind . . ."

"Just a few more questions," Case said.

"No more questions." He put his pen down, making it clear our interview was over.

As I began to close my iPad, Case forged ahead. "Were you at your booth all morning?"

Tom banged his fist on the table, startling us both. "What does that have to do with anything?"

Case and I shared a surprised look. His alarming response caught the attention of his administrative assistant, too. When she popped her head in the door, Tom stood, straightened his tie, and walked toward her. He offered a quiet apology before shutting the door and returning to his desk. "I'll ask it again," he said quietly. "What does that have to do with anything?"

"We're asking that question of everyone we know who had dealings with Hugo on Saturday," Case said.

"*Dealings* with him?" He pressed his lips together for a moment, as though trying to contain his anger. Still talking in a quiet voice, he said, "I already told you the extent of my *dealings*. It was a brief conversation!"

Case picked up the manila envelope he'd set on the floor by his feet and took out the top photo. Pushing it across the desk, he said, "Did Hugo mention this photo he took of you with Pete Harmon?"

Tom looked at the photograph, then glanced at us. "I've never seen that photo before."

"Did you know it existed?" Case asked.

In another show of temper, Tom raised his hand as if to slam his fist on the desktop again. Instead, he adjusted his tie. "Look, I'm telling you, I've never seen this photo before."

"That's not what I asked," Case said.

"Well, that's my answer."

I rolled my eyes at Case.

"Did you receive any threats stating that a photo of you would be published if you didn't pay?" Case asked.

Tom rose, his face coloring hotly. "I don't appreciate being treated like a suspect. You need to leave my office now." He pointed toward the door, but neither of us moved.

Case pushed the photo toward him. "I'm going to suggest you answer the question. If you're not willing to talk to us, our next stop will be the bank CEO's office. I'm sure he'd be very interested in what you were doing counting money in Pete Harmon's car."

Tom stood stock-still for a moment, then sat down heavily. "If I talk," he said quietly, "you have to swear it goes no further than this office."

Case took his time sliding the photo back inside the envelope. "If you give us straight answers, I won't have any reason to pay a visit to the CEO."

Tom glared at Case for a long moment, then finally gave a curt nod. "Fine."

"How did you learn about the photo?" Case asked.

"I received a letter in the mail here at the bank stating that there was a photograph of me and Pete Harmon. No photograph came with it, just a flat statement of fact and instructions about how I was to pay."

"Do you still have the letter?" Case asked.

"No. I destroyed it."

"What were the instructions?" Case asked.

"I was to send cash to a P.O. address."

"Did you pay it?" I asked.

"Not at first." Tom rubbed his eyes with his thumbs. "Then I received a second letter giving me a deadline. That's when I decided to pay it."

"Why did you give in?" I asked.

"Because someone I trusted advised me to. The last thing I need is for that photo to get out."

"Who advised you?" Case asked.

"That's confidential."

"We know Pete offered a twenty-five-thousand-dollar payoff to any member of the city council who agreed to vote for his land deal," Case said. "I can only assume that Pete was also being blackmailed. Did he advise you to pay the ransom?"

Tom's eyes narrowed. "What part of 'confidential' don't you understand?"

"Did you accept Pete's offer?" Case continued, unfazed.

"No," Tom answered. "You can ask Mr. Harmon, and he'll tell you the same."

"We will," Case said. "One more question. Were you at the Savings and Loan booth all morning on Saturday?"

"This again," he ground out. "I took one break to use the restroom, and that was it."

"I have a question," I said. "You're a vice president. Why were you working at the bank's booth?"

"Actually, I'm a senior vice president," Tom answered stiffly. "We're not a large company. Not many employees offered to spend their Saturday in a hot tent."

"So you offered to work?" Case asked.

"I didn't know Hugo would be at the art fair, if that's what you're getting at."

There was a knock on the door, breaking the tension in the room. "I've answered your questions," Tom said, rising. "Let's end it there."

"Thank you for your help," Case said, handing him a business card. "If you think of anything else that Hugo said to you on Saturday, please give me a call."

Tom took the business card and made a show of dropping it into his waste bin.

"I don't like Tom Silvester," I said, as we left the bank and started up Oak Street.

"I can tell," Case said. "Your face gives you away, Goddess."

I wrinkled my nose at him. "What I was going to say was, I don't believe Tom would've offered to work that art fair out of the goodness of his heart."

"What's your theory?"

"He knew Hugo was going to be there."

"So he was there to kill him?"

I shrugged. "Maybe."

"By the way Hugo was acting that morning," Case said, "it seemed like he was trying to catch Pearson off guard to talk to him. My guess is that he would've done the same with Tom. I don't think anyone knew that Hugo would show up there." He took my hand in his, and we walked along together. "Let's review what we learned."

"Okay. We know Tom received two threatening letters, just like Pearson did. We know he paid to keep his photo off the internet, again like Pearson. We know he spoke with Hugo on Saturday. And we know he was at the art fair and took a break from the booth."

"So preliminarily," Case said, "let's say he had the means, motive, and opportunity. That firms him up as a suspect."

"And he was quick to throw Pearson under the bus," I added. "I'm going to call my friend Darlene and see what she can tell me about that break Tom took, and then we should talk to Beau Clifford. What do you want to bet he received some sort of threat, too?"

"If his story is the same as Tom's," Case said, "then we've got three men with motives."

I didn't like that he still counted Pearson as a suspect. "What about Pete Harmon? We can't forget he's in those photos, too. And just because Pearson didn't think Pete would go to the festival doesn't mean he didn't go."

"Let's save Pete for last," Case said as we sidestepped

a group of tourists. "There's still one thing that bothers me. Why was Jewel's photo included?"

"Either she's a suspect or she has information," I said. "The problem is, how do we get her to talk?"

"I don't know, but I feel like we've overlooked something. When I get back, I'm going to review all the notes and see what I can find. And what about your classmate friend from the nature walk? Maybe she and her husband saw something on Saturday that we missed."

"That was Marylou. I'll look her up on Facebook and see if I can arrange a meeting."

My phone beeped. I checked it and saw a text message from Nicholas: *Do you know where Oscar's star toy is? I can't find it.*

His text message made me smile. I couldn't have loved him more if I'd tried. I texted back: *On my way to Spencer's now. When I get there, I'll help you look.*

"When do you want to go see Beau?" I asked Case.

"Let's go tomorrow after lunch. Send me your notes from today's meeting, and I'll let you know if I find anything new. If not, I'll pick you up in front of Spencer's at one o'clock." He raised my hand to his lips and kissed my fingers, a romantic gesture that warmed me all over.

"What are you doing later tonight?" I asked.

"Studying." He gave me a shrug. "That's what happens when you date a college boy."

I watched him walk away with a confident stride, then noticed several women's heads turning to watch him.

He's all mine, ladies. Eat your hearts out. I walked in the opposite direction with a smile on my face.

Before I reached Spencer's, I looked up the bank's phone number and asked for Darlene Cagney. "Darlene,"

I said when she came on a few minutes later, "this is Athena Spencer. How are you?"

"Wondering why the Goddess of Greene Street is calling me in the middle of the day," she said with a smile in her voice. "What can I do for you?"

"Answer a couple of quick questions."

"Sure. Let me close my office door, and then you can fire away."

I waited until I heard her voice again to say, "This is strictly confidential, okay?"

"You have my word. Are you working on the Hugo Lukan murder?"

"Unofficially looking into it."

"Got it. How can I help?"

"Last Saturday at the festival, when Tom Silvester took a break from the booth, do you remember how long he was gone?"

"The first time maybe ten minutes. The second time it was over half an hour."

"So he was gone twice."

"Yep. The bum left me alone right at the peak of the festival, sometime around eleven o'clock. I was steaming mad when he got back, and he didn't even apologize, although that shouldn't have surprised me."

"Then it happened well before the police arrived."

"Oh, most definitely."

"The second time he left, did you see which direction he headed?"

"Let's see. The first time he headed toward the Porta Potties. The second time he headed in the opposite direction. Maybe toward a food booth or something."

"Was he walking toward the dunes?"

"In that direction, yes."

"Was that when he was gone half an hour?"

"At least half an hour. He was gone so long I was getting worried."

"If I needed you to give the police a statement about Tom's half-hour break, would you do that for me?"

"Absolutely."

"Thank you. And may I ask what your relationship with Tom is like?"

"Let's just say I tolerate his behavior."

"Meaning?"

"He's a bad-tempered chauvinist with a huge ego. And here's something else about Tom. He came very close to being fired. He was taking on risky loans, and the CEO found out. But Tom talked his way out of it, so he was given another chance."

That explained why Tom was worried about the CEO finding out about the photo.

"So, tell me," Darlene said eagerly, "is Tom a suspect?"

"If I tell you, I'll have to kill you."

She laughed. "Okay, I get it."

I stopped outside Spencer's. "Thanks for your help, Darlene. One of these days we'll have to meet for coffee, and I'll explain everything."

I ended the call with a smile. Tom Silvester, the bad-tempered, egotistical loan officer, now had no valid alibi, and I had a witness I could take to the detectives. Progress.

CHAPTER ELEVEN

Standing outside Spencer's, I put in a call to Case. "You'll never guess what I found out from my friend Darlene."

"Fill me in."

"Tom not only left the booth twice on Saturday, but he was gone over half an hour the second time. *And* he was heading in the direction of the dunes. I also learned that he was caught approving risky loans. According to Darlene, he's already on thin ice with the bank CEO, which means he definitely wouldn't have wanted that photo to get out."

"Good work. I'll put that in the notes."

"Okay. I've got another call. I'll see you tomorrow." I checked my phone and saw my mother's name on the screen.

"Thenie, have you spoken to your baby sister yet about

what's bothering her? She was at the diner for lunch and in such a gloomy mood we couldn't get her to talk."

"Sorry, Mama. I've been so busy I forgot."

"Would you do that, please? She's worrying me."

"I'll try my best."

Inside the store, I found my son unloading a box of rainbow-colored plastic sun-catchers.

"Did you find Oscar's toy?" I asked him.

Nicholas shook his head. "I've looked in all of his hiding places, but I couldn't find it. It just disappeared."

"Maybe Oscar took it over the fence."

"He hasn't done that in a long time. Anyway, Grandpa's going to give me a new toy for Oscar, so he'll have something to hunt when Denis comes over."

"That's kind of Grandpa." I glanced around the store and saw my dad talking to customers in the back. Drew was ringing up a sale at the front counter, but I didn't see my sister. "Do you know where your aunt Delphi is?"

"I think she's meeting with some customers in the conference room."

Yikes. The only time Delphi ever took customers off the sales floor was to do a coffee grounds reading. I walked over to the small conference room just beyond the office and paused to listen outside the door.

"Does that mean you'll be traveling tomorrow?" Delphi was asking someone.

"Yes," a man answered. "I'll be taking the ferry to Saugatuck."

"Please don't go," Delphi warned. "The coffee grounds are very clear on this."

"But he has to," a woman replied.

"Wait," Delphi said. "I'm getting something."

I stepped into the room to see my sister rubbing her

temples, her eyes closed, a coffee cup in front of her. A middle-aged couple was seated across from her, and just as I feared, they were looking at each other in alarm.

"Delphi, sorry to interrupt, but there's an important phone call for you," I said.

"I'll be there in a minute." She opened her eyes and said to the man, "There are serious shallows ahead."

"What does that mean?" the man asked.

"Do not trust the ferryboat pilot."

"You don't understand," the man said. "I *am* the ferry boat pilot."

"I'm off my game," Delphi moaned, walking back and forth in front of the desk in the office. "I'm misreading the signs. I can't focus. What am I going to do?"

"Maybe it's because you're keeping this big secret from our family," I said, shutting the door. "Mama wants to know what's wrong with you. She won't leave me alone about it."

"Now you know how I feel."

"Yes, I do know how you feel, Delph. I kept Case a secret from Mama, which only made things worse. The best thing I ever did was tell her the truth."

"You didn't tell her the truth," Delphi exclaimed. "You said Case was a Greek fisherman from Florida. You made him wear a disguise."

"Okay, but the truth came out eventually."

"The truth *always* comes out eventually," Delphi said, narrowing her eyes at me. She sat down in one of the chairs facing the desk. "And the truth will come out about you, too."

"This isn't about me, Delphi."

"Then let's make it about you. How about this? You tell me the truth about Goddess Anon, and I'll tell Mama about Bobby." She folded her arms, sat back in her chair, and nodded toward the desk. "Sit."

Two thoughts struck me as I sat down. Either I continued to play coy until Delphi wore herself out trying to trip me up, or I confessed and trusted that my scatterbrained semi-psychic sister would keep my secret. Would she be happy that I was Anon, or would she be angry? Would she be angry enough to blow my cover just to get even with me?

No, that wasn't Delphi.

As she stared me down, I finally made my decision. If I knew my sister, she wouldn't give up her pursuit. She believed her intuition over everything. I also knew that she was loyal, loyal enough to stay silent and keep my little secret between us.

"You're right, Delphi," I said, sitting behind the desk. "I am Goddess Anon."

Her eyes remained locked onto mine, like she was reading me. "Give me your hands," she said and stretched hers across the oak top. I could barely keep my eyes from rolling.

She studied me hard as we held hands. I was expecting a lecture on the importance of sisterhood and honesty, truthfully any number of responses except the one she gave me.

"No, you're not."

I pulled my hands back into my lap. "Excuse me?"

"I know you too well, Thenie. You wouldn't just come right out and admit that you were Goddess Anon, but you know what you *would* do?"

I sighed. "Tell me."

"You would say you *were* Goddess Anon so that I'd agree to confess to Mama." She shook her finger at me. "You're sneaky, but I see right through you. Plus, your aura is a dark green right now. You're totally lying."

Maybe it was just the dark green curtains on the wall behind me? But I didn't tell her that. And I didn't lie to her. I just let her keep talking.

"So, forget it, Thenie. I am *not* telling Mama *anything*."

"Then stop acting like such a downer at the diner," I said. "Will you at least try to talk to Bob about your situation?"

"No. I mean . . . I don't know. I mean—" She threw her hands in the air. "I don't know what I mean." She sank back and dropped her head into her hands. "It's not just Bobby. Right now, he's the least of my concerns."

"What's wrong?"

She looked up at me with a troubled gaze. "I don't know how to tell someone something that's going to hurt."

"You have to be tactful. Or don't say anything at all."

"That's what I've been doing, and it's eating me up." She sighed miserably. "Thenie, I saw something when I read Elissa's coffee grounds, and I didn't tell her the truth. I haven't wanted to tell you because I know you believe in Pearson Reed's innocence, but I saw a black knight. That's very symbolic to me."

"What does it mean?"

"Guilt."

"Pearson Reed?"

She nodded. "Now you see why I couldn't tell Elissa. I tried to give her a hint about the black knight, but I don't know if she understood."

"You've got it wrong, Delphi. Pearson Reed isn't guilty of killing Hugo. He might be guilty of something else, but not of murder."

"I knew you'd say that." Delphi stood up. "Just forget what I told you, then."

"Athena," my dad said, sticking his head in the doorway, "Elissa Reed is here. Do you have time to talk to her?"

I glanced at Delphi, and she got up. "Let me slip out first."

"Sure," I answered. "Wait a few minutes, Pops, and then send her back."

Delphi pointed her finger at me. "Don't tell her what I said. If it's going to come from anyone, it should come from me."

"I won't say a word." Mainly because I didn't believe it.

"Athena," Elissa said a few minutes later, stepping into the office, "I'm sorry to bother you, but I was passing by and thought I'd let you know that Pete Harmon is going to hold a press conference tomorrow at four o'clock."

I rose from behind the desk. "Come in and sit down."

"Thanks, but I don't have time. I'm going around town spreading the word that we're going to rally outside Harmon Oil at three thirty with our protest signs."

"So, Pete's holding a press conference at four," I said, writing it on a sticky note.

"Yes, he is. Apparently, he didn't care for the editorial in yesterday's newspaper in favor of renovating the park, so I'm assuming he's going to make a case for *his* project."

"Four o'clock is usually a busy time here, but I'll try to be there," I said. "At the very least, I'll spread the word through the Greek Merchants Association Facebook group page."

"I knew I could count on you," she said.

"I'll get on it right now."

"Good. Then I'll see you tomorrow." She hesitated in the doorway, then said, "I hate to keep bothering you, but is there anything new on the murder investigation?"

What could I tell her? That we'd found two men with motives, one of whom was her husband? "Actually, we're investigating two potential suspects right now, and we're also looking for anyone at the festival who saw Hugo down by the woods."

"Maybe I can help with that. I'll put the word out and see what happens."

As soon as Elissa left, I got on my computer and logged into my Facebook account to do a search for my high school friend Marylou Porter, whom I'd talked to at the beach after Hugo's body had been found. I located a Marylou in Sequoia, took a chance, and sent her a private message asking her to call me about Hugo's murder. After I'd finished, I got onto the Greek Merchants Association group page and wrote a post about the press conference.

"Mom?"

I glanced up to see Nicholas's smiling face peering in the doorway. "Hi, honey. What's up?"

"Denis invited me to come over tomorrow afternoon after lunch. He has a playroom at the Studios of Sequoia, and he wants me to see it. He's says it's really cool. Can I go?"

"Do his parents supervise?"

"He said his mom will be at her art studio on the second floor. The playroom is up on the third floor."

"If it's okay with Elissa, it's okay with me."

"Cool, Mom. Thanks."

I heard a *ping* on the computer and went back to check the screen. A message had come in from Marylou Porter: *Happy to talk to you. How about meeting tomorrow at 7 p.m. at Jivin' Java coffee shop?*

I wrote back: *See you then.*

Wednesday was going to be a crazy day.

After a busy morning at Spencer's, at one o'clock Wednesday afternoon, Case and I took Nicholas to the Studios to meet Denis. I wanted to verify with Elissa that she would be there, so the three of us headed up the curving staircase to her studio on the second floor.

"I'm so glad you came by," Elissa said when she saw us. She was wearing a gray paint smock and standing near a tall, blank canvas. The room was filled with beautiful paintings of the lake and the dunes, paint supplies, and a table full of different-sized brushes. "I've got a surprise to show you. But first let me take you up to Denis's playroom."

We followed her to a large, sunny room on the third floor. The room had a big TV monitor on one wall, a bright orange vinyl sofa against the wall opposite the TV, and a card table and chairs beneath a large window that looked out onto the backyard and lake.

Denis was seated on the sofa holding a Game Boy. "Niko," he called, "come here."

"The boys will be fine up there," Elissa said as we started back downstairs. "I'll check on them periodically, and don't worry about picking Niko up. I'll bring him back before supper. Now, let me show you my latest painting."

She opened the door of a storage closet in her art studio and brought out a five-foot-tall canvas. "I just finished it," she said, turning it to face us. And there on the canvas was a beautiful, full-color rendering of the statue of Athena, her arm outstretched in greeting, just like the statue at Spencer's.

"It's gorgeous," I exclaimed in awe.

Case moved in for a closer look. "You painted this?"

"I took photographs of your statue and painted it from the photos," she said, her face glowing with pride. "I'm going to auction it off at the art auction next Saturday. We're featuring the painting as the star of the show."

"I'll be sure to put the word out," I told her. "How much would a painting like this normally sell for?"

Elissa turned to study the painting. The detail was stunning. "I've never painted anything like it," she said, "but it's one of my finest works. It should fetch a pretty penny."

"I would hope so," I said. "It's enchanting."

The Warrior Goddess stood tall and proud, and there was an expression on her face even more detailed and determined than that of the actual statue. I was once again reminded of my namesake, which filled me with a sense of pride and much-needed motivation.

Case and I left the Studios and headed across town to the area of the big-box stores. We pulled into Jumbo-Mart's enormous parking lot and looked for a place to park, but the store was so busy we ended up at the far end of a row.

"Have you ever been here before?" Case asked as we walked toward the building.

"Not once. I'm almost ashamed to say this, but my mother does most of the grocery shopping at our house. Her castle, her rules kind of thing."

When the double glass doors swished open, we walked inside and stared around in awe. Groceries, fresh produce, clothing, home furnishings, outdoor furniture, and appliances were all packed into a huge industrial warehouse, with customers swarming everywhere. I'd never seen such a gigantic beehive of activity.

"Excuse me, may I see your membership card?" a young man just inside the door asked.

"We're just here to see your store manager, Mr. Clifford," I said.

He pointed behind him. "Step over to the service counter. They'll help you there."

We did as he suggested and spoke with a young woman, who said, "Let me see if he's in."

While she picked up a phone to make the call, Case nudged my arm and looked up at the security camera slowly shifting in our direction. "Looks like we're being watched."

I glanced around and saw security cameras everywhere. Way across the floor on the second level, I could see a wall of one-way glass mirrors indicative of a security department. They weren't taking any chances with safety.

"Mr. Clifford is out right now," the young woman said as she hung up the phone.

"Do you know when he'll be back?" Case asked.

"No," she said. "I'm sorry."

"Don't you two leave just yet," an elderly woman broke in, her bright blue eyes alive with enthusiasm. As thin as a rail, with curly white hair, she wore a bright yellow JumboMart smock over a pair of brown slacks. "Why don't I give you a visitor's pass so you can tour the store? I'll even show you around. I highly recommend it."

She seemed to be signaling something with her eyes, as though she really wanted to talk to us.

"That would be great," I said, just as Case said, "That won't be necessary."

"Come on, honey," I said, looping my arm through Case's. "It'll be interesting."

"Interesting again?" he asked quietly.

"You have to admit, we've been curious about Jumbo-Mart."

He lowered his eyebrows, as if to say, *Do you* really *want to take a tour?*

"Come with me," the woman said, and we started off on our tour. While our guide narrated, I walked around looking at the selection of bulk goods, wondering what she'd been signaling. It wasn't until she led us to a back hallway that I found out.

In a whisper, she asked, "Are you investigating Mr. Clifford?"

Her question stunned us both.

"You're the Goddess of Greene Street, are you not?" she asked. "You solved Harry Pepper's murder."

"Yes, I'm Athena Spencer, and this is my partner, Case Donnelly."

She shook our hands. "My name is Jessie Mae Farmer, and I'm something of a novice sleuth myself. It's a pleasure to meet you."

"Thank you," I said. "But what makes you think we're investigating Beau Clifford?"

"You didn't hear it from me, but you're not the first ones to come looking for him."

"The police were here?" I asked.

She wrinkled her nose. "Heavens, no. But a few weeks ago, a man—a very big man, mind you—huge black trench coat and dark glasses, came around asking for Mr. Clifford. He gave me the shivers. They met up in his office, behind that glass up there." She pointed up at the tinted windows. "Afterward, Mr. Clifford came out looking as pale as a ghost.

"I couldn't figure out at first what the meeting was about, but, as I said, I'm something of a novice sleuth. My friends used to call me Jessica Fletcher, would you believe? I even solved the case of the cheating husband. Some of my finest work. Then I divorced him." She laughed at her own joke.

"What was the meeting about?" I asked, trying to get her back on track.

"Let's see what you think," she said with a wink. "The same day that Mr. Clifford met with the big man, our deposit was off by four hundred dollars. Now, what do you suppose that means?"

"I don't know," I said. I glanced at Case, and he gave me a dubious look, as if to say, *Is this woman being helpful, or is she off a bubble?*

"You couldn't know," she said with a lift of her eyebrows. "You need the final clue."

"And what's the final clue?" Case asked, clearly just humoring her. I could only imagine what he was going to say about her later.

"The final clue came after he called me up to his office and gave me a lecture on how to balance my drawer at night. Now, I've been working a register for as long as I can remember. I don't need a lecture on how to balance a drawer, and I certainly don't need the money. That's what

I told him. But who else could he blame it on? I'm the old lady, the elderly nutjob, or so he'd have everyone believe. But I know what I saw, and I know I'm not too old to figure out what was going on.

"The final clue was right there in front of my eyes. He tried to hide it, but I caught it, right there on his computer screen. No wonder the four hundred went missing, I thought. No wonder the big guy came calling. And never in a million years would I have suspected him of it."

CHAPTER TWELVE

"Horse racing?" Case asked.

"That was my first reaction," Jessie Mae said. "Horse racing? Was that what he was doing up in his office all day? So I used my head. I waited until Mr. Clifford was gone and came back up to take a look at his computer. Sure enough, he gambles. And what do you think that tall man in the black coat was here for? To collect on a gambling debt is what I figured. Mr. Clifford stole money to pay down his gambling debt and then tried to blame it on me. I'm surprised I wasn't fired."

"Actually, Mrs. Fletcher—" Case said.

"Farmer. Jessie Mae Farmer."

"Mrs. Farmer," Case continued, "your story is interesting—"

"And exactly what we needed to know," I said. "Now,

would you do us another favor and take a look at a photo?"

I pulled the manila envelope out of my tote bag and took out the picture of Pete Harmon with Tom Silvester. "Do you recognize either of these men?"

She shook her head. "Never seen them before. The man who came looking for Mr. Clifford was built like a huge stone statue. And he didn't have a beard or mustache."

I put the photo away, then took her hand in mine and patted it. "Mrs. Farmer, you've been very helpful. We can't thank you enough for the information you've provided."

Jessie Mae beamed with pride. "And you don't need to say a word about keeping this to myself. I know how these investigations work. I'm just delighted that I could help."

We followed her back up the long hallway, then cut through the huge store and exited to the parking lot. Case was grumbling under his breath as we got into the Jeep, muttering about wasting our time.

"It wasn't a complete waste of time," I said. "We learned something about Beau that could explain why he would take Pete Harmon's bribe money."

"We need a motive for murder, not thievery. We still don't know if Hugo was blackmailing Beau. We're going to have to come back when we're sure Beau is at the store."

"They open at ten a.m." I said. "Let's do it tomorrow."

"I have to take a test tomorrow morning."

No wonder he was being a big grouch.

Case's phone dinged. He took it out of his pocket and

read the text message. "It's from Lila. She's at the office, and she has information for us."

I checked the time. "I have less than an hour before I have to be at Harmon Oil for the protest rally."

"That should be plenty of time to talk to her."

When we arrived at the office, Lila was sitting in Case's chair, twirling one long lock of blond hair, a satisfied smile on her face. Wearing a sequined turquoise T-shirt with white capris and white high-heeled sandals, she rose at once and came to give us hugs.

"You're going to be so happy when you find out what I've been up to," she said. "As I mentioned before, I am a very well-connected woman, and one of those connections happens to be someone who does business with Pete Harmon. That someone, whom I promised would remain confidential, happened to know that Harmon was, in fact, at the dunes with a surveyor when the festival was going on."

Case and I stared at each other as Lila beamed. "I knew that would shock you."

It not only shocked me, it made me happy. Now we had someone else with the means and opportunity. But did he have a motive?

"And I'm not done," Lila said. "I spoke with someone at the surveyor's office and found out that Pete is going to have a surveyor stake out the new buildings he's planning next week. Is he confident or what?"

"How did you get the information?" I asked.

"It's called money, darling," she said. "I slipped a woman at the surveyor's office a nice chunk of it, and she spilled the beans happily." Lila brushed her hands together. "That's how it's done."

I was more than annoyed by Lila's free use of her money, but I knew what Case would say: *You can't argue with results.*

"Now, how else can I help?" Lila asked.

Case glanced at me. "You wanted to interview Beau Clifford at JumboMart tomorrow at ten. Why don't you take Lila with you? It'll be a good experience for her."

I would have gladly throttled Case at that moment. "I don't think she has *enough* experience, Case. You know how tricky those interviews can be."

"I'll let you do all the talking," Lila said. "I'll just be there as a distraction." She glanced from me to Case and back to me. "Come on. It'll be fun."

Just like the protest march hadn't been.

"Okay," I said. "Be ready at nine thirty tomorrow morning."

By three thirty, Spencer's had quieted down enough that I was able to leave to go to Pete Harmon's press conference, which Elissa had told me about. When I arrived, a group of protesters had already gathered, and as before, some were standing by a table handing out signs and others were already walking back and forth in front of the main gates. I noticed a much larger crowd standing around the podium. The news van was there again, as was Charlie Bolt from the *Sequoian Press*, but they were no longer focusing their cameras on the protest.

"What's going on?" I asked Elissa as I approached the table.

She gave me a pained look. "I'm worried. With all the negative press about Pearson in the news, I'm afraid our movement is losing steam."

"Don't give up yet," I told her. "It's still early in the investigation."

At four o'clock, Pete Harmon, wearing a pale gray suit and tie, and accompanied by a team of well-dressed men, strode out to the podium in front of the building and tapped on the microphones that had been set up. A crowd had gathered in front of the podium along with several news reporters and a cameraman from the local TV station. I stepped away from the protest marchers, who had begun to chant, "No harmin' the lakefront," and made my way through the congested crowd.

"Good afternoon," he began with a smile. "As you may have heard, Harmon Oil Company will soon be offering this community a chance for real growth and opportunity."

He was roundly booed by the marchers, but the noise was quickly drowned out by the raucous roar of cheers from the crowd around me.

"Thank you," Pete said. "Now, let me tell you about plans to make a lakefront parcel of land shine like the diamond it is. Imagine a beautiful marina, with a wide expanse of boardwalk running the length of it, where people can stroll along and view the boats that will be moored in the modern slips. Imagine a state-of-the-art refueling station, where all of you boat owners can go to fill up your engines any time day or evening."

I lifted my hand to get his attention but was swallowed up by a frenzy of waving arms and clapping hands.

"Imagine an attractive, low-profile, sandstone building, fully landscaped, on the far edge of the property, where Harmon Oil will soon be headquartered. And imagine all the money the city will collect on the taxes for these new ventures. Then, if you will, imagine new computers in the high school and middle school. Imagine all the happy students and their parents. And last but not least, imagine the eyesore that is now Parcel Ninety-Five, banished forever."

At that he got a huge round of applause.

"Do you mean you won't be asking for any tax incentives from the city?" I called out.

"We don't get tax incentives now," he retorted with a smile. "Why should we start?"

His comment got a smattering of laughs and more applause.

"Are you saying you won't ask for them?" I called.

He ignored me. Then someone else called, "Why don't you spend money restoring the dunes to their natural beauty instead of making them uglier?"

Yet another person called, "Why destroy something that should be for the people of this city purely for profits?"

"Why continue to let this area rot," Pete replied, "when we could be creating hundreds of jobs?"

"Hundreds?" I called out. "Explain how."

"That property is ripe for redevelopment," he continued, "and I'm the man to do it."

His supporters clapped harder, the cheers grew louder, and my attempts to further my questioning were completely washed out. Unlike the Talbot press conference where I was able to make a stand, spread a message, and even force my way to the table, Pete Harmon was unaffected by the opposition. He seemed to revel in it.

"Please continue to show your support when the city council votes on my bid to purchase the land," he said.

Another round of applause had me trying to get nearer to the podium.

"Thank you," he said abruptly, and, with his little sup-

port group, strode back inside the building before he had
to answer any questions.

"It was a less-than-satisfactory press conference," I
told Case as I drove back to Spencer's. "Pete painted a
pretty picture but wouldn't answer any questions. The
crowd loved it. He's getting way more support than I'd
expected."

"I'm not surprised. It's possible he packed the conference with supporters."

"That's so not fair."

"Does that surprise you?"

"It shouldn't," I answered. "Have you discovered anything new in the notes?"

"Not yet. I've been studying since I got home. Do you
want to go over questions for Beau this evening, same
time, same place?"

"I'm meeting Marylou at seven at the coffee shop. I'll
come over afterward."

"I'll have wine at the ready."

I had so much going on that I left work at six o'clock
that evening, leaving Dad, Delphi, and Drew to handle
Spencer's. Fortunately, there wasn't much activity after
six. When I arrived home, Nicholas greeted me, fairly
bouncing with happiness.

"We had a great time, Mom. Denis has such cool
games. Mrs. Reed even let us paint on easels. I'm painting a picture of Oscar. But one thing was very strange.
When I asked Denis if we should put the games away before we left, he said I wasn't allowed to go into the closet,
like he was afraid I'd take something."

"I'm sure he didn't mean that," I said, ruffling his hair.

"Well, it kind of hurt my feelings. I wouldn't have said that to him."

"That's because I did such a spectacular job of raising you."

He rolled his eyes. "Anyway, Denis wants to come over to Spencer's Friday afternoon to play with Oscar. Is that okay?"

Delphi stuck her head into the bedroom. "Athena, can I see you for a moment?"

I was surprised to see her home so early. I held up a finger to signal for her to wait. "Niko, my answer is yes. Denis can come over. Now I need to talk to Aunt Delphi. Go wash your hands before dinner."

"Sorry," Delphi said. "I didn't mean to chase Niko out, but it's kind of an emergency." She glanced back at the door to make sure no one was there, then said in a whisper, "I want to go out with Bobby this evening, but I don't want Mama to know. Can you help me?"

"I'm supposed to meet a friend at Jivin' Java's at seven o'clock, so you could say you're coming with me. Do you remember Marylou Porter from school?"

"Vaguely. But what reason would I use to come with you?"

"I seem to remember that Marylou has a sister your age, so let's say we're going to meet up with them."

"Does she really have a sister my age?"

"She could have."

Delphi smiled. "That'll work." She threw her arms around me and gave me a hug. "Thank you, Thenie."

"You're welcome. Now let's go eat dinner."

* * *

At seven o'clock that evening, Delphi and I entered Jivin' Java's coffee shop and glanced around at the tables. Seated on the other side of the room, Marylou waved at me.

"Okay, I made my appearance," Delphi said. "I'm going to take off now."

"Don't be late tonight, or you'll get the third degree from Mama."

Delphi looked alarmed. "She'll know something's up when we don't come home together."

"Not necessarily. Remember, we Spencers are good storytellers. So let's say I have to meet Case when I'm done here to work on an interview I have tomorrow, and you're going to hang out with Marylou's sister named—"

Delphi smiled. "Marlene."

"Okay, her sister Marlene, until, say, ten o'clock?"

"That works for me." She glanced back at the door and smiled. "Here's Bobby now."

"Tell him I said hi."

After Delphi left the coffee shop, I slipped between the crowded tables to the coffee bar along the side of the shop and placed my order for two coffees. When they were ready, I walked back to Marylou's table and set the cups down. "Thanks for meeting me."

"Thanks for the coffee," Marylou said with a smile. "So, what is the Goddess of Greene Street up to?"

I sat down across from her. "It seems I can't escape my new title."

"Why would you want to? I've seen several of the old gang from school, and we're all very proud of you. So what are you working on now? The photographer's murder?"

I took the lid off my coffee and blew on it to cool it down. "I'm looking into it for a friend."

"And how can I help?"

"I wondered if you'd noticed anything at the festival Saturday morning that I might have missed. When you went down to the woods for the nature walk, did you see anyone besides our group near the trail?"

"There were a lot of people walking around. I wasn't really paying attention."

"Was there anything that stood out?

She sipped her coffee. "When my husband and I went down to the shoreline a little earlier, I saw two men talking together well past the *No Trespassing* sign, and neither of them matched the description of the photographer who was in the newspaper."

I didn't have the iPad with me, so I made notes on my phone. "Would you describe the men for me?"

"One was tall and had a black mustache. He had on a tan shirt with black pants. The other one had dark hair and a beard and was dressed very casually in a T-shirt and shorts."

Using my phone, I did an internet search for Pete Harmon and found a photo of him. "Does this look like the man with the beard?"

She leaned over for a closer look. "Yes. That's him! He has a devilish sort of face. I'd know it anywhere."

"You just identified Pete Harmon, owner of Harmon Oil." I did a search for Tom Silvester and found a grainy photo from an old newspaper article. "Does this look like the other man?"

"Like a younger version maybe, but it's the same mustache."

"You said they were talking?"

"They were until they saw me watching them, and then they moved away. I didn't pay any attention to them after that, so I can't tell you what they did next."

"That's okay," I said, returning to my notes. "This is very helpful. And I have one more favor to ask. If I need you to go to the police station and give a statement about seeing Pete Harmon at the festival, would you do it?"

"I'd be glad to."

We spent another half hour catching up, then went our separate ways. I headed down to the marina, where the *Pamé* was docked, to talk to Case.

"You've got a big smile on your face," he said when he let me in, "so I'm assuming your meeting was productive."

"It was." I hung my purse on the back of a kitchen chair and sat down. The tiny kitchen table was loaded with books, study guides, and notepads. The long, narrow counter was filled with much of the same. Only the kitchen sink was visible—barely—stacked with ceramic bowls and dirty silverware. "Looks like you've been productive, as well."

"I haven't studied this hard since college finals," Case said, trying to clean off a spot at the table for me. "And I'm still way behind the other guys in class."

"You'll do just fine," I said.

"I don't have the same level of experience," he told me, sitting down at the table, "which puts me at a disadvantage."

"But you have me," I teased, "and a pretty good track record so far."

Case leaned over and gave me a kiss. His hand came up and caressed the back of my neck, pulling me in deeper. That's when his phone beeped.

"Pizza's on the way," he said, which effectively ended the romantic moment. "Would you like to have dinner with me?"

"Thanks, but I've already eaten."

"No problem. How was the meeting with Marylou?"

"I'm glad you thought of talking to her, because it paid off. She saw Pete Harmon down by the lake on Saturday morning talking with a man who fit the description of Tom Silvester."

Case stood while I was talking and began to rummage through his cabinets. "You're kidding."

"Nope. That means we now have two eyewitnesses, one for Pete and Tom, and another for Tom alone, and both are willing to talk to the detectives."

"Perfect." He brought a bottle of wine to the table and poured two glasses. Picking one up, he held it up. "Here's to progress."

We clinked glasses and sipped the wine. "Speaking of progress," I said, "have you made any?"

"Unfortunately, no. But once I take this test, I'll be able to concentrate more on the case."

"And hopefully I'll learn something when I talk to Beau tomorrow."

Case got the iPad and pulled a chair around next to mine. "Let's review the questions I put together."

As I read down his list, he pointed to one. "Forget asking about his gambling addiction. I don't want to get Mrs. Farmer fired."

"But we need to establish a reason for him to take the bribe money."

"It's too risky, Athena. You're going to have to work around it. And don't forget to pick Lila up at nine thirty tomorrow morning."

"Work around that, work around Lila . . ." I let out a heavy sigh.

"It won't be that bad," Case said.

"Really? Then after our interview, I'll have Lila come over and help you study. How does that sound?"

"Cruel and unusual."

"Exactly. That's why I want you to promise not to force Lila on me anymore."

Case leaned in to kiss me, but I dodged him.

"Promise, Case," I said.

"Only if you promise to stay after I have a bite to eat."

"Don't you have to study?"

"I've done nothing *but* study. I need an Athena break."

That I could get on board with.

When Lila walked out of her house Thursday morning, I was tempted to step on the gas and speed away. Never one to dress conservatively, she had outdone herself. With her blond hair bouncing over her shoulders, she wore a skintight baby-blue knit dress with cutout shoulders and matching spike heels that would've tipped me over.

"Don't look so shocked," she said as she climbed daintily into my SUV. "This outfit is relatively conservative."

"We need to portray ourselves as professionals, Lila."

"Oh, come on. Lighten up."

Lighten up? "Men make fools of themselves over a sexy woman, Lila, and I need solid answers from Beau, not mumblings from a drooling idiot."

"You'll get your answers. Just stand back and watch me work."

I grumbled to myself all the way to JumboMart, then had to sit in the parking lot telling Lila about Jessie Mae Farmer, what we'd learned from her, and what information we could and could not use. Then I had to explain what Lila was to do, which was basically to smile any time Beau looked at her. "In other words, distract him," I said.

"I know what to do," she said. "Let's go, partner."

CHAPTER THIRTEEN

When we stepped inside JumboMart, Lila was not awed. Lila had been there before. She even had a membership card.

"Come on," she said. "I know the way to the offices."

She led me across the store and up a hallway to an elevator that we took to the second floor. We stopped outside Beau Clifford's office, and Lila knocked on the door. Hearing, "Come in," she opened the door and walked in, with me trailing behind like her assistant.

Beau was seated before a computer monitor, but upon seeing two women striding toward him, he stood up immediately. Dressed in a green plaid button-down shirt and jeans, his light brown hair parted on one side and combed back, he appeared to be about forty years old.

"Mr. Clifford," Lila announced. She walked straight up to his desk and offered her hand. "Lila Talbot, Talbot

Enterprises. And this is Athena Spencer, my partner at the Greene Street Detective Agency."

Beau's mouth opened in astonishment, his gaze traveling from her face down her body and up again before darting over to me. As though dumbstruck, he asked, "How can I help you?"

"Mr. Clifford," I said, stepping forward, "I'm investigating Hugo Lukan's murder—"

"*We're* investigating Hugo Lukan's murder," Lila corrected. She turned to smile at me, clearly ignoring my warning look. "Go ahead."

"Wait just a minute," Beau said, sitting down. "I don't know Hugo Lukan. I've never so much as spoken to the man."

"Well, he certainly knew you." Lila snapped her fingers at me. "Athena, photos."

I'd get even with Case for this. Pressing my lips together, I took the manila folder out of my tote bag and pulled out the photo of Beau and Pete. I placed it on the desk in front of Beau and waited until he'd looked at it.

"What's going on?" he asked, glancing up at me in shock. "Where did this come from?"

"This is a photo Hugo took before he was murdered," I said.

"I don't understand."

"Hugo was looking into a conspiracy within the city council," I said, "and wanted my partner Case Donnelly's help. He sent several photos to Case in that regard, and yours was one of them."

He seemed confused. "A conspiracy?"

"That's what he called it," I said. "And from what we've learned, that conspiracy involves Pete Harmon buying your vote for the duneland project."

Beau looked down again at the photo, his mouth open as if to speak, but no words came out. He seemed to be in shock.

"Let me ask you this," I said. "Did you take the money Pete offered you?"

He held out his hands as though to pause the interview. "Look, I don't know you, and I don't appreciate being questioned like this. If you want answers, go see Mr. Harmon. That's all I have to say."

"Are we to assume, then, that you will be voting *against* Harmon on the lakeside project?" Lila asked, surprising not only Beau but me, as well.

"How I vote is none of your business," he retorted.

Looking perturbed, Lila folded her arms beneath her breasts and pushed them up to catch his attention. "Are you married, Beau?"

He quickly refocused his gaze on her face. "What does that have to do with it?"

"Do you have children?" Lila asked.

"I am happily married with two daughters."

Lila smiled. "Wouldn't your kids love a big, beautiful park with a sandy beach and forest trails?"

"Of course, they would."

"Then you'll vote against the Harmon Oil project," she said.

"I didn't say that," he replied. "You don't understand the tax benefits and additional school funding the Harmon Oil project will bring."

Lila placed both hands on his desk and leaned toward him. "Are you aware of a tax loophole that has been exploited by the Harmon Oil Company that would eliminate up to eighty-five percent of those funds?"

Clearly Lila had done some homework. I stood back and waited for his response.

Beau wiped sweat from his forehead and sank back in his chair. "I'm not saying another word."

Lila leaned over, closer to him. "Beau," she said softly, "it's in your best interest to talk to us. We know about the bribe."

He folded his arms over his shirt and glared at her.

Lila glanced at me, her eyebrows pulled together, like she couldn't believe her method wasn't working. She lifted her shoulders with a huff, as though he was a hopeless cause.

Time for me to step in and get the interview back on track. I picked up the photo and held it up in front of him. "I've already shown this to the police, so it's just a matter of time before they come knocking on your door."

"This is ridiculous," he said in a tight voice. "I joined the city council to make a difference for my kids. I never wanted to be involved in all this nonsense."

"You're already involved." I took out the other two black-and-white pictures and laid them on his desk. "You, Pearson Reed, and Tom Silvester are all implicated in Pete Harmon's plan to buy your votes."

As he stared at the photos in surprise, I finally felt like I had the upper hand. "Tell us what you know about the bribery scheme."

Beau got to his feet. "Take these pictures and leave before I call security."

He was visibly shaking, and I could tell it wouldn't take much to convince him to confess. All he needed was one final push. I just had to work around the gambling matter.

"Look, we need your help," I said. "I can tell you're not a bad guy. You got in way over your head, and now you need a way out. Let us help you. Tell us the truth and help us find Hugo's killer. We know it's related to Pete Harmon and the money he offered you."

"Sorry," he said defiantly. "I can't help you."

Lila gave him a knowing smile. "I'll bet you did take that money."

His Adam's apple bobbed as he swallowed. "Excuse me?"

"You're a betting man, aren't you?"

Lila, no.

Beau just stared at her.

She toyed with a diamond ring on her finger. "I'm guessing you've lost enough money on your gambling habit to make Pete's offer quite attractive."

Beau's mouth fell open as he dropped back into his chair. "My *gambling* habit? Where did you get that idea?"

"I'll bet if I searched your internet history right now," Lila said, "it wouldn't be long before I found a gambling website. Is that a bet you'd like to take?"

He glanced at his monitor, and his face flushed with embarrassment. "How did you—Where did you get that information?"

My thoughts raced back to Jessie Mae Farmer. I crossed my fingers and said a prayer that Lila wouldn't reveal her name.

Lila kept talking. "Don't worry about what we know or how we know it," she said. "Just answer our questions, and no one else has to know."

"There's a lot of information to be had on the web," I added, "and our partner, Case Donnelly, is an expert inter-

net researcher. We know more about you than you realize."

Lila looked at me as though she were impressed, and I
returned the glance. It was impromptu and clumsy, but
we were actually working as a team.

"What do you want from me?" he asked in a desperate
voice.

Although she had jumped the gun, Lila's tactic had
worked. "We want straight answers," I said.

"What more can I tell you?"

I opened the iPad and pulled up the list of questions.
"Tell me about Pete Harmon."

"I don't know what else to say. He wanted my vote. He
offered me cash."

"How much?" I asked.

After a moment's hesitation, Beau said ashamedly,
"Twenty-five thousand."

"Did you take it?"

Beau dropped his head into his hands. "If I'd had any
idea that I would get involved in all this mess, I never
would've run for city councilman." He paused to take a
deep breath, then looked up. "If I talk, you have to drop
this whole gambling matter. Not a word about it to anyone. I'll get help, I promise, but if my wife finds out, I'll
be out on the street."

"Tell us the truth, and we won't tell your wife," Lila
said immediately.

"Did you take the bribe from Pete Harmon?" I asked
again.

He looked down in shame. "I had to. I was drowning
in debt."

"Was the money exchanged specifically for your
vote?" I asked.

He nodded, and I noted it on the iPad. "Did anyone else on the council take money from Harmon that you know of?"

"Yes."

"Who?"

"Tom Silvester and Pearson Reed."

My stomach dropped. Pearson had lied again? "Did they actually tell you they took the money?"

"No, but I heard them arguing about it."

I typed that into my notes. "Do you remember their conversation?"

"Not word for word. And they stopped arguing when I joined them."

"Did you hear Pearson say he took the bribe money?" I asked.

"Words to that effect."

I typed this in with a big exclamation point at the end. I didn't want to believe it, but Pearson was still a suspect. I was trying to gather my thoughts when Beau continued.

"One more thing," he said. "Tom Silvester made it clear that I was not to mention it to the remaining two council members."

"Do you have any idea why they weren't offered money, too?"

"They've been very vocal at the meetings about the lakefront land remaining a city park. You should ask Pearson about them. He knows more than I do."

"Was Pete Harmon at that council meeting?"

"Yes. He's been attending them for at least the last three months."

"Were you ever contacted by email or mail and asked for money to keep your photo off the internet?"

"Absolutely not."

"Did Hugo ever ask to talk to you in private or ask to help you in any way?"

Beau gazed off into the distance as though he was searching his memory. "He left a bunch of messages for me, but I never called him back."

I was at the end of the list. "Were you at the art fair last Saturday?"

"No. I had to take my girls to a soccer game that day."

"Can anyone verify that you were at the game?"

"My wife, my kids, the neighbors . . . Please, believe me. I was there." Looking more like a little boy than a store manager, he put his hands over his face. "I can't believe I'm mixed up in this. I just want it to go away."

Although I didn't fully trust him, I felt bad for the man.

"What do I tell the police if they come to see me?" Beau asked.

"I suggest you tell them the truth," I said, "and reconsider your vote."

"It's too late for that," he said in a defeated voice. "I accepted the money."

"Pay it back," Lila said.

He shook his head. "I can't."

"If you vote no," I said, "there's nothing Pete Harmon can do about it."

He laughed dryly. "You don't know Pete Harmon."

"Then you'll have to live with your conscience." I pulled out one of Case's business cards. "If you think of anything else that will help our investigation, please contact us."

We left Beau looking shaken and wan. As soon as we were outside his office, Lila gave me a high five.

"You were terrific," she said as we walked toward the elevator.

"You did very well yourself. How did you find out about the tax loophole?"

She laughed and draped her arm around me. "Darling, anyone with a computer can be an expert researcher. Besides, I have connections and know how to make people talk."

"Now if only we could make Pete Harmon talk."

"Let me work on it," Lila said with a wink.

We both stepped into the elevator. Even though Lila was a spoiled drama queen, I was starting to believe that if anyone could get Harmon to talk, she could.

I didn't hear from Case until after lunch, when he called to find out how our interview went. I stepped into the garden center's office and closed the door.

"First things first," I said. "How was your test?"

"Difficult, but I think I aced it. I should get the results by Friday. Now, put me out of my misery and tell me how Lila did."

"She surprised me, Case. She actually came through."

"That's a relief. I worried all morning."

"Believe me, so did I."

Case laughed. "So, tell me what you learned from Beau."

"He had an alibi for the morning of the festival. I haven't talked to his wife or his neighbors to verify it, but I do believe he was at his kids' soccer game. And surprisingly, he said he didn't receive any threatening letters, so he didn't know anything about his photo until I showed him."

"If you can trust that he was telling the truth."

"True, although his reaction was completely believable. And I think he would have told me if he'd received any blackmail threats. But the most shocking information he gave me was that all three of them, including Pearson, took Pete Harmon's bribe money."

"I tried to warn you about Pearson."

"*If* what Beau said is true," I said. "For what it's worth, we have only his word on it."

"You believed Beau's alibi."

He had me there.

"If Beau's information is correct," Case said, "then Pearson lied to us. There's no way we can trust him going forward."

"I'm going to go see him, Case, and tell him what I heard. Maybe he can explain it."

"You can try."

"I have to try."

"What's your feeling about keeping Beau on the suspect list?" Case asked.

"I'd put him at the bottom. He has an alibi that we can test, and if he's telling the truth about the photo, he didn't have a motive for murder."

"That leaves us with Tom, Pearson, and Pete."

"I still think there's an explanation for Pearson. And we haven't figured out what part Jewel played in all this, either."

"Athena," Drew said, sticking his head into the office, "can you come help on the sales floor? We're getting a rush."

"I have to go, Case. I'll call you after I talk to Pearson."

I spent the rest of the afternoon working at Spencer's

and didn't think about Hugo or Pearson until I took Nicholas home for supper that evening, and then I couldn't quit thinking about them. If I could've, I would have gone to see Pearson that evening, but I knew it would raise red flags in Elissa's mind, and I didn't want to do that. I finally decided to go the next morning as soon as my office work was finished.

I had just sat down on my bed with my laptop to write my blog that evening when my sister Maia tapped on the door frame. "Hey, are you busy?"

"Nope. Come in."

She came in with her laptop open and sat beside me. "I found out something I thought you'd find helpful. Hugo Lukan's third wife, Carrie, has a very interesting post on Facebook. Check it out."

I set my computer aside and put hers on my lap. There, on her screen, in all-capital letters, it read, *I HATE MY EX*, and then went on to ask if anyone could help her get rid of him. She finished with a few laughing emojis, but the post was anything but funny.

"How did you hear about this?" I asked.

"One of our yoga instructors told me about it. Carrie Lukan used to work at Zen Garden. She didn't last long, though. No one liked her very much. Anyway, you might want to check it out."

I scrolled down through the comments. Apparently, her friends didn't think the post was a joke, either. The most recent comments were people telling her to take the post down, out of respect. Earlier comments were full of suggestions on how to dispose of a body, how to poison someone, how to create an alibi, and so on. Carrie commented back with thumbs-up on almost every single reply.

"Wow," I said as I read through the comments, "she really hated Hugo."

I scrolled down through old posts. For a while her Facebook page was devoted to him, then it turned ugly. She had basically catalogued every wrong he'd ever done to her.

"She even posted a picture of him with his eyes blacked out," Maia said. "What do you think?"

"It looks like it started as pure fantasy," I said. "But why would she leave this up if she actually killed Hugo?"

"I don't know. But Carrie does have a boyfriend—and look at this comment."

"'Let your boyfriend do the dirty work,'" I read. "I'll check into it. Thanks for letting me know."

Late Friday morning, I sat down across from Pearson at his desk at the printing company and began to lay out the dilemma for him.

"Do you remember a conversation that you, Tom Silvester, and Beau Clifford had at the end of the last council meeting regarding Pete Harmon's bribe?"

Pearson's cheeks flamed crimson. "I . . . remember something about it."

"Do you remember telling Beau that you'd accepted the bribe?"

"That's wrong. I never said I'd accepted it."

"I just want to confirm with you that you didn't take the money."

"Athena, I need you to help me. Why would I lie to you?"

"I don't know. Maybe because you're afraid I'll say something to Elissa."

Pearson shook his head. "No, I have no secrets from my wife. And just so you know, in my fifteen years as city council president, I've never accepted a bribe, and I certainly wouldn't accept it at the detriment of SOD. Beau simply heard me wrong. Pete offered me money, but I didn't take it."

"Okay, I'll take your word for it. If you don't mind, I have a few more questions from my interview with Beau."

Pearson sighed and rubbed his forehead. "You understand that Beau Clifford is not the most reliable of sources."

"Pearson, you haven't been the most reliable, either. You've kept the truth from us on more than one occasion, even though we're doing this investigation as a favor to you and your wife."

"I thought you were investigating the murder," he countered, "but it seems like you're more interested in picking up where Hugo left off."

"It's all connected," I said. "I can't help you without knowing the truth about the bribes. If you were involved in dealings with Pete Harmon, I need to know right now."

"It's true I've kept a few things from you, but it was to help keep your investigation focused. I'm not a murderer. How else can I prove that to you?"

"I believe you, Pearson. But I need your absolute honesty going forward."

"You've got it," Pearson said.

"What are your thoughts on the other two city council members, the ones not photographed by Hugo, as far as the bribery is concerned?"

"As far as I know, they were never offered money."

"That's what Beau thought, due to their vocal stance

on the city keeping the lakefront property. Is that a fair assessment?"

"Yes. They've been behind the Save Our Dunes group ever since it formed."

"Were they at the Art in the Park festival?" I asked.

"No, they couldn't make it. I can vouch for that. And I'm sure Pete Harmon knew it would be futile to approach them."

"Then, why did he approach you? You and Elissa started Save Our Dunes."

Again, his cheeks colored. "That's a good question. I wish I had an answer for you."

I wished he had an answer, too. As it stood, I felt very conflicted. I wanted to believe him, but it still felt like he was hiding something from me.

"Is there anything else I can help you with?" Pearson asked.

"No," I said, standing. "That's all I wanted to know. Thanks for seeing me."

"Want to meet at the pizza truck for lunch?" I asked Case on the phone as I walked back to Spencer's.

"Can't," he said. "I'm waiting for a delivery. Why don't you stop at the deli for sandwiches? I have some good news to share."

"How exciting! I'll see you in an hour."

Shortly after noon, I stopped outside the deli and glanced up to where our sign was going to hang, trying to imagine it in the empty space. I felt a spark of excitement run up my spine at the thought of it. The spark fizzled just a little, however, when I noticed Lila's silver Tesla parked in front of the deli. Even though she was beginning to prove herself as a worthy member of our team, I still had my reservations about her.

Taking the high road, I bought three ham-and-cheese sandwiches and bottles of water and took them upstairs, where I found Case spreading all four photos out on the desk for Lila to study. She looked surprised when I offered her one of the sandwiches.

"You got this for me?" she asked. "Thank you."

It was a short, surprising pause in her heiress routine, and for a split second I could see traces of humility as she accepted the food. Buying her a sandwich had been only a simple gesture of goodwill, but I could tell she appreciated it. The high road felt pretty fine.

Lila unwrapped her sandwich and took a small bite, then tapped Jewel's photo. "How does this Jewel person fit into the picture?"

"We don't know," Case said. "She wasn't much help when we interviewed her. We know she was a friend of Hugo's, and she works for Pete Harmon."

"Then maybe she can tell you how to get Pete to talk to you," Lila said.

Case and I looked at each other. "We tried that," I said.

"Well, I haven't tried." Lila wiped the corners of her mouth with a napkin. "Anyway, what was the good news you said you had to share, Case?"

"My exam results came back," Case said. "I passed the test. Now I can send in my application for my private detective's license."

"That's a reason to celebrate." I lifted my water bottle. "Here's to the Greene Street Detective Agency becoming a reality."

"Greene Street Detective Agency." Lila bit into her

sandwich and chewed hungrily for a minute. "We have to do something about that name."

Case swallowed his bite and looked at her. "What about the name?"

"It just doesn't have any"—she twirled her finger in the air—"pizzazz."

"Pizzazz?" He looked at me.

I lifted my shoulders in a shrug. He'd been the one who'd wanted to involve Lila. I turned to direct my question at her. "What do you think we should call it"

"Oh, I have some ideas," she said, "but we can discuss that later. What's our next move on this case?"

"Our next move," Case said, clearly caught off guard by the sudden switch in subject. "Athena, you spoke with Pearson. What did he have to say about taking the bribe?"

"He said that Beau heard him wrong. He didn't take the bribe, and he's firmly behind the Save Our Dunes group, which makes sense since he helped form it. He also said the remaining two city council members have been very vocal about being behind SOD at the council meetings, and that would explain why they weren't offered the bribe money."

"But it doesn't explain why Pearson was," Case said.

"I pointed that out to him, but he didn't have an answer. I hate to say this, but the interview wasn't as reassuring as I'd hoped. I left with the feeling that Pearson wasn't being totally forthcoming."

"So, if I have this right," Lila said, "you have one out of three men from the photos who claims that he didn't take the bribe, and you have only his word for it. In my experience with men, I wouldn't trust him."

"I *don't* trust him," Case said. "And I won't until the

murderer is caught. Everyone is a suspect until we can rule them out."

I didn't say a word. It was getting harder and harder to defend Pearson Reed.

"Our next challenge is getting Pete Harmon to talk to us," Case continued. "I did a lot of research on him but wasn't able to come up with much that we can use, surprisingly. He owned and operated a marina up north for fifteen years that he inherited from his father. His father's company, the original Harmon Oil, also owned quite a few gas stations all along the coast. The only thing I could find was that the refueling station and marina went bankrupt. Nothing in the papers or online about why. He's kept a low profile ever since. I've put in a few calls to his office to see if he'd talk to me, but he isn't interested."

"We could talk to Jewel again," I said. "Maybe she can get us in to see him."

"She seemed pretty adamant about staying out of it," Case said. "I'm not holding out much hope for that route."

I finished the last of my sandwich and wiped my hands on a napkin. "Pete can't stop us from showing up at his office."

"You can show up," Lila said, "but that means nothing. Trust me. When my husband didn't want to talk to someone, he made certain they didn't get past the reception desk."

"Then, how do we get to him?" I asked in frustration. "Stalk him like Hugo did?"

"I think I know someone who can help." Lila checked the time on her cell phone. "If you're not busy, we can go see him right now."

"You'll have to go without me." Case balled his napkin up and tossed it into the trash. "I have to wait for the new computer to be delivered."

"That's probably better anyway," Lila said. "It'll be easier to get the two of us in."

I gave her a puzzled glance. "Get us in where?"

Lila popped open her compact and powdered her nose. "Prison," she said to the mirror. "Just wait until my ex sees both of us waiting for him. This will be fun."

CHAPTER FOURTEEN

Lila parked in the visitors' lot and escorted me through the Lakeside Correctional Facility as if it were a home away from home, waving and charming her way through several layers of security before finally entering the visitors' area.

There were a number of tables scattered at random throughout the wide, brightly lit room. Guards stood outside each door, while a separate guard monitored the visitation room from within. Lila sat casually with arms crossed and a mischievous grin on her face. I sat next to her in impatient silence, having nothing to do but twist my hair in curls around my finger. We had both given up our purses and jewelry at the security gate.

Finally, the door buzzed and opened, and a man walked in wearing a bright orange jumpsuit. The image struck

me at once. This formerly stylish, vain man of seemingly
unlimited money and power had been reduced to a pale,
disheveled version of his former self. Grayson Talbot Junior, or Sonny as my family had dubbed him, the son of a
real estate mogul, now stood before us as a prisoner,
caught up by his own greed.

I remembered a meeting I'd had at his mansion when I
was trying to save Little Greece from demolition. I remembered sitting across from him and his lawyer at a
large cherrywood conference table, feeling small and in-
adequate, desperately trying to keep my composure and
speak my mind. And Case, who'd come along to help me,
had been whisked away by the woman who now sat at my
side.

In the end I'd won the battle against the Talbots, and
now I felt a sense of accomplishment as Talbot Junior
shuffled toward us, his demeanor shifting as he caught
sight of Lila, and then again as he did a double take after
spotting me. He laughed to himself, shaking his head and
muttering something under his breath.

"You can give the inmate a quick hug, but no touching
once he sits down," said a blunt, burly guard as Talbot
joined us at the table.

"Ha!" Lila said. "You won't have to worry about that.
I don't seem to remember any touching, even when we
were married."

Talbot immediately resumed a fight that must have
started years ago. "How could I touch someone who was
never around?" His face looked sunken, his hair graying
at the temples, but his voice was still as piercing as ever.

"I was around long enough for you to ignore me," Lila
fired back.

"Maybe I didn't know it was you, covered in that clown makeup, hidden behind a dense fog of expensive perfume. I see you haven't changed, my dear."

"The insults don't stop hurting because we're divorced, darling."

"Is that so, Ms. Lila Talbot? I knew you'd get everything in the settlement, but I never figured you'd keep the last name, too."

"Are we going to do this now," Lila asked, "in front of our esteemed guest?"

Sonny eyed me with a wry grin. "Athena Spencer."

I was surprised they'd even remembered I was there.

"And why is she so 'esteemed?'" he asked, looking me over.

Lila smiled and put her arm around me. "She's the one who put you here."

His grin immediately dissolved. "Did you bring her to humiliate me? If so, I think I have some push-ups to finish." Sonny raised his hand to the guard, threatening to end our conversation before it even started.

"Oh, please," Lila said. "Like you could complete a push-up."

"If you two don't mind," I interrupted, "there was a reason we came to see you, Grayson. Lila, can we stay on topic?"

Lila took the hint. Shifting daintily in her seat, she said, "If we could put our differences aside momentarily, Gray, we're here to ask for your help with an investigation."

"Why would I help you with anything?" he shot back.

Lila stood abruptly. "You were an insufferable, abusive letch of a man when I was married to you, and you're even more so now. I don't know why I even came here."

He folded his arms over his chest and looked away. "To gloat, I assume."

"To help us take down Pete Harmon," she snapped back.

Noting the commotion, the guard had made his way to our table, but Talbot waved him away. "You said Pete Harmon?"

Lila lifted an eyebrow. "I thought that would get your attention."

Eyeing her warily, Talbot asked, "What do you want to know?"

Before another argument could break out, I took the lead. "What can you tell us about him?"

Talbot made himself more comfortable. "What has he gotten himself into now?"

"Pete Harmon was caught on camera trying to bribe several members of the city council to get their votes," I said. "We're not sure how successful he was."

"Caught by whom?" Talbot asked. "I haven't heard anything about this."

Lila huffed in exasperation. "Will you stop interrupting and let her explain?"

"That's okay, Lila," I said. "Harmon was being followed by a photographer. Hugo Lukan."

"I've heard about the Lukan murder," Talbot said. "Is Harmon a suspect?"

"We believe he is," I said. "The problem we have now is getting Pete to talk to us."

Talbot scratched his chin. His face was thin and bristly. He sat back with a furrow between his brows. "That won't be easy. Pete Harmon is slippery."

"He's *slippery*?" Lila repeated.

"Slick," Talbot answered. "Hard to catch. Tell me, why was Pete trying to bribe the council members?"

"He needs their votes in order to buy the lakeside property behind the old Victorian mansion on Greene," I explained.

"The Sequoia Park property," Talbot said, as though reminiscing. "Highly sought after and extremely valuable. I spent three years trying to acquire that land, but Pearson Reed wouldn't even let it go to a vote. I finally gave up and took over my father's project."

"You mean destroying Little Greece?" I asked. "That project?"

"Yes, well, I failed at that, too, thanks to you. I assume Pearson turned down the bribe. If I couldn't get him to budge, Pete Harmon wouldn't stand a chance. The sad part is that as long as Pearson is on the council, that old parkland will continue to lie empty. They don't have the money to redevelop it." Talbot shook his head, still lost in the past. "I tried every way I could to change his mind, even bribery, but the man is a Boy Scout, totally clean. I couldn't get a thing on him."

That was good to hear. "Meanwhile," I said, "Pete Harmon is trying to convince the town that his project will provide a tax revenue that will benefit the community."

Talbot smiled. "That's smart. It's probably a lie, but a smart move. Good PR for him."

"It *is* a lie," Lila said. "He's using your old lawyers to wiggle his way around the tax laws."

"See what happens when you put a monster away?" Talbot asked with a smile. "A bigger monster takes his place."

"We need a way to get to Harmon," I said.

Talbot held up a finger. "Wait a minute. Pete would need three votes. I'm guessing Tom Silvester took the bribe. He was never shy about selling his vote. So that's one. Who are the other two?"

"Beau Clifford," Lila told him. "He's new to the council and has a really crazy gambling habit, so we used that to—"

"Lila, that's more than your ex-husband needs to know."

"Got it. Beau was the second vote," she said. "And Pearson Reed was the third."

"Not Pearson," Talbot said. "No way."

"He's denied accepting the money," I said.

Lila cocked her head at me. "And you still believe him?"

"We can discuss that later," I said. "There are two other city council members whom we haven't questioned."

"And why haven't we questioned them?" Lila asked.

"Because there's no evidence against them, and, according to Pearson, they are fully committed to keeping the land a park."

"But if Pearson refused the money," Lila said, "then someone else might have accepted."

"I highly doubt that," Talbot said. "As I remember, the other two members are staunch environmentalists. Unless Harmon found a way to get to one of them, they will most definitely vote against him."

"That leads us back to Pearson," Lila said.

Ignoring her comment, I asked Talbot, "How do we get to Harmon?"

"I may know a few tricks that will get you through the door, but you'll never get a straight answer from him. You're better off trying to find a whistleblower, someone close to him, an administrative assistant or a former employee who can scrape up some dirt. What exactly do you want to know?"

I began to enumerate. "We need to know whether he has an alibi for last Saturday, whether he received a blackmail letter, and what he finds so appealing about that particular parcel of land."

"I can tell you about the land," Talbot said. "All the boat traffic goes through that bottleneck. There's nowhere else along the coastline left to build on. And the next marina and fuel station is too far north to be convenient, so a refueling station there would be a gold mine."

Sonny Talbot directed his attention toward me. "There *is* one thing you can try, and that's to force Harmon to the table. I don't know if it will work, because Pete went bankrupt covering it up, but there was a scandal. After his father died, Pete took over the Harmon Oil business. In order to cut costs, he began dumping waste into the lake and surrounding woodlands. An environmental inspection was performed, and the resulting lawsuit almost destroyed the company. He managed to hang on to the gas stations but lost everything else. You won't read about this anywhere. This was before the information age. Everything was easier to cover up back then."

"So, how do I use that information?" I asked.

"Tell him you'll make an issue of it, take it to the newspapers. He won't like that."

"I can do that."

Talbot smiled. "See? I can be a nice guy when I want to be."

When he wasn't trying to kill me.

"Thanks for the information," I said. "I appreciate it."

"Believe it or not," Lila said, "so do I."

"One more thing," Talbot said. "Watch your back. Harmon doesn't play nice."

"Like you trying to bury me under a building?" I asked.

Talbot smiled. "Yes, exactly like that. If you're not careful, he just might bury you under those dunes."

We left him gloating over his helpfulness and returned to the free world, where I put in a call to Case. "I think we have a way to make Pete talk."

Friday afternoons were busy at the garden center, so I wasn't able to arrange to go see Pete Harmon. We agreed to go Monday instead. In the meantime, I had to come up with a landscaping plan for the Studios of Sequoia so I could have all the shrubs planted before the auction.

I got out my landscaping guide and began to research native shrubs to plant around the back of the house. I finally decided that my game plan would be to put a tall American cranberry bush viburnum on one outside corner, and a silky dogwood tree on another. In between, I would fill in with the three-foot-tall New Jersey Tea bush and wolfberry bushes. In front of them I'd plant the low Potentilla fruticosa for floral impact.

I drew it out and showed my dad, who gave it two thumbs up. I texted Elissa to let her know I'd be ready to plant by the next week, and then I took my iPad and walked out to the back to see what shrubs we had in stock. The rest I'd have to order.

Out of the shrubs burst a streak of gray and black, followed by a blur of red and blue. Oscar squealed as he ran by. Elissa's son, Denis, clipped my arm as he followed, knocking the iPad from my grip. I watched in horror as it hit the ground.

The storage barn doors flew open, and I could hear Denis shriek in glee as Nicholas ran out after him. The two boys came down the path toward me, but this time I stood my ground. I caught the eye of my son, who saw my glare and came to a screeching halt. Denis, however, continued past me, rounded the corner, and disappeared.

"What in the world is going on?" I asked Nicholas. I bent down, picked up the iPad, and breathed a sigh of relief as I brushed off the dirt. There were a few scratches on the corner, but the screen was intact. "This isn't a playground, Niko. You can't run around like that back here. Look what almost happened."

Nicholas inspected the iPad. "I'm sorry, Mom. We were playing hide-and-seek with Oscar."

"The game ends now," I said. "Tell Denis you have to go back to work."

"Can you tell him?" Niko asked. "I don't want him to get mad at me again."

"Again?"

Nicholas looked away. I got an unsettling feeling in my stomach and asked, "What happened?"

My son looked around as if afraid Denis might overhear. "I asked him if he took Oscar's star toy. He got really mad and stopped talking to me. And he wouldn't help me look for it, either."

"Where is he? I'll tell him you have to work."

We searched the outdoor area and did a quick sweep through the storage barn, but Denis was nowhere to be found. The unsettling feeling in my stomach continued. Denis was proving himself to be a menace, and I wasn't so sure I wanted my son hanging around with him any-more.

Nicholas led me down the path toward the back of the property and stopped at the fence bordering the alley. The gate was open. "His bike is gone," Nicholas said. "Do you think he heard us talking and left?"

"It's nothing to worry about if he did. I'll talk to Elissa to make sure he's okay."

"Tell her Denis stole Oscar's toy."

"Do you have proof that Denis stole it?"

"No, but I have a feeling he did."

I ruffled his short brown hair. "Every good private eye knows you shouldn't accuse someone without proof. Besides, Oscar has other toys. He won't mind. Now, run inside and see if Grandpa has work for you."

I watched him gallop away, wondering whether his feeling about Denis was correct. Then I fired up the iPad and went back to work, deciding that if other toys went missing, I'd have to talk to Elissa.

On Saturday morning, Nicholas and I walked into the diner for breakfast and found Delphi and my mother having a standoff. My sisters sat by silently, clearly hoping Mama wouldn't involve them.

"Please, Delphi, just go out with him once," Mama pleaded. "He's perfect for you."

"I'm not interested in dating," she fired back.

"Of course, you are. You're a young, vibrant woman. Why wouldn't you be interested in meeting an eligible bachelor? You're not keeping something from me, are you?"

Delphi huffed in annoyance. "Who is this guy?"

"He's Cynthia Pappas's son. He was married for a brief time, but it didn't work out, through no fault of his."

"Or so you say," Delphi muttered.

"He's very good-looking and has a charming personality," Mama said. "I met him yesterday when Cynthia brought him to the diner for lunch."

Delphi stared at her in alarm. "Oh my God, does he know you're playing matchmaker? He does, doesn't he? How embarrassing, Mama."

"*Glykiá mou,*" she said. *Sweetie.* "I wouldn't embarrass you for the world. This was a casual conversation. I suggested he might like to meet you this evening, and he said he would be delighted. Now, how can you disappoint such a nice young man?"

Delphi looked at me for backup, catching me off guard. "Isn't it kind of quick?" I asked. "Delphi is only just hearing about it, Mama."

"I don't even know his name," Delphi moaned.

"David Pappas," Mama said immediately. "Please say you'll go. I'd hate to have to call and disappoint him. Do it for me, Delphi."

Delphi glanced from Mama to me, but unfortunately, I didn't see a way out. My storytelling gene was turned off.

"All right," Delphi growled. "I'll go. But from now on, check with me before you set me up on a date."

"*Efxaristó,*" Mama said. *Thank you.* "I promise you won't be disappointed."

"I lied."

After a busy day at Spencer's, it wasn't until after supper that I was finally able to sit down to write my blog.

Seated at my tiny desk, I had just opened my laptop when Delphi popped into my bedroom.

Sinking down onto the edge of my bed, she said it again. "I lied today, and I'm ashamed."

I swiveled my chair around to face her. "What did you lie about?"

"This afternoon I told David I was coming down with a head cold and couldn't go." She flopped backward onto the bed. "Am I going to burn in eternal damnation?"

"Why did you lie?"

"For two reasons," she said. "Because David was very nice over the phone, and I didn't want to hurt his feelings. And because I promised Bobby I wouldn't go out on another blind date. I can't hurt him like that again."

"Then why did you agree to go?"

"Are you kidding me?" She raised herself on her elbows. "You know better than anyone how hard it is to say no to Mama. Now it's only a matter of time until she finds out."

I leaned closer to study her face. "Oh, wow," I said with exaggerated concern.

"What?" Delphi asked. "What's wrong?"

"You don't look well." I felt her forehead with the back of my hand. "You're burning up."

She felt her own forehead. "I am?"

"Nope, but if Mama asks, you're spending the evening in bed nursing that fever."

"You are my savior," Delphi said with a big smile.

"All you have to do is sneeze in front of Mama and blow your nose. I'll back up your story."

Delphi rose to a seated position with a smile. "I knew I could count on you. I'm going to my room to practice sneezing."

"Don't overdo it," I called as she trotted out of my room.

A dramatic sneeze was my response. At any rate, she had given me an idea for my blog.

IT'S ALL GREEK TO ME
Blog by Goddess Anon

PANTS ON FIRE

"Truly, to tell lies is not honorable, but when the truth entails tremendous ruin, to speak dishonorably is pardonable." —Sophocles

When is it okay to lie?

This question came up recently when a friend of mine, okay me, told a lie to get out of doing something I really didn't want to do. Why didn't I tell the truth? Because it would've hurt the other person's feelings, and I just couldn't bring myself to do that. In that instance, I firmly believe lying was the right thing to do.

I also believe it's okay to lie when telling the truth would be stupid, as in, your child asks if you ever did anything bad and got away with it and you basically lay out a game plan for the child to do the same thing. Not smart.

Also, it's always better to lie if someone asks you how s/he looks, and your honest answer could end your friendship. "I just had my hair done in this new style and I love it. What do you think?" and she looks like an alien being. If you care about your friendship, you lie.

And then there's the occasion when you bump into an acquaintance, make small talk for a minute, and then before you part, you feel obliged to say, "We should get together sometime," when you can barely make the conversation last three minutes as it is. Lying does end the meeting on a friendly note rather than awkwardly saying, "Well, I have to run. Take care now," and making a hasty escape. And no one really expects you to get together anyway.

So, I guess the answer to my question is that it's okay to lie when you have a really compelling reason to do so—oh, and when you won't get caught.

Aye, there's the rub.

Adio sas,

Goddess Anon

Sunday afternoon started out as every Sunday afternoon did, with a gathering of the entire family. Uncle Giannis, Aunt Rachel, and their sons, Drew and Michael, were there. Aunt Talia and Uncle Konstantine were there. And, of course, Yiayiá and Pappoús were there, along with the six of us.

Now that Case had been invited to the family gatherings, we had managed to squeeze in one extra chair across from mine, but today his was currently empty. Case had called that morning to inform me of a last-minute interview with the two remaining city council members. He'd said it was the only convenient time they could meet.

Convenient for Case was more likely.

Delphi sat down first and stretched her arms out casually, as if to enjoy all the extra space from Case's empty chair next to her, while the new seating arrangement had me sitting even closer to my loudmouthed uncle Giannis.

As we were getting ready to eat, the doorbell rang. For

a moment everyone looked around in confusion, as though thinking, *We're all here. Who could it be?*

Could Case have come to dinner after all?

I sprang into action first, running to the foyer, pulling the door open—and staring in surprise at Bob Maguire, who stood in the doorway dressed in civilian attire. Delphi was right behind me and immediately flushed bright red, quite a contrast to her ebony hair.

"Bob!" she exclaimed, gaping at him partly in disbelief, mostly in horror.

"Hi, Delphi. Hi, Athena."

"Come in, Bob," my dad called, coming to greet him. "Clear the doorway, girls. We have a guest." Having seen Maguire pop into the garden center to talk to Delphi on more than one occasion, he had obviously put the pieces together. "Good to see you," my dad said, offering his hand. "Hera," he called to my mom, "you remember Officer Maguire."

My mother, who was watching from a distance in some bewilderment, suddenly jerked to attention. "Yes, I do," she said, hurrying toward the doorway. "You were kind enough to help when Selene was in trouble. Come in, come in. You're just in time for dinner."

Maguire glanced surreptitiously at Delphi, who was still flushed. She turned to me with imploring eyes that said, *What do I do?*

My dad continued to play the good host, escorting Bob into the dining room as Mom, Delphi, and I followed behind. "Bob, please have a seat here next to Delphi." As she awkwardly circled the table to join Maguire, my dad continued. "Delphi, why don't you introduce Officer Maguire to the rest of the family?"

Delphi shot me a terrified glance as she sat dutifully next to Maguire. Meanwhile, everyone at the table leaned in with delighted anticipation.

"You can call me Bob," Maguire said when she'd finished. "And I didn't mean to interrupt your meal."

"No trouble at all," Dad said, clapping him on the back, clearly enjoying the shocked look on my mother's face.

Poor Maguire sat beside Delphi, who seemed afraid to turn her head toward him. He was instantly swallowed up by the family chatter.

Yiayiá served the roasted lamb and braised chicken while my aunts and uncles grilled Maguire about his duties on the police force. Mama was suspiciously quiet, keeping her eyes glued to the tiniest flinches and gestures between Delphi and her guest.

When the discussion shifted to Pete Harmon's bid to acquire the land, Uncle Giannis turned to Maguire. "Bob," he said, "what do you think about Harmon's project to take over the land?"

Trying to be diplomatic—he obviously hadn't yet ascertained how the family felt—he said, "It would be great to see that land open to the public once again."

"That's what I'm talking about," Uncle Konstantine said, lifting his glass of beer. "Cheers to that, Bob."

Bob clinked glasses, for the first time revealing a sincere, dimpled smile. He turned to Delphi and shared with her a relieved glance.

"Harmon Oil Company sucks big-time," Cousin Michael said from the card table, to which Niko laughed out loud, and Michael's mom, Aunt Rachel, shushed him.

With that subject on the table, a loud discussion followed, while Maguire and Delphi sat side by side, casting discreet, longing glances at one another. I spied Mama watching their movements like a hawk, hardly taking her eyes off the two as she ate, drank, and wiped her mouth with a cloth napkin.

Somehow we made it through dinner, dessert, and Greek coffee. It wasn't until Delphi and I escorted Maguire to the door that he said, "I'm sorry I intruded on your meal."

"Don't be sorry," I said. "Everyone enjoyed your company. Right, Delph?"

"Yes, we did," she said, seemingly unaware that she was batting her eyelashes at him. "That was a very brave thing you did for me. I'm sorry I was so awkward."

"I was the awkward one." He smiled down at her sweetly. "Tell your family I said thank you for the gracious meal."

I leaned close to say, "I'm sure that's not all we'll be talking about."

Delphi looked around, and upon seeing no one but me, turned and gave Bob a kiss on the cheek. Bob told her he had some news to share with me, so Delphi floated away on a cloud, her sandals slapping along the floor as she left.

"You are braver than I thought for showing up at Sunday dinner, Bob," I told him. "I'm impressed."

"I appreciate that," he said. "But actually, I had no idea your family was having dinner." He glanced over my shoulder, then said quietly, "I came to see you."

* * *

After everyone had gone, I went up to my room and called Case to tell him about Maguire's visit. "Bob got a look at the coroner's report. Hugo had apparently put up a fight with his attacker, because there was blood and skin cells under his fingernails."

"And Pearson had scratch marks on his arms," Case reminded me.

"Bob told me the DNA sample has been sent to the lab in Lansing, so they'll know for sure if it's a match in two to four weeks."

"Then I guess our investigation is suspended until further notice."

"We don't have two to four weeks, Case. Elissa told me that the auction is suffering because of the negative attention Pearson is getting. We've got to do something now."

"What do you suggest?"

"We continue," I said. "We meet with Pete on Monday and check him for scratch marks."

"Seriously, Athena, how do you propose we do that?"

I sat down on my bed, thinking hard and coming up with nothing.

"That's what I thought," Case said.

"We can still interview him."

"How did Bob fare with your family?" he said, changing the subject.

"Let's just say he was officially inducted into the Karras-Spencer conglomerate."

"Poor Bob."

"Exactly what I said to myself. If my family didn't scare him off, nothing will."

"They didn't scare me off."

"Says the man who didn't show up for Sunday dinner. How did your interviews pan out, by the way?"

"Both city council members had alibis, and both alibis checked out." And upon my silence, he added, "I'm sorry again for ditching dinner. I'll make it up to you."

"Yes, you most definitely will."

After a Sunday that seemed to stretch on for a week, Monday morning couldn't come quickly enough. I wanted to get on with the investigation before the police zeroed in even further on Pearson. With every piece of evidence stacked against him, I couldn't help but compare his situation with my sister Selene's, when she'd been accused of murder. I'd felt then much the same as I did now—something wasn't adding up. So, after my morning work was finished, Case picked me up in the Jeep and we drove out to Harmon Oil.

Harmon Oil Company was located in a concrete-block, two-story building on the southeast side of town on a lot surrounded by a heavy hurricane fence. We entered through the gates and parked in a section of the parking lot marked for visitors. Entering through the glass door, we headed for the receptionist's desk and asked to see Pete Harmon. We gave our names and stated our business as investigating Hugo Lukan's death.

The receptionist picked up her phone, spoke to a woman named Marci, then hung up and said, "Mr. Harmon isn't able to see you today."

"Can we set up an appointment for tomorrow?" I asked.

"Mr. Harmon won't be available for several weeks."

Weeks? Just as Lila had said, they were giving us the runaround.

"Can you put a call in to Pete's administrative assistant?" Case asked.

"I can leave a message for her," the receptionist said.

"Please do," Case responded. "Tell her we have more questions about the death of Hugo Lukan, and we believe Mr. Harmon can help us with them."

The receptionist hesitated a moment, then picked up the phone again. She relayed the message and ended with, "Thanks, Marci." To my surprise she said, "Have a seat in the waiting area. Someone will be with you shortly."

"Excuse me," I said. "Who is Marci?"

"Pete Harmon's administrative assistant."

"I thought Jewel Newsome was his administrative assistant."

The receptionist tilted her head questioningly. "Is Jewel a friend of yours?"

"Actually, no. Just someone I met recently."

She smiled as though she was enjoying sharing the news. "Jewel was let go."

"As of when?" I asked.

"As of four weeks ago."

Four weeks ago? I glanced at Case with raised eyebrows. If Jewel had lied about that, what else she had lied about?

In less than five minutes, Pete Harmon himself stepped off an elevator and strode toward us. An imposing man, Pete was wearing a cornflower-blue blazer, a white button-down shirt, and black jeans, accentuating his black goatee and black hair.

Very brusquely, he said, "Come with me," and led us down the hall to a cozy, expensively furnished conference room. He shut the door behind us, motioned for us to sit at the long cherrywood table, then circled it until he was standing behind us.

I looked at Case, and he swiveled his neck to keep an eye on Harmon, who was closing the blinds against the bright morning sun. He proceeded around the table, unbuttoning his blazer before sitting down, eyes focused like a laser beam, a tiny smile hiding behind the beard, as though he found the situation amusing.

"Speak," he commanded.

Woof?

CHAPTER FIFTEEN

I knew his command hadn't sat well with Case when he shot me an annoyed glance.

"I'm Case Donnelly, and this is my partner, Athena Spencer. We're investigating Hugo Lukan's death, and to that end, I have some photos I'd like for you to review."

"First of all," Pete said, "I know who you are and why you're here. Second, let me see your private investigator's license."

"We're here for a friend," Case said. "Nothing official."

"Wrong answer. You should've said you're investigating on behalf of Pearson Reed, which means you are private citizens working in opposition to the Sequoia Police Department. And why do I say that? Because they consider Mr. Reed the prime suspect in Hugo's death. Correct? Of course I'm correct. What else is correct? This. I

put in one call to the chief of police, and your investigation stops dead in its tracks."

His rapid-fire delivery had my nerves jangling.
"That's not true," I said, trying my best to appear unfazed. "We're not working in opposition to the police. In
fact, we've even shared our evidence *with* the police."

"And yet you're still on the hunt for another suspect."
He rose from his chair, buttoned his blazer, and headed
for the door. "I suggest you drop this whole investigation
before you embarrass yourselves. You wasted your time
coming here."

I didn't know about Case, but I wasn't ready to throw
in the towel that quickly. "How about clearing up a question first about you offering money to three city councilmen in exchange for their votes on acquiring lakefront
property?"

"Not a chance, Miss Spencer," he answered coolly.

"We know you offered the councilmen bribes," I retorted. "How do you defend that?"

He smiled. "Prove it."

"We have photos that show you handing envelopes of
money to them," Case said.

Without batting an eye, Pete said, "I'd like to see those
photos."

Case took the three black-and-whites out of the manila
envelope and spread them on the table. Pete studied each
one, then straightened. "How did you get these?"

"I can't reveal that information," Case said.

Pete leaned over the table and placed his fingertips on
the polished wood surface. "Let me rephrase that. How
did you get these from Hugo?"

"How do you know they came from Hugo?" I fired
back.

Pete smiled. "It was an extremely easy deduction."

Case continued on. "In addition to the photos, we have a councilman on the record stating that you offered him cash in exchange for his vote."

Pete sat down in his chair and leaned back, the fingers of his right hand tapping the tabletop impatiently. "On the *record?* Did you call in a court reporter? Give me a break, Donnelly. Get to the point or get out."

"Did Hugo ask you for money to keep these photos off the internet?" Case asked.

With a haughty lift of his bearded chin, looking extremely confident, Pete said, "In the first place, my attorney would tell me not to answer that question. In the second place, this is the first time I've laid eyes on these photos."

"How about we take that as a yes?" Case asked.

Pete shrugged. "I receive many threats. Hugo's was never any concern to me."

"Did you pay Hugo the money?" Case asked.

"I had no reason to."

"Where were you the morning Hugo was murdered?" Case asked.

He made it obvious that he was more interested in straightening his tie than in answering questions. "None of your business."

Stand back. Greek temper on the rise. "You know what *is* our business?" I asked. "Saving the lakefront from your disastrous new project."

"So," he said, his mouth twisting into a cynical smile, "in addition to being the Goddess of Greene Street, you're also going to become the Savior of Sequoia?"

My blood began to boil. "All we have to do is prove

that you're bribing members of the city council, and your operation will come to a grinding halt."

"I very much urge you to try," Pete answered. "See how that works out for you."

"I hope you understand how far we're willing to take this," I said. "Either we get answers, or we'll share some damaging information with the press about Harmon Oil that could ruin your business." I hadn't planned on using my ace card so soon, but Pete's arrogant attitude had really gotten under my skin.

Case sat back in his chair and crossed his arms. I couldn't tell if he was upset with me or was giving me the signal to proceed.

Pete studied me for a long moment, making me squirm inside. "I was wondering when the threats would begin."

"It's not a threat, Mr. Harmon," I replied. "It's leverage."

"Same thing. Your entire investigation is based on threats. First you threatened Tom Silvester with reporting our little envelope exchange to his boss, and then Beau Clifford with exposing his gambling habit. No wonder you got the answers you wanted. You play dirty."

I stared at him in surprise. "Excuse me?"

"Please, Miss Spencer," he said with mock humility, "explain how this *leverage* you mentioned will work, because my company has undergone thorough vetting in preparation for our latest land development project. Tell me, what kind of information could you possibly have that would ruin me?"

"I spoke with a friend of yours," I said. "Grayson Talbot Junior. He told me a lot about you and your past business dealings."

Pete's expression didn't change. He still held that conceited grin in place, but for a split second I thought I detected a muscle twitch in his jaw. Had I finally hit a nerve? "He's not a friend of mine," he said evenly.

"I was being facetious," I said. "He told me about that toxic waste you dumped illegally and the lawsuit that resulted."

Pete laughed. "You're getting your information from convicted felons now? That should go over well with your clients." He stood up and began to stroll around the table. "But please, I urge you to follow through with Talbot's claims and see how far that gets you. In case you haven't realized it, I'm a hero in Sequoia." He stopped in front of the door. "Now, unless you have any more baseless threats, I think I should be getting on with my day."

"You may believe our threat is baseless," Case said, "but we *will* follow through. That's what we do. We dig. And we won't stop digging even if they arrest Pearson Reed, even if the city council votes for your project."

"And it's not just a threat," I added. "It's a promise. If you won't cooperate, we will share your dirty little secret with the press and make sure that it goes public. One way or another, we'll make good on our promise."

Pete turned at the door to glare at us, his lips pressed together in barely concealed anger. "All right," he ground out, "let's say I'll humor you and tell you I was at home Saturday morning. My wife will verify my alibi."

Wives always verified their husband's alibis. "Were you at home *all* morning?"

"All morning."

"Is there anyone else who can verify it?" Case asked.

"All I need is one alibi witness."

"Then you weren't down at the festival grounds with a city surveyor?" Case asked.

Pete walked up to the conference table opposite us and leaned his hands on the surface. "Who said I was there?"

"Two eyewitnesses," I said. "They're willing to testify."

He stroked the dark strands of his beard before answering, "I didn't attend the festival, but I was in the vicinity *briefly*. You can speak to the city surveyor if you'd like."

Amazing how quickly his story changed.

"You were seen around eleven o'clock near the entrance to the trail where Hugo was murdered," Case said. "That puts you at the scene of the crime at the right time."

"That's impossible," he said sharply.

"That you were seen," Case asked, "or that you were there around eleven o'clock?"

"This is starting to sound like slander."

"We have credible witnesses," Case said.

Pete straightened, his face flushed with anger. "You're in way over your head, Donnelly. Don't play with fire unless you want to get burned."

Play with fire and you get burned. I glanced at Case in surprise.

"Speaking of threats . . ." Case tipped the envelope and let the last piece of evidence Hugo had sent him slide out. He took it from the envelope and smoothed it out. "What do you make of this note?"

As Pete bent over for a look, Case said, "Sounds familiar, doesn't it?"

Turning on his heel, Pete strode toward the door. Before leaving, he turned to point his finger at me. "If you accuse me of sending a threatening letter, I'll dare you to prove it. If you accuse me of bribery, I guarantee none of those men will back up your claim. If you accuse me of murder, I will come at you with an army of attorneys. The legal fees alone will sink you and your entire family. The garden center, the Parthenon, your precious, priceless *Treasure of Athena*. Nothing will be spared.

"And you, Case Donnelly, your insignificant little private eye venture will fold before you even get that license in the mail. If you don't believe me, challenge me, and we can continue this conversation in court."

The icy intimidation sent shivers down my spine. His eyes pierced through me, and a smile curled his lip at the corners as he gauged my reaction.

"If you're not concerned about our investigation," Case asked, "why do you know so much about us?"

"Because I have eyes everywhere."

"You didn't have eyes on Hugo when he captured your secret parking lot meetings," I fired back.

"You're absolutely right, and I can thank Hugo for helping me see the blind spots in my security. That won't be a problem anymore. And just like Hugo, *you*"—he jabbed a finger at us—"have made a powerful enemy."

As he reached for the door handle, I noticed that his white shirt cuff had inched back, revealing a dark red wound on his wrist. Yanking open the door, he left us alone in the conference room. The bustling sounds of the office building filtered in as Case and I stared at each other.

" 'Don't play with fire?' " I asked.

"We called his bluff, and he didn't like it. And I'd bet any money he wrote that note to Hugo."

"Case, I think we have our number-one suspect."

As we walked down the hallway, Case leaned his head toward me and said quietly, "Harmon doesn't play around. We need to move this investigation along."

"I'm going to speak with Maguire and let him know what Harmon said," I told him, "just to have a record of it."

"Good idea."

"Did you notice the wound on Pete's arm?"

"I didn't." Case held the door for me as we exited the building.

"It was a long, dark red scratch right below his wrist."

"Like this?" Case turned over his wrist and lifted a bandage from his skin.

"Ouch. What happened?"

"The buckle on Jewel's leather strap happened," he answered. "Sharp edges."

"Okay, so maybe it's a coincidence, but I still say Pete Harmon is our killer."

We had just gotten into the Jeep when a big SUV pulled into a parking spot and Tom Silvester got out. We watched as Tom headed toward the building.

"He must be going to see Pete," I said. "I sure would love to be a fly on the wall."

"Are you in a hurry?"

"What do you have in mind?"

"A little stakeout. Let's see how long before Tom comes out."

As we settled in to wait, I said, "Do you realize that thanks to Sonny Talbot, we now know that Harmon had the means, possible motive, and certainly the opportunity?"

"We should thank Lila for suggesting we talk to Sonny," Case said.

"We should," I agreed. "She's turning out to be useful after all."

Case smiled and reached for my hand. "Athena Spencer just said something nice about Lila Talbot. This is truly a special moment."

My fingers entwined in his. "Funny man. But thanks to Lila, we also found out that Jewel lied about working at Harmon Oil."

"It would be good to know why she did that."

"The simplest answer is that she was embarrassed about being fired. But it makes me wonder what else she lied about."

Case rubbed his freshly shaven face. "She certainly knows more than she revealed to us. And after dealing with Pete Harmon, I can see why she wouldn't want to talk about him. But perhaps armed with the knowledge we have now, we'll be able to persuade her to share what she knows."

"That reminds me, I also want to talk to Hugo's ex-wife Carrie."

"Because?"

Oops. "My sister Maia learned about a Facebook post written by Carrie Lukan that talked about killing Hugo."

Case lifted his eyebrows. "And why am I only learning about this now?"

"There's a chance I may have forgotten to tell you."

With a smile, Case shook his head.

"What's so funny?"

"What are the odds that we went to all of this trouble tracking down four suspects only to find out that Hugo's ex-wife did it?"

"You laugh, but you should see the post. It's pretty detailed. So I thought I'd talk to Carrie and see if she's worth a spot on our suspect list."

Case pointed toward the glass door, where I saw Tom leaving the building. "That was a fast meeting."

We watched him cross the parking lot, get into his SUV, and drive away.

"Let's see where he goes," Case said and started the engine. We followed Tom back to town, where he drove to the Michigan State Bank and got into the drive-through lane.

"If I were a betting man," Case said, "I'd guess that Tom was just handed another envelope full of money."

"It makes sense that he would deposit the money here and not at the Sequoia Savings and Loan, but I thought Pete already bought his vote."

"Remember Pearson telling us that Pete would be giving them small cash installments? That must have been another installment."

"If Tom received another payment," I said, "then it would be time for Beau to get one, too."

"And Pearson," Case added, "if he accepted the first bribe."

I heaved a sigh of exasperation. "Case, I wish you could've heard how Talbot talked about Pearson. He called him a Boy Scout and said there was no way he'd accept a bribe for that lakefront property."

"Money makes people do the unthinkable, Athena."

I didn't want to argue about it, not until I could find a way to prove Pearson's innocence.

We waited until Tom had finished his transaction, and then we followed him all the way across town to the JumboMart. We watched as he parked in the employee parking lot and entered the store, and then Case said, "Looks like he and Beau are going to talk. I guess we know who Pete's errand boy is."

"Again, to be a fly on the wall."

"Would you like to take bets on where Tom's next stop will be?"

Within ten minutes, Tom was in his SUV heading toward the downtown area. He turned on White Street and proceeded straight to Quick As an Ink, Pearson's printing company.

I had no words to express my dismay.

On our way back to Spencer's, I phoned Maguire and asked him to stop by for an update on our investigation. He agreed immediately, no doubt hoping to see Delphi again. When he got there, I poured him a cup of coffee and invited him to sit down.

"Catch me up," he said, taking a seat on the other side of the desk.

"We just interviewed Pete Harmon," I said. "We've now talked to all four men in the photos. Three of the four—Pete Harmon, Tom Silvester, and Pearson Reed—were seen at the festival, and I have witnesses who are willing to testify to seeing Tom and Pete talking down by the trail where Hugo was killed."

Maguire finished making notes on a small notepad and glanced up. "So, three suspects for sure."

"And one of those suspects—Pete Harmon—threatened us if we proceeded to investigate him."

"Threatened you how?"

"In the same way that someone threatened Hugo with that anonymous note. His words were, *Don't play with fire unless you want to get burned.* Sound familiar?"

"Pete Harmon is a ruthless businessman, Athena. I did a little digging of my own and found out that he's sued a large number of people over the years."

"Then we should definitely take him seriously."

"You bet. He'll sue you in a New York minute. The good news is that he's never caused anyone bodily harm, if that's what you're worried about."

"Unless he's the murderer."

Maguire acknowledged my comment with a nod.

"Are you going to share this information with the detectives?" I asked.

"I can try. I've shared the photos Hugo sent you, but so far they haven't been willing to listen to other theories."

"Why doesn't that surprise me?"

"Athena?" I heard.

Delphi stuck her head in the door and instantly smiled. "Hi," she said shyly.

Maguire smiled back. "Hi."

"I think we can safely say our meeting is over," I said. "Come in, Delphi."

They were barely aware of me quietly letting myself out.

Delphi didn't go with me to have lunch at the diner. She claimed that Mama would be in interrogation mode now that Maguire had made an appearance at our house. Mama, however, didn't even bring up the subject.

"Maia," I asked my sister, pausing halfway through my *avgolemono* soup, "can you find out where Carrie Lukan is working now?"

Mama tapped her spoon on the table. "Maia, would you put down your phone and answer your sister?"

"I was just looking it up," Maia said crossly. She read something on her phone, then said, "She teaches classes at Yoga One Studios. If you leave now you can make it before her one-thirty class."

"Would you do me one more favor?" I asked Maia. "Find out what Carrie's boyfriend's name is?"

"No problem. My friend Sophie at Zen Garden knows Carrie. I'll text Sophie right now and ask her."

After several more minutes, I had the name. Having a big family paid off.

At one o'clock, I headed back to Spencer's to let my dad know I'd be out for a while and then took my white SUV for the ten-minute drive to the yoga studio. Inside the studio, I found Carrie setting out yoga blocks in a large, airy room. Similar in style to Zen Garden, the room had light wood floors and open shelves on the back wall, where yoga mats, blankets, bolsters, and blocks were stored.

"Carrie, hi," I said to the slender blond woman. Physically fit, she was a little shorter than me and appeared to be around forty years old. "I'm Athena Spencer, and I've come to ask you some questions."

"Wait. I know you," she said. "Your sister is a yoga instructor, right? I've seen your picture in the newspaper. You're the Goddess of Greene Street. You investigate murders." Her eyes opened wide as she realized my mission. "Oh my God, you're here about Hugo."

"Right."

She didn't look pleased. She turned away from me and began to set out more blocks. "He was a lying, cheating bastard, and I have nothing else to say about him."

"Carrie, I know about your Facebook posts."

That got her attention.

CHAPTER SIXTEEN

Carrie gave me a skeptical glance. "So you know. And?"

"Your posts sound really"—I didn't want to say crazy—"angry."

"So what? I was just venting."

"When you are asking people what kind of poison works best to kill someone, that's more than venting."

She finished setting out the blocks, picked up a clipboard, and began to read over it. "Okay, so I got a little involved. That doesn't mean I murdered Hugo. Now, if you'll excuse me, I have to prepare for class."

"I'll stop bothering you in a minute. First, I have two quick questions for you. Where were you the Saturday morning of the art festival?"

At that she stopped checking her clipboard. "You're asking for my *alibi*? Are you *kidding* me?"

"Do you have something to hide?"

"Of course not. I just can't believe you think I might have done something to my ex."

"Anyone who sees your Facebook page might think the same. And I don't rule anyone out unless I have proof."

"Fine," she huffed. "I was out on the lake with my boyfriend."

"If I call Brad right now, will he verify that?"

She looked stunned. "How do you know his name?"

"I did my homework."

She turned her attention back to the clipboard. "You can't call him. He's at work now and can't be reached."

"Come on, Carrie. That had to sound lame, even to your ears."

"Look," she said angrily, "I didn't kill Hugo. The newspaper article said he was strangled. How could I have strangled him? Do I look strong enough to subdue a man?"

"Are you saying you and your boyfriend weren't at the festival?"

"I'm saying I didn't kill Hugo, and you can't prove I did."

"And Brad? Does he have an alibi for that Saturday morning?"

"He has me." She strode to the door and pointed to the hallway. "That way to the exit."

I strolled casually toward the door. "You really should take down your Facebook posts, you know. I wouldn't be surprised if the police came calling."

"Are you going to tell them about it?"

"I think the detectives would want to know."

She seemed to fold at that. Taking a deep breath, she

said, "Okay, fine, here's the truth. I didn't see Hugo that morning. I didn't even know he went to the festival until I read about his murder in the newspaper. Brad and I rented a boat and went out on the lake. And that's all I can tell you. If you'd like, I'll give you the name of the boat rental company and you can check their records."

I pulled out my phone and handed it to her. "Type out the name for me."

After she'd handed it back, I said, "About what time did you rent the boat?"

"We were at the festival for around an hour and then left. So I'd say about eleven o'clock."

"Good enough. I'll call the boat rental company to verify that when I leave here."

Her shoulders slumped in relief. "Thank you. And I promise, as soon as I get home, I'll delete all the posts. I never imagined anyone would take them so seriously."

I wanted to bang her head against the wall. "Okay, then. Thanks for the information."

"One more thing," she said. "If you're looking for suspects, look up Jewel Newsome."

"How do you know Jewel?"

"How do I know Jewel? Well, let's see. She was a friend of mine until Hugo slept with her—while we were still married, by the way. Then, after I kicked him to the curb, he moved in with her, and when they broke up, he came back, begging me for a safe place to stay. He called her a psycho, which I could have told him from the start."

"Did you let him stay with you?"

"No, and a week later he was dead. So if you want to track down Hugo's killer, start with her."

"What do you know about Jewel?"

"She's a psycho."

"Anything else?"

"Yeah, her boobs are fake, her jewelry is garbage, and she is a very, very bad friend."

"Okay, I get it. Thanks for your time."

As soon as I got back into my car, I called the boat rental company and verified her story. Then I phoned Case. "I spoke with Carrie Lukan and I've already verified her alibi, so I'm going to say she's in the clear."

"Good work."

"She did have an interesting take on Jewel," I said, and relayed Carrie's story.

"Hmm," Case said. "I think we need to take a closer look at Jewel sooner rather than later."

When Nicholas and I arrived at the diner Tuesday morning, Mama, Selene, and Maia were once again gathered around a laptop chortling over my blog entitled, "Smile for the Camera."

"I've seen you give me a phony smile," Maia said to Selene.

"Really?"

Maia pointed at her. "You're doing it now!"

"I'm not the only one who does it." Selene glanced over at me.

"Sorry," I said. "I haven't read the blog." I went to the kitchen pass-through window to say good morning to my grandparents.

"It's about why we smile in different situations," Selene said, as I took a seat at the counter, "like when someone says something offensive, and you don't want to call them out on it."

"Or when someone compliments you and you know it's true," Maia added.

"I smile a lot," Nicholas said, setting down his glass of chocolate milk.

"And right now, you're smiling with a chocolate mouth," I said, and handed him a napkin.

"Yesterday's blog was better," Mama said. "How often have you lied to protect someone's feelings, Selene?"

"Only when I had to."

"Does that mean I can lie, too?" Nicholas asked.

"No, it doesn't," I said.

Giving me a wink, Mama said, "I think your son and I should have a little talk."

I didn't want to tell her that was my job. I just smiled instead.

At Spencer's, I got on the computer to check on orders and was relieved to see that the shrubs I'd ordered for the Studios were going to be delivered the next day. I got on the phone next and lined up the guys who planted for us so I could get everything in the ground before Saturday. Then I phoned Elissa to let her know.

"I'm glad you called," she said. "I wanted to ask if you'd come down to consult with me on the outdoor décor. I know what I'd like, but I don't know if it's right for the patio."

"I'd be happy to come over. Are you free later today?"

"I'll be working in my studio all afternoon. Feel free to drop by anytime."

She hesitated then, and I had the feeling she wanted to ask me about the investigation. "I'll see you later today," I said quickly, and ended the call, feeling like a coward.

"Knock, knock," my dad called, strolling through the open doorway.

"Pops, you don't have to say 'knock, knock' if you're already in the room," I teased.

"Don't mind me. I'm just here for the coffee."

"And how many cups is that so far?"

He set his mug down by the coffee machine and peered at me over his glasses. "I forget."

"Two cups a day is your limit," I reminded him. "Doctor's orders."

Dad gave me a long sigh but kept his thoughts to himself.

"While you're here," I said, "I'd like to get your opinion on something."

"Always happy to share my opinion." He sat down across the desk from me and crossed one leg over the other. "Shoot."

"I went to see Sonny Talbot the other day."

His eyes widened a bit. "How did that go?"

"Actually, it went well. Lila Talbot got me in to see him. She thought we could get some useful information about Pete Harmon, and she was right. I just don't know what to do with it now."

"Fill me in."

"Apparently, Harmon Oil once operated a refueling station up north. They were caught dumping waste into the lake and subsequently had to file bankruptcy after covering up the scandal. Now that Pete Harmon is intent on building another refueling station here in Sequoia, I fear the same thing will happen. Case is looking into the old case, but even with his researching skills, I'm afraid we won't find anything."

"If that information were to go public, Thenie, you shouldn't have any trouble stopping Harmon from purchasing that land. Why not take the story to the press?"

"I told Harmon I would do just that if he didn't cooperate."

"Oh boy." Dad took off his glasses and wiped them
with a tissue. "I'll bet that didn't go over well."

"He wasn't happy, but it worked. We were able to verify that he was at the festival on the day of the murder and
that he received a blackmail letter." Not wanting to upset
my dad, I left out the part about Harmon's threat.

"Good work," Dad said, "but you still haven't answered
my question. Why not take that story to the press?"

"I'd need documentation first, and that will take some
time to acquire, if I can find any at all."

"Athena, do you want to stop him from acquiring the
land or not?"

"Absolutely, but right now all I have is Sonny Talbot's
word on what happened. A convicted felon's word. No reporter worth his salt would print a story based on that."

Dad put his glasses back on. "Have you forgotten
everything you learned in Chicago? What journalist
wouldn't love to get Sonny Talbot back in the news, especially when it comes to the Harmon land deal?"

"And every good journalist knows you have to have
facts to back up a story."

"Then let the reporter get the facts and go for it. Stop
Harmon in his tracks. You wanted my opinion, so there it
is. Don't you have an in with the reporter who covered
the statue's unveiling? Charlie something?"

He was talking about the reporter for the *Sequoian
Press*. Case had been the one to give me the title Goddess
of Greene Street, but Charlie was the one who'd made
sure that the public knew about it.

"Yes, I do, Pops. Charlie Bolt. I'll have to give him a call."

"Knock, knock," Case said as he strode into the office.

I put my head in my hands. "You don't have to say 'knock, knock' if the door is open."

Dad just smiled at me.

"Sorry to stop by unannounced," Case said. "I was on my way to the office. How are you, Mr. Spencer?"

"I'm fine," Dad said as he stood and shook Case's hand. "Just stopped by for a cup of coffee."

"No more," I said firmly.

"Worth a try," Dad said on his way out.

Case came around the desk and pulled me up for a kiss, smelling of musky aftershave and tasting of peppermint.

"What was that for?" I asked breathlessly.

"Do I need a reason?" He smiled.

I leaned in for another kiss and heard Nicholas clear his throat.

"Doesn't anyone knock around here?" I asked.

"Sorry," Nicholas said. "The door was open. Case, come with me. I need your help."

Case glanced at me in bewilderment as Nicholas turned and bounded away.

"Duty calls," Case said. He gave me one last peck on the lips and followed my son.

Curiosity getting the best of me, I left the office and trailed after them through the barn, watching as Nicholas burst out the back door toward the outdoor garden center. I caught the door behind Case and joined the two outside.

Almost at once, there was a rustling noise behind the knockout roses, and out sprang Oscar, his beady, masked black eyes studying the three of us, no doubt hoping one of us had peanuts. After assessing the situation with his snout, he ambled over to where Nicholas stood and flinched in surprise as Case reached down to pet him.

"It's okay, Oscar," Nicholas said. "He's a friend."

After a few friendly pets, Oscar was practically purring as he rolled over onto his back for a belly rub. My son turned his attention toward the flagstone pathway and said, "Look here."

"What's going on?" I asked.

"See this?" He pointed to a muddy shoe print. He removed one of his athletic shoes and set it inside. "It's different than mine, and it leads this way." He slipped his shoe back on and waved us forward. "Come on."

Following a trail of muddy prints, he led us down a path through the azalea bushes, with Oscar following along like a puppy.

"Oscar's toys keep disappearing, so I set a trap," Nicholas told us. "Before we opened this morning, I got the hose out and watered down the area where the toy thief jumped the fence." Nicholas stopped at the back of the property in front of the white picket fence and pointed. "See here? He stepped right in the mud."

"Who's your suspect?" Case asked, as he and I studied the shoe prints.

"Denis Reed," Nicholas answered immediately. "I think he rides his bike here and steals things. Now you need to help me prove it."

Case knelt down and inspected Nicholas's muddy trap. "It looks like he stepped here before climbing the fence."

"Exactly," Nicholas said, beaming with pride. "I made sure the gate was locked so Denis would have to climb over to get in and out. I know it's him. All we have to do is look at the bottom of his shoe. If it matches, we have our proof."

"That's solid detective work," Case said, standing up. "Now, how do you think we should check his shoe?"

"I don't know," Nicholas answered. "I don't want to accuse him unless I have proof. Right, Mom? That's why I need your help, Case."

"Okay, kiddo," Case ruffled his hair playfully. "This will be my first official investigation."

"I get paid on Friday," Nicholas said. "I can pay you then."

He wore such an earnest expression I had to hide my laugh.

"Don't worry about it this time," Case said. "First one's free."

"I think I know where Denis put the toys, too," Nicholas continued. "In his playroom at the Studios. He wouldn't let me see inside the closet, so the toys might be in there."

"First let's check the shoe print," Case said. "We'll have to get him to take off his shoes next time he's here to see if they match. Maybe if you're inside and you both take off your shoes, your mom can sneak one of Denis's out here."

"That's a great idea!" Nicholas gazed at Case with admiration. "Can you get a warrant for that closet?"

"I don't think this is that kind of case," I said. "Why don't I just ask Elissa if she can check the closet?"

"No, Mom. Case needs to investigate first."

"Okay, I'll make sure he does."

"Case, let's take photographs," Nicholas said in his best professional voice.

I watched as Case helped my son photograph the

prints. It was heartwarming to see them bond, and I couldn't help but smile. It seemed my son took after me in a love of solving mysteries. In the meantime, I had a dilemma. Should I continue to let Denis come over and possibly steal more toys, or should I tell Elissa what we suspected and take the chance of ruining not only our friendship, but Denis and Nicholas's, too?

And there was my next blog subject.

We were on our way back inside the garden center when Case's phone rang.

"Case Donnelly," he said, then listened intently. "Can you meet us at our office today?" He held his hand over the phone and said to me, "Are you free at one o'clock?"

"I'll make sure I am."

"We'll see you at one. The address is five thirty-five Greene Street, above the deli."

He hung up and stuck the phone into his pocket. "That was Beau Clifford. He has something important to show us. He said it can't wait."

CHAPTER SEVENTEEN

Case's office was starting to look like a real place of business. A new desktop computer sat on his desk, a sleek copier stood on a stand in the corner, and a ream of paper and various office supplies took up a shelf above it. Case had even brought in some of his books and study guides for the bookcase.

"What do you think?" he asked, leaning back in his desk chair.

"Looks very professional." I handed him the manila envelope with the photos in it. "This is for your new filing cabinet."

"You mean *our* new filing cabinet."

There was a knock on the outside door, and then a man's voice called, "Hello?"

"Come in," Case called.

I heard the door close, and a moment later Beau

walked into the office carrying a white envelope. I introduced him to Case, and the two men shook hands. Case invited him to sit in one of the chairs across the desk from him, and I took the other chair.

"What can we help you with?" Case asked.

"This came in the mail yesterday." He slid the envelope across the desk. As Case pulled out a letter, I got up and went around the desk to see it.

Typed in a large font in the middle of the page, it said: *Unless you want a photo of you taking money from Pete Harmon to be posted on the internet, mail $5,000 to P.O. Box 117 within seven days. You know what will happen if you don't.*

I looked at Case in surprise. How could Beau have received a blackmail letter two weeks after Hugo's death?

Case picked up the envelope and turned it over. It had been sent to Beau in care of JumboMart, and there was no return address on it. He stuck the letter in his copier and pressed Start. "I'm going to make a copy to keep in my files."

"What do you make of it?" I asked Case.

Case returned to his desk chair. "It can't be from Hugo. It was postmarked one day ago."

"Who else would know about Beau's photo?" I asked.

Case pursed his lips and said nothing.

"What do I do?" Beau asked. "I don't want that photo put out there."

"You have seven days before anything will happen—*if* it happens," Case said. "Someone could be calling your bluff. In the meantime, let us work on it."

Beau dropped his head into his hands. "I can't believe this. I never should've agreed to meet with Pete Harmon."

Case tapped his pen on the desk, thinking. "Has Pete made contact with you since you and Athena talked?"

Beau shook his head. "Tom Silvester came to see me, though. He brought another payment from Pete. I told Tom I wouldn't take it, that Pete had already secured my vote." He ran his fingers through his hair. "I know I took a chance declining the money, but I don't want anything else from Pete Harmon."

"What do you mean, you took a chance?" I asked.

Beau sighed. "Pete doesn't like to hear no."

"What did Tom say?" Case asked.

"He wasn't happy. He probably didn't want to be the one to report that back to Pete. He told me, 'In for a dime, in for a dollar. Just take the money and don't look back.' But I couldn't."

"Good for you," I said.

"Have you contacted the police about this letter?" Case asked.

"Absolutely not," Beau said. "I just want this to go away."

"We'll have to show this to the detectives."

"What if they want to talk to me? What if they show up at my work? Or my house? What if my wife finds out?"

"You can't keep this a secret forever," I said.

He pointed at me. "You told me my wife wouldn't find out about this."

"No," I replied. "We said *we* wouldn't tell your wife."

At that, Case stood. "Give us a few days to work on this, and then we'll be in touch."

"What does it matter at this point?" Beau's shoulders sagged. "I can't pay the ransom. I don't have the money. And now if my wife finds out . . ." He paused, as though he wanted to say more, then turned and walked to the door. "Talk to the police if you want. I have to go home and speak with my wife."

As soon as Beau was gone, I rose and went to stand by the window, gazing down at the people on the sidewalk below. "Who besides Hugo would threaten Beau with blackmail?" I turned to look at Case. "Have we gotten this all wrong? I feel like we're chasing our tails now."

"I think I know exactly who our blackmailer is." Case sat down and swiveled his chair toward me. "Let me ask you this. How would Hugo have found out about Pete's bribes in the first place? Who was the one person who could've known all of Pete's dirty secrets? And who got fired by Pete just before the blackmailing started?"

I slapped my palm on the armrest. "It's Jewel. But why would she just now try to blackmail Beau?"

"For two reasons," Case said. "She needs more money, and her scheme worked before." He leaned back in his desk chair. "There's been no mention of any of the men who were blackmailed anywhere on the internet that I could find, and no photos have come to light. Why is that?"

"Because she's been getting the extortion money."

"Exactly," Case said. "Pearson and Tom both admitted to paying it, and based on this new information, I'll bet that Pete Harmon also paid her."

"Now that you mention it, Jewel did seem pretty desperate for money when we questioned her, so desperate that she was willing to give up information that could ultimately lead us back to her."

"But not desperate enough to give up information about Pete, or that she was fired," Case said.

"Do you think she cooked up this plan after she got fired?"

"Probably. All along we've assumed that Hugo had been the one blackmailing these men, but that didn't make sense because he asked for my help. Then there's this." Case reached for the manila envelope I'd just brought down. He dumped the contents on the desk, moved aside the black-and-white photos, and pointed to the picture of Jewel seated before a laptop computer. "This photo didn't make sense before, either, but it's starting to now. Think about the timeline. Jewel was fired from Harmon Oil four weeks ago, and the blackmail letters started arriving not long after that."

"Somewhere in that timeline, we know that Jewel and Hugo broke up," I said, thinking aloud. "He must've found out about her blackmail scheme, and that's when he came to you."

Case leaned over to scrutinize Jewel's photo. "There must be something in this picture, some kind of evidence that Hugo wanted to discuss with me. But what is it?"

I went around to stand beside his chair, and we both studied the photo. A few items lay scattered across a desk. A desk lamp was on, casting a glare onto the laptop's screen.

"Why would Hugo take a photo of her at the computer," Case mused, "and use his cell phone instead of his professional camera?"

"And why did he take it when she wasn't looking?"

"Because he didn't want her to know," Case said.

"I wish we could see what's on her laptop screen," he said.

After a moment of thought, I went for my purse and

pulled my cell phone out. "Sit down at your computer. Let's reenact it."

Case sat down and swiveled his chair toward his new monitor, pretending to type on the keypad. I backed up against the window with my phone and took his picture, then showed it to him. "What do you think?"

Case took my phone, used his fingers to enlarge the photo of him, then squinted at the monitor in the picture. "I can just make out what's on my screen. If we could do the same with Jewel's photo, we might be able to read it."

"We'll have to have it professionally enlarged."

"Maybe not." Case used my phone to take a picture of Jewel's photo. Then he pulled out a cord from his drawer and plugged my phone into his computer. After a few moments, the picture was uploaded and displayed in full view. The words were fuzzy, and the screen was pixelated, but I could make out the first line. In a bold font it said: *Pearson, if you think I won't publish the photo on the internet—*

I glanced at Case in surprise. "It's Pearson's second blackmail letter."

"She's got her fingers on the keypad, Athena. Hugo must have suspected that she was up to something and caught her in the act."

"Now the photo makes sense, and the timeline fits."

Case put the photos back into the manila envelope. "Hugo wanted to talk to Pearson at the art festival, saying he had some explaining to do and wanting to help him. Now that makes sense, too. He was going to warn Pearson about Jewel's scheme."

"Hugo tried to talk to Beau, too," I said. "And sad to say, neither one would give him the time of day."

"He could've also made contact with Tom Silvester at the festival."

I suddenly felt very badly for my initial feelings toward Hugo. I had written him off as untrustworthy, just like everyone else had. "He was trying to do the right thing," I told Case. "Hugo was trying to stop Pete Harmon and expose the city council, but instead was murdered, maybe because of Jewel's blackmail scheme."

Case slid the note back into the envelope and filed it in the new filing cabinet. "I think it's time to confront Jewel."

I turned my head at the sudden loud *thump* in the stairwell. I thought at first maybe Lila had come to surprise us again, but her heels would've been a dead giveaway on the wooden steps. At a second *thump*, Case rose quietly from his chair and placed a finger over his lips as he moved through the room. And all I could think of was that Pete had come to make good on his threat.

CHAPTER EIGHTEEN

I followed behind Case as he carefully turned the doorknob to the outer hallway and opened the door just wide enough to peer outside. He glanced back at me, shook his head, then swung the door wide and stepped out. I heard a *screech* and glanced around him to see Jessie Mae Farmer from the JumboMart drop two bags of groceries and clutch her chest.

"Dear Lord in heaven," she cried, "I just about had an aneurism. Next time say something before you jump out."

"Mrs. Farmer, what are you doing here?" Case asked as he helped her pick up the bags.

She drew a deep breath in and blew it out. "You just took ten years off my life." She took a bag from Case and settled it on one hip. "I heard about new tenants moving in, but I had no idea it was you. I rent one of the apartments down the hall. What a coincidence, wouldn't you say? Although it's been said there are no such things as coincidences." She peered around at me. "How are you doing, dear?"

"I'm fine," I said, stepping up beside Case. "Sorry for the scare."

"I lived through it." She moved over so she could see our door. "I'm assuming this is your private-eye office. Good location. But you need a sign on the glass. What are you calling yourselves?"

"The Greene Street Detective Agency," I said.

"I like it. Has a nice ring to it."

"I like it, too," I said, giving Case a pointed look.

He carried one of the bags to her apartment and helped her take it inside. When he came back, he turned the dead bolt on the office door. "Let's keep this locked when we're here. I don't want to sound paranoid, but we should be cautious, even when we're out."

I followed him back into his office and picked up my purse. "I've got to get back to Spencer's. I've got a meeting with Elissa in half an hour."

"Why don't we pay Jewel a visit when you're done?"

"I can't today. I promised my dad he could take some time off. He's been working long hours lately, so I'll be closing up shop tonight. How about tomorrow after lunch?"

"You've got yourself a date."

Back at Spencer's, I checked in with my dad, picked up my iPad, and headed down to the Studios to talk to Elissa. The day was mild and partly sunny, the perfect day for a stroll down Greene Street. Being nearly mid-week, there weren't as many tourists in town, so the sidewalks weren't as congested as they were on the weekends. It gave me a clear view of my surroundings and fortunately, nothing seemed out of the ordinary.

I passed the quaint section of Greene Street known as Little Greece, which had nearly been razed by the Talbot Corporation in order to make way for a giant condominium complex. I'd fought hard to keep it from being demolished, and I was prepared to do the same for the lakefront land. I wasn't sure the Save Our Dunes group would raise the money they needed to persuade the city council to keep the land as a park, so I was glad to have a backup plan. And that reminded me.

I pulled out my phone and made a call to my reporter buddy. "Charlie," I said when I reached him, "this is Athena Spencer."

"The Goddess of Greene Street," he teased. "What can I do for you?"

"I have a juicy story I think you're going to love. It's full of intrigue and corruption—"

"You needn't go any further. I'm all ears."

I gave Charlie a complete rundown on the scandal that had nearly ruined Pete Harmon, and I could almost hear him rubbing his hands together.

"You're right," he said. "It is a juicy story. I'll get right on it. I have to warn you, though, it might take a few days—I'll have to make a trip up north to do some digging—and there's a chance nothing will come of it, but I'll give you a heads-up if the story pans out."

"That's all I ask, Charlie. Our only time constraint is that the story has to come out before the next city council meeting, which is a week from this coming Wednesday."

"Then I'd better start digging."

I hung up with a smile. Play with the goddess's fire, Pete, and *you'll* get burned.

Twenty minutes later, I reached the Studios, on the southern end of Greene Street. I climbed to the second floor and found Elissa sitting before an easel, dressed in an artist's smock, her short, dark hair brushed away from her face.

She was painting a picture of the dunes, the same view she could see from her rear window. But in her version, there was a charming flagstone path that meandered past granite park benches, and giant planters filled with butterfly weed, purple love grass, and blue coneflowers.

"How pretty," I said quietly, so as not to startle her.

She turned and smiled. "Thank you. Another piece for the auction."

"Your vision of the park is exactly what I'd imagined."

"It was nearly that beautiful once upon a time. And this lake view"—she indicated her painting—"is what we can do if we're given the chance." She put her brush in a jar of solution and wiped her hands on a towel. "I appreciate your stopping by."

"No problem. The shrubs I've selected for you are being delivered today, and I've lined up our landscape guys for tomorrow."

"That's wonderful. One less thing to worry about."

"Are you worried about the auction?"

She nodded. "We sent out invitations to our past customers, but I just learned yesterday that several of our biggest customers from Chicago aren't coming. I've had local buyers back out as well, and I fear it's because of the news about Pearson being a murder suspect. The number of people who'll be bidding for some of the more costly artwork is way down. And this is our last chance to make our goal before the council votes."

"How much do you still have to raise?" I asked.

"Well," she said, thinking out loud, "because of the abrupt halt to the art fair, we were only able to raise six thousand that day. That means we've raised eighty thousand in the three years we've been in operation, so we still have another twenty to go before Monday. That's why we're so anxious about the auction. We need big spenders."

I didn't see how SOD could possibly raise that amount at one art auction, but then I'd never attended one before. And once again I knew that contacting Charlie Bolt had been the right move. I just had to hope he'd be able to uncover enough to make a story before the city council met.

"I can't wait to see what you'll do with the patio," Elissa said. "We need it to be stunning. Let's go out back, and I'll tell you what I have in mind."

We proceeded down the staircase and out the back door. After studying the design that I had laid out, Elissa stood in the center of the big cement patio and pointed to the outside corners. "What would you think about a large planter on each corner?"

"I think it'd be charming. I'd also put smaller pots on each side of the large ones and then fill them all with native flowers and grasses. In fact, what would you think about using the same flowers you put in your painting?"

She pressed her hands together in delight. "That would be wonderful. And I like your idea of hanging lanterns. We could use the same lanterns that you have at Spencer's around your patio area."

I finished making notes in my iPad and glanced around.

"What about a water feature up by the house and a granite garden sculpture at the lower end of the patio?"

"I like it."

"We've got a selection to choose from. Can you come down to Spencer's later today? That way I can put it on the truck with the shrubs and trees."

She checked her watch. "I've got a few other things to do here, and then I can come down. I'll bring Denis with me. He so loves to play with Oscar."

It was on the tip of my tongue to tell her about Denis possibly being our toy thief, but I just couldn't bring myself to accuse him. What if Nicholas was wrong? Instead, I said, "Have you considered getting Denis a dog?"

Elissa tapped her chin. "Maybe. I'll have to talk to Pearson and see what he thinks." She sighed. "He's been so depressed. With the murder investigation hanging over his head and the art auction coming up, I know he's worried, and frankly, so am I. The detectives haven't been around in days, and we're holding our breath, hoping they're looking for the true killer and not still trying to prove that Pearson is guilty."

Which was probably the exact opposite of what they were doing.

"Case and I are still actively investigating, Elissa. We have several suspects whom we're tracking, and hopefully we'll have something definite soon."

I hoped that was vague enough to offer her comfort without getting specific.

She gazed at me for a moment longer, then seemed to snap to it. "Okay, I'll get things wrapped up here, and then Denis and I will come down to Spencer's in about an hour."

I'd have to tell Nicholas to hide Oscar's toys.

* * *

"Mom, we have to think of a reason why Denis and I need to take off our shoes. Case and I got a photograph of the muddy shoe print, and now we need to compare it so we have proof that Denis stole Oscar's toys."

I had just returned from the Studios, and Nicholas had come into the office with me.

"The problem is," I said, "I'll be with his mother. I won't be able to sneak his shoe out to fit it in the shoe print." I thought for a moment. "What if we asked Aunt Delphi to ask both of you to take off your shoes while you're inside the store? Then she can sneak his shoe outside, and if the pattern matches the one in the dirt, we have our culprit."

Nicholas gave me a high five. "See? We can be a detective team, too. I'll go tell Theia Delphi right now."

When Elissa and Denis came down an hour later, Nicholas had his plan in place. Elissa left Denis with him and accompanied me outside to where we kept the garden sculptures.

"This statue of a blue heron is lovely," she said, stroking the neck of the four-foot-tall cast-iron bird.

"If you want to continue with that theme, we have another statue of an egret that would complement it," I told her.

"Yes! Let's do it."

At that moment, Nicholas pushed the back door open and both boys came flying out in bare feet, running up the path through the shrubs.

"Denis, where are your shoes?" Elissa called, but the boys were too far away to hear.

The plan was working.

* * *

The next morning, I dropped Nicholas off at Spencer's, then went down to the Studios to oversee the planting of the shrubs and trees. When the workers had finished, Elissa came out to see how everything looked.

"I love it," she said, standing in the middle of her newly designed patio. "I love what you did with the large planters, too. With that and the hanging lanterns, this space will really shine."

"I'm glad you like it."

She plugged in the fountain, a pretty waterfall with colored lights behind it, and exclaimed in delight, "I can't wait for Pearson to see it." Her expression clouded over for a moment, then she inhaled deeply and went on. "Let's hope for a great turnout."

"I put out your flyers, and I also distributed them to the Greek merchants. Hopefully that will bring more people in."

"That's wonderful. Thank you."

"This," I said, sweeping my hand across the view of the dunes, "is worth the effort."

"If only everyone in town thought so," she said with a sigh.

If the news about Harmon Oil got out, I had a feeling everyone *would* think so.

"Athena," Elissa said, "I need to talk to you frankly."

My heart came to a standstill.

Elissa was chewing her lower lip, her fingers twisted together. "You keep telling me that the investigation is moving along, but I feel like you're not being up front with me. If the investigation is moving, why hasn't Pearson been cleared?"

I was at a loss for words. After trying to decide how

much to tell her, I said, "To be honest, the investigation isn't going as well as we'd hoped. We have two strong persons of interest that we believe had the means, motive, and opportunity. We just haven't been able to come up with enough evidence to convince the police to investigate them."

She looked away, rubbing her forehead. "That isn't the news I was hoping to hear."

"I'm sorry. But don't think we've given up. We still have more interviews to conduct, so all is not lost, okay?"

Looking very down in the mouth, she said, "Okay, and thanks for being honest with me."

My cell phone rang, and with relief I saw Case's name on the screen. "I've got to get back to Spencer's," I told Elissa, letting the call go to voice mail. "I'll let you know if we find anything helpful."

"Thanks again for everything," she said in a dispirited voice.

I called Case as I strolled north on Greene Street. "I just had a frank talk with Elissa about her husband. She's pretty down in the dumps."

"No doubt," he said.

"So, what's up?"

"Do you want to meet for lunch at the pizza truck? Then we can head over to Jewel's house after we eat."

"Pizza sounds delicious."

I was surprised to see Lila at the plaza standing in front of the Mexican food truck. With her blond hair pulled back in a loose, sexy bun, she was wearing a yellow tank top, black and white yoga pants, and yellow wedge sandals, making her look like a giant bumblebee.

In my white T-shirt and blue jeans, with my long straight hair, I felt drab by comparison.

"Lila stopped by the office and wanted to know what was new with the investigation," Case told me when I found him sitting at a picnic table. He looked very yummy in a form-fitting black T-shirt and snug blue jeans. His hair was thick and wavy, and a faint five o'clock shadow gave him a very masculine look that made me catch my breath.

"I caught her up," he continued, "and she wants to go to Jewel's house with us."

"Don't you think having three people confront Jewel will make the woman a little nervous? She wasn't that co-operative to begin with."

"You're right," he said. "We'll have to leave Lila in the car—if she still wants to come."

"Leave me in the car for what reason?" she asked, placing three orders of tacos and a container of nachos and salsa down in front of us.

So much for having pizza for lunch.

I tried to be tactful. "Our interview with Jewel is going to be tricky. Having three people there could present a problem."

She waved away my concern. "Sweetie, I'm a master when it comes to tricky situations. Remember, I lived with Grayson for five years."

I still couldn't see the three of us in Jewel's little studio, throwing questions at her. I waited for Case to speak up, but, disappointingly, he stayed silent on the subject.

Back at the office, Case checked his email and suddenly thrust his fists into the air with a loud "Yes!"

"What happened?" Lila asked.

"I was granted a private investigator's license. It'll be mailed out today, so I should have it in two days."

"Congratulations!" Lila and I said together. She wrapped her arms around Case and gave him a noisy kiss on the cheek, then drew me in and squeezed us both in giddy excitement. "We're officially private eyes!"

We?

"And now we can get a sign hung outside," she continued. "Before you know it, we'll have clients. I say we all go out to dinner tonight and celebrate."

Yippee.

"Just one thing," Case said. "Now that we can officially open our office, Lila, you and Athena will be working under my license. That means we need to establish some ground rules."

Thank God he was finally speaking up.

"Okay, Mr. Private Eye," Lila said with an indulgent smile, "let's hear them."

"The fastest way for me to lose my license is to break the law, so the most important rule is that you work within the limits of the law. If you're not certain about something, ask and I'll let you know whether it's allowed or not."

"Got it," Lila said.

"Number two. Don't investigate alone for obvious safety reasons."

I didn't say anything, but I had an issue with that rule. I'd been an investigative reporter on my own for years and knew how to take precautions. But I didn't want to discuss the matter in front of Lila. She needed that rule.

"Number three," Case continued, making eye contact with Lila. "We want to be considered professionals, so we have to act appropriately."

I knew that one was for Lila.

She made a face like she'd tasted something sour. "You're sounding exceedingly bossy. I had enough of that with Grayson."

"Don't worry," Case said. "I don't want to be anyone's boss. We're a team, but if we want to keep it that way, you'll have to follow the rules."

I couldn't help but chuckle to myself at Lila's exasperated expression.

"That means you, too, Athena," Case said.

"Me? What rules have I broken?"

"You have a tendency to forge your own path," he said. "Just make sure you don't forge it alone. I don't want either of you putting yourselves in danger."

I crossed my arms over my T-shirt. "Finished?"

"For now."

"Then here's to the Greene Street Detective Agency," I said, holding up my water bottle.

Case tapped his bottle against mine.

Lila held up her index finger. "Wait a minute. I'd like to propose a different name. How about the Talbot Detective Agency?"

I nearly choked on my water. Case paused with the bottle to his mouth.

"It has a wonderful ring to it," Lila continued, "and everyone knows the Talbot name."

"Yes, but most people think the Talbot name stands for greed, coercion, and attempted murder," I said, making sure each point hit home.

"Exactly," Lila said cheerfully. "There's a stigma attached to the name. Imagine how uncomfortable I feel walking around town. The stares and whispers—they're too much sometimes. I want the Talbot name to be known for justice. Plus, since I bankrolled the whole operation, I'd like a little say in how we run things."

I glanced at Case to get his reaction, but I couldn't gauge it. His eyes were focused on Lila, but he seemed to be looking straight through her. Finally, he inhaled, as if he'd been underwater and was just coming up for air. "To justice," he said.

"To justice," we echoed.

"Now let's go see Jewel."

We locked up the office, walked to the parking lot at the marina, and climbed into Case's Jeep, which now had the doors removed.

"How fun!" Lila called from the back seat. "I love this car."

Good, I thought. *Then hopefully you won't mind staying in it while we talk to Jewel.*

But that didn't happen. Case parked the Jeep in front of Jewel's tiny house, and we all got out. This time, I noticed, there was a black pickup truck parked in the driveway rather than the compact car we'd seen the first time we were there.

The three of us trooped up to the front door, rang the bell, and waited for Jewel to answer. Case rang the bell again and then knocked, but no one appeared.

"We'll have to go around back," Case said. To Lila he said, "She works in a converted garage making jewelry."

"Jewel. Jewelry." Lila chortled. "With a name like that, what else would she do?"

"The problem is," Case told her, "we don't know who the truck belongs to. It'd be safer if you waited in the Jeep while we check it out. That way you can keep an eye on the front of the house and text me if anyone comes around."

She studied Case as though wondering whether he was being truthful. She glanced at me, and I gave her a nod of encouragement.

"Okay," she said with a huff. "If that's what you want."

We waited until she was in the Jeep, then we walked back to the garage. Case knocked on the service door, then tried the handle, but it was locked. I cupped my hands around my eyes to peer through the dusty side window.

"Case, come look! It's been cleaned out."

He looked inside, then muttered under his breath, "She's gone."

"Then who owns the pickup truck?"

Suddenly we heard Lila shouting, and both of us went running toward the front. We found her standing at the bottom of the front steps with her hands on her hips, and a big, beefy man standing in the doorway.

He pointed toward the street. "You need to leave right now!"

"Not before I speak to Jewel!" Lila yelled.

"No way!"

"Then I'm not moving."

This was her answer to a "tricky situation?"

"Lila, what are you doing?" Case asked quietly, drawing her away.

"I saw a woman looking out the front window," she said with a scowl aimed in the man's direction. "And this *caveman* won't let me speak to her."

The man stepped out onto the porch carrying a large moving box. He looked like a biker with his long, scraggly beard and flaming skull T-shirt plastered against his gut. He directed his comment at Case, "Get this *lady* out of here."

"We're private investigators," Case said, stretching the truth for Lila's sake. "We're working on a murder investigation."

Carrying the box, the burly man stepped down from the porch. Giving Lila a glare from under thick eyebrows he said, "Get outta my way." When she refused to move, he sidestepped her, muttering under his breath.

"We'd like to speak with Jewel," Case said, as we followed the man to his truck. "Is she inside?"

"Maybe," he called.

Trotting along after us, Lila called, "She definitely is. I saw her."

To my surprise, Case gave Lila a warning glance, but that didn't stop her. "What are you hiding?" she demanded. "Why won't you let us speak with her?"

The man set the box in the back of the truck and brushed off his hands before turning to scowl at Lila. "This is Jewel's house, and she don't want to talk to you."

"Then can we ask you some questions?" Case asked.

"You can ask me all the questions you want," he called over his shoulder as he headed back to the house, "but you ain't getting inside."

"Sweetie," Lila said to Case, "let me handle this. I know what to do now." She marched ahead of us, opening her purse and removing her wallet.

"She's going to bribe him," I told Case as we hurried after her.

CHAPTER NINETEEN

"How much will it take to convince you to answer a few questions?" Lila was asking the man as we caught up with her. "Fifty? A hundred?"

"Lila, stop," Case called.

The man turned in the doorway and glowered down at her. "You sure don't act like a private eye." He gave her a smirk. "Don't look like one, either."

"Seriously," she said, "what will it take?"

"You ain't got enough money to make me betray a friend." He slammed the door in her face.

She swung to look at us, a furious look on her face. "He's a caveman. You're a caveman!" she called through the door.

Case started back toward the Jeep, calling out sharply, "Let's go."

Surprised by the sudden change in his tone, I hurried after him, Lila close on my heels. We'd barely gotten our seat belts fastened when he took off.

"Where are we going?" Lila asked.

"You're going home," Case ground out.

I glanced at Lila through the sideview mirror and saw her mouth open in shock. "Excuse me?"

"I'm taking you home."

The wind blew in from the open sides of the Jeep, blowing her blond hair around her face. She was speechless, maybe for the first time in her life.

Case took a sharp right and continued east toward Lila's mansion.

"Maybe we should go back," I said to Case. "It's important that we talk to Jewel."

"It's very important," he answered. "That's why I'm taking Lila home."

She huffed loudly. "I don't even know what I did. What did I do?"

Case didn't answer right away. I could tell he was trying to cool down before saying something he'd regret. Finally, after Lila repeated her question, he answered evenly, "It was a mistake to bring you."

"Don't say that," Lila replied in a little girl's voice. "I was just trying to help."

"I know you were, and that's the problem. You took over." He inhaled deeply and let it out again, as though reaching inside for the calm to continue. "If you can't be a team player, Lila, and act professionally, then I don't want you coming along."

Lila's eyes grew wide with indignation. She folded her arms under her breasts, turned her head to gaze out the window, and sat there in stony silence.

I leaned back in the passenger seat, struggling with my own thoughts. After weeks of dealing with Lila's lunacy, I'd waited a long time for this moment, thinking it would be supremely satisfying. But watching her struggle for her dignity, huffing to herself because she still didn't understand, and searching for words to combat Case's accusation, I felt truly sorry for her. And now that I was actually starting to appreciate the kind of advantages she could offer, I couldn't help but try to ease the situation.

"Case," I said quietly, "she's not being any less professional than I was on our first interview."

"I could've gotten that guy to talk," he answered, not bothering to keep his voice down. "He's our only lead to Jewel."

"If he would've accepted the money, you wouldn't be so upset. Remember, you gave Jewel money for her answers."

"That was different," he said. "I didn't lead with my wallet. That's not how this works."

"I'm sorry," Lila butted in, "but that's how it works in my world. Money gets you what you want. Isn't that why you agreed to be a partner with me in the first place?"

Case sighed loudly. "Maybe this whole thing was a mistake."

At that Lila pulled a pair of sunglasses from her purse, shrouded her eyes, and again folded her arms. "Take me home then."

He dropped Lila off without another word, then reached for my hand and squeezed it gently, as if saying, *It'll be okay*, as we made our way back to Jewel's house. He passed the truck still parked in the driveway, drove around the block, circled back, and parked on the side street with a view of Jewel's house. "Now we wait."

I unbuckled my seat belt and made myself as comfortable as possible. I gave Case a sideways glance, waiting patiently as his thoughts caught up with his actions.

After a few minutes of silence, Case finally spoke. "You think I was too harsh?"

I put my hand on his shoulder. "Maybe a little."

He rubbed his temples like he was trying to ease a migraine. "What was I thinking to take her on as a partner? And now she wants to change the name of the detective agency?"

"You know," I said, "last week I would've been over the moon about you putting Lila in her place, but since then she's helped us out quite a bit. She just needs a little more training."

"Who's going to train her?" Case asked. "You shoot me daggers any time I suggest she help you out, and I doubt she'll want anything to do with me now."

"You could apologize."

"I can't even think about doing that right now."

I rubbed my thumb along the top of his hand. "You know what they say. Time heals all wounds."

"Thanks, Goddess Anon," he said dryly. "You now have your next blog topic."

"Trust me, give it some time. She'll accept your apology, and I promise not to shoot any more daggers your way."

After a few more minutes spent in silent reflection, we saw the beefy guy, whom we had now dubbed "the caveman," finally finish loading boxes. He hustled Jewel into the truck and started the engine.

"Here we go," Case said.

Staying well hidden, we followed him south to a section of town that was run-down, with houses in need of paint and scraggly lawns. He turned down an alley and parked his truck behind a one-car garage. Case pulled up just before the mouth of the alley, where we could watch him.

In a few minutes, the caveman began to unload boxes and carry them into the garage. Soon after, we saw Jewel dart into the garage after him, and then the garage door closed.

Case got a fix on the house, and then we drove up the street past it. "I'll have to do a stakeout. When our caveman friend leaves, I'll go up to the house and try to take Jewel by surprise. I doubt she'll be expecting me."

"What if she won't talk to you?" I asked.

Case smiled. "I'll show her the picture Hugo took at her computer. She'll talk."

Delphi and I stayed at Spencer's until it closed at eight o'clock, giving Dad and Drew another evening off. Nicholas was excited to show me the photograph he and Delphi had made of Denis's shoe, which was a match to the shoeprint in the mud. It was all the proof we needed, but I still didn't know how to confront Elissa with it. I knew I couldn't put off that conversation forever, but for the time being, I let it go.

Nicholas stayed until suppertime, then I sent him home with my dad to eat. I didn't get to write my blog until after nine o'clock, but that extra time had given me the opportunity to work on it in my head. And since I couldn't get Lila off my mind, she became my next blog subject.

IT'S ALL GREEK TO ME
Blog by Goddess Anon

MONEY CAN'T BUY EVERYTHING

In my circle of acquaintances there is a woman who believes that money can solve just about any situation she encounters. When she runs up against a problem, the first thing she does is reach for her wallet. And she has the wealth to do so.

Am I jealous? Just a tad. But then I think of all the things she can't *buy with her money, and I feel sorry for her. Number one is friendship. This woman, let's call her Billie, doesn't have a single close friend. I suspect it's because she tried to buy them, too.*

Number two is patience. Instead of automatically reaching for her wallet, how about trying another method, such as talking, reasoning, using her intelligence? Which leads me to number three: integrity. It isn't something to be purchased, like a bag of apples. You have integrity by being straightforward with people, not by advertising your wealth.

Number four is manners. Billie has obviously never stopped to consider how rude she is to assume people's behavior is for sale. And number five, of course, is love. As the Beatles sang, "Can't Buy Me Love." We love people for who they are, not for what they can buy us. Billie hasn't got that down yet, either. She's single and will probably remain so unless her money attracts someone. In that case, I pity her.

I could also mention respect, common sense, trust, class, and character as traits that can't be bought, but I'm out of time. What do you consider the most impor-

*tant out of that whole list? I'll be interested in your
comments.*

    As always,
    Goddess Anon bidding you adio.

The next morning, Nicholas and I were on our way to
the diner when Elissa called in a panic. I placed my phone
on speaker and heard, "Athena, Pearson's been arrested!"

My stomach gave a lurch. I was no longer hungry.
"Call your lawyer, Elissa. Have him meet you at the police station."

"I don't have anywhere to leave Denis." She sounded
as though she was hyperventilating.

"Drop him off at the garden center. We'll take care of
him."

"Great," Nicholas said, as I hung up the phone. "I
guess I'd better hide Oscar's toys."

"Be nice to him today," I said. "His dad was just arrested. I'm sure he'll be frightened and confused."

Nicholas looked at me in surprise. "Okay, Mom. I
will."

When we arrived at the garden center later that morning, Nicholas sprinted past my dad on his way to find
Oscar and his toys.

"What's going on?" my dad asked.

"Pearson's been arrested, Pops. Elissa is going to leave
Denis here while she's at the jail, and I might be in and
out today. I hope that's okay."

"We can handle things here. Take as much time as you
need."

I poured myself a cup of coffee in the office and sat

back in my desk chair, trying to calm my nerves before calling Case.

"What's up, Buttercup?" he asked.

"Pearson's just been arrested."

"You're kidding."

"I wish. Elissa's panicking, and I feel like I've let them both down."

"Stop, Athena. You haven't let anyone down."

"But we're no closer to finding the killer than we were before, and I don't know what else we can do."

"We've been working this case for almost three weeks, and all of the evidence we find keeps leading us back to Pearson Reed. Maybe the police did find the killer and you just don't want to accept it."

I sat forward. "No, nope, not happening. I can't give up yet. We still have to talk to Jewel. She knows something she's not telling."

"That's why I've been sitting out in front of the caveman's house since six this morning," Case said. "I'm not going to let her out of my sight."

I could hear him yawning. "How are you holding up?"

"Pretty good, but this coffee won't keep me full for long. Will you be free at lunch?"

"You bet. Give me a call when you get hungry, and I'll stop by with sandwiches."

I hung up and let out a breath of relief. Just knowing Case was on the job made me feel better.

Twenty minutes later, Elissa came in with Denis in tow. "Thank you, Athena," she said hurriedly. "Denis, behave yourself, and I'll see you later."

"Is Kevin going to meet you there?" I asked, referring to my ex-boyfriend/attorney Kevin Coreopsis.

"He said he would. I hope he's there already."

Denis watched with big eyes as his mother left. "What's going to happen to my dad?" he asked, chewing his nails. "The police put handcuffs on him and took him away."

"They're going to ask him some questions, and they will probably keep him overnight. They won't hurt him, but it's going to be a scary time for both your mom and your dad. Will you be strong for your mom?"

Denis nodded. "I'll be strong for my mom. But why did they have to put handcuffs on him? He wouldn't hurt them."

"It's just a law," I said, hoping he'd accept that. "Now, here's Niko, who's helping his grandpa with a display. Niko, why don't you show Denis how he can help you?"

I left the boys with my dad and went back to the office, where I once again paced, going over every detail we'd uncovered so far. We had four people caught on camera by Hugo, five photos in all, counting Jewel's. I felt as though we could rule Beau Clifford out, but I was no longer sure about Pearson.

At two thirty, Case called back. "Is that offer of food still open? I haven't had lunch."

"You bet. Tell me what you'd like, and I'll be there as soon as I can."

Twenty minutes later, after a stop at a nearby fast-food restaurant, I drove back to the caveman's neighborhood and found Case's Jeep parked down the street. I pulled in behind him and picked up the sack of food.

Slipping into the passenger seat, I handed him the sack. "Here you go. Roast turkey and chips."

He unwrapped the sandwich and bit into it hungrily.

And just as he was chewing his first bite, the caveman exited the house.

We both slid down in our seats until he'd gotten into his truck, then Case peered over the steering wheel. He handed me his sandwich and said, "Let's go."

"We're going to follow him?"

"I don't want to approach his house if he's only making a run to the store."

We stayed a distance behind him as he made his way across town. When he turned in at the Harmon Oil Company, pulled into the employee parking lot, and got out of the car, we looked at each other in surprise. "He works for Harmon," we said together.

"He must be working the afternoon shift," Case said.

"I'll bet this is where he met Jewel."

We waited until he'd gone inside, then we headed back to his house. Case parked in the same parking spot on the street and finished his sandwich, taking his time to make sure the caveman didn't return. Then he prepared to go up to the door.

"Do you want me to wait?" I asked.

"I want you to come with me."

CHAPTER TWENTY

Standing at her door, Case knocked, waited a few moments, then rang the doorbell. In a minute, the door opened a crack, and an eye peered out at us.

"Jewel," Case said, "we need to talk to you. It's important."

She opened the door wide enough so that we could see her furious face. "How did you find me?"

"I'm a private investigator," he said. "I know how to find people."

"I don't have anything more to say to you."

Before she could slam the door, Case said, "We know Pete Harmon fired you."

That made her pause.

"We know about your blackmail scheme, too," he said, "and we're going to the police right now unless you talk to us."

She gave him a defiant glare. "I don't know anything about a blackmail scheme."

"We have the letter you sent to Beau Clifford," Case said. "We know about the post office box, too. There's no point in denying it."

She stood eye to eye with Case, staring him down for a long moment, as though trying to decide whether he was serious, then she opened the door wider and stepped back. Her dark hair was pulled back, revealing the same earrings she had on in the picture Hugo had taken. She was wearing jeans and a blue T-shirt, with white sneakers on her feet. "Come in, then," she said grudgingly.

We stepped straight into a tiny box of a living room, where an old green tweed sofa and love seat had been jammed in with a TV set that looked like it had seen many years of use. Instead of offering us a seat, however, Jewel crossed her arms and glared at us.

"What do you want?"

"May we sit down?" I asked.

She shrugged.

We sat on the sofa and she finally perched on the edge of the love seat, her fingers drumming nervously on her crossed arms. She said nothing.

"You know why we're here," Case began.

With a defiant lift of her chin, she said, "Why should I tell you anything? Hugo might've trusted you, but I don't."

"You can trust we've done our homework," Case countered, "and you better believe we have enough evidence against you to bring to the detectives."

"I had nothing to do with Hugo's death."

Case gave her a piercing look. "I think you know that's not entirely true."

Jewel glanced away, still drumming her fingers against her folded arms, but now she was chewing her lower lip.

"We want to know how this whole blackmail scheme started," he said. "You can tell us, or we can let the detectives figure it out."

She turned her head to give him a glowering look. "I overheard Pete setting up meetings. That's how it started. I was curious."

"What sparked your curiosity?" Case asked.

She picked at a thread on the love seat. "Pete never scheduled his own meetings. That was my job. So I picked up the phone and listened in. That's when I heard him explaining how he was setting things up so that no one would ever find out."

"What things?" Case asked.

"The payouts, the bribe money."

Case continued asking questions. "Did you know what the bribe was for?"

"Yeah, votes for his land acquisition."

"Did you know who he was talking to?"

"Not at first, but then I overheard enough to figure it out. He set up meetings with three men. You already know who they are."

"And after you heard Pete make appointments with each man," I said, "is that when you decided to send Hugo to catch them in the act?"

She just stared at me, blinking.

I looked over my notes. "You told us that Hugo got close to you so he could get close to Pete Harmon. But that wasn't the truth, was it? You told Hugo about the scheme and sent him to do your dirty work."

"That's not true," she said. "When I told Hugo what

I'd learned, he was the one who decided to photograph Pete. I didn't want him to do it at first."

"What changed your mind?" I asked.

"Pete fired me," she said. "After that, I had nothing to lose. I told Hugo to go for it."

"Why was Hugo so interested in what Pete was doing?" Case asked.

Jewel finally sat down across from us and crossed one leg over the other, sullenly rubbing at a spot on her jeans. "He wanted revenge."

Finally, we were getting somewhere. I typed *revenge* into my iPad.

"Hugo wanted to see Pete suffer even more than I did," Jewel began. "He'd been investigating the Harmon Oil Company for a newspaper back when Harmon Oil first had legal issues. Pete covered up the whole thing and damaged Hugo's reputation in the process, planting false allegations and scandalous rumors about him, ruining Hugo's first marriage. Basically, his whole life was scarred by Pete Harmon."

My fingers could barely keep up.

"What did Hugo intend to do with the photographs?"

"He had a plan, but he wouldn't tell me about it. He said it was better that I didn't know."

"Was it about blackmail?"

She shook her head.

"When did you decide to blackmail the men?" Case asked.

"When I didn't have a paycheck coming in and my rent was due. The jewelry business is a joke and Hugo didn't have any money, so I figured out how to make some quick cash off those photos." She shrugged. "It seemed like a good idea, but Hugo found out and hit the roof."

"That's when you broke up," I said.

She nodded. "He wanted me to pay back the money."

"You know Beau Clifford isn't going to pay you the five thousand," Case said.

She lowered her head and finally gave a nod.

"Did you know that Hugo received a death threat because of those blackmail letters?" I asked.

The words must have sent a shiver down her spine, because she gave a shudder and rubbed her arms for warmth. Then, as though a light had come on, as though she'd finally realized her role in Hugo's demise, she turned pale. In almost a whisper, she said, "The death threat was meant for me."

"Maybe that's why Hugo hit the roof," I said. "Your little scheme put you both in danger."

"He was trying to explain himself at the art fair," Case added, "trying to undo the damage you'd caused."

In a whisper she said, "And then someone killed him." After a moment, she said in a shaky voice, "I didn't mean for anything to happen to Hugo." She looked toward the window, her hands balling into fists, the muscles in her jaw tightening. "I could just wring his ugly neck."

"Who?" I asked.

"Pete Harmon," she said through clenched teeth. "If it hadn't been for him, none of this would've happened."

"You're going to have to make restitution to everyone who sent you money," Case said. "Be prepared to give a statement to the police about it."

Her eyes grew wide. "I can't pay that back."

"You can try," I said. "Pay a little at a time. You need

to do this for Hugo. Pete's not the only one who ruined Hugo's reputation. You did, too."

Tears ran from her eyes, making streaks through her makeup. "If you turn me in, I'll deny it."

"We're not going to do anything," Case said as he stood. "You're going to turn yourself in." He slipped Jewel's photograph out of the envelope and showed it to her.

She began to cry openly as she looked at the photograph Hugo had taken. "Why didn't you show this to me before?"

"We didn't know how you were involved," Case explained. "But now we do. Hugo didn't want us to investigate the bribery. He wanted us to investigate the death threat. And he wanted us to investigate you."

"I didn't mean to hurt anyone," she sobbed.

"You set Hugo up," I said. "You used his computer to write those blackmail threats. You took money from three people. How is that not hurting anyone?"

"Hugo used me first," she cried, her mascara now bleeding under her eyes.

Case held up his hand to stop me from arguing with her. He placed Jewel's photo back into the envelope and said, "If you don't turn yourself in, we'll make sure the police come to pay you a visit."

Jewel lowered her head, sniffling. "I'm sorry. I'm so sorry." She turned away, ending our conversation.

When we got outside, I said, "Do you trust her to turn herself in?"

"Like I told her, we'll make sure she does."

"Do you want me to explain this to Maguire?"

"I think it's time we talk to the detectives. Do you have to get back to Spencer's?"

I checked my watch. "I have forty minutes left, but I really need to have a talk with Pearson. Why don't you drive us downtown? Then you can talk to the detectives, and I'll go to the jail and see if I can get in."

"That'll work. I'll call Beau on my way and tell him he doesn't need to worry about the blackmail letter. I'm sure he'll be relieved."

It took ten minutes to get through the security checks, then another ten to wait for Pearson to be brought in from his jail cell. I was seated in a room with a long row of cubicles and a heavy-duty glass partition running down the middle. Matching cubicles sat on the other side of the glass.

Pearson looked like a beaten man when he shuffled in wearing ankle cuffs. He sat down and picked up the phone. "Have you talked to Elissa?"

"I saw her this morning, before she came here, but we didn't get into anything about the investigation. What did your lawyer say?"

"There's going to be a bond hearing tomorrow. Kevin's going to try to get me out then."

I didn't have high hopes. It was almost impossible to get someone freed when they were facing a murder charge. "Was Elissa here when you spoke to Kevin?"

"She came just before Mr. Coreopsis got here. She's not doing well. She was already extremely anxious about the auction, and now"—he gestured around him—"this." He sighed wearily. "Do you have any good news for me?"

"Case is talking to the detectives right now. He's going to try to present enough evidence so that they'll reconsider the charge against you."

"Evidence against whom?" he asked.

"Tom Silvester and Pete Harmon."

Pearson shook his head sadly and looked away.

"Do you know what evidence they have against you?" I asked.

He ran a shaking hand through his hair. "Besides the cuts on my arms, the police have an eyewitness who saw me enter the trail around the time of the murder. I told the detective that it was when I went looking for my son, but he didn't act like he believed me."

"Did you see anyone else on the trail?"

He shook his head.

"What about the polygraph test? Didn't that prove you were telling the truth?"

"It was inconclusive."

"That's not good."

"But that's not the worst of it." Pearson rubbed his eyes. "They found one of my golf clubs at the murder scene, and my fingerprints are on it. They're calling it the murder weapon."

CHAPTER TWENTY-ONE

An eyewitness who put Pearson on the trail at the time of the murder. Cuts on his arms. An inconclusive polygraph test. And now a possible murder weapon? The evidence was stacked so highly against Pearson that all the doubts I'd kept at bay came flooding in like a tidal wave. "How did your golf club end up at the crime scene?"

"I don't know for sure, but my guess is that Denis took it to play with. I told Detective Walters that, but he scoffed as though he couldn't believe I was blaming my own child."

Normally I'd be infuriated by the detective's narrow-mindedness, but after everything Case and I had learned, it was hard to ignore the facts. "Why would your son take your golf club into the woods?" I asked, barely covering my skepticism.

"As I explained to Detective Walters, Denis has taken them before. He goes into the woods and pretends he's chopping his way through a jungle. I had my golf bag in my trunk during the art fair. I must have left my car unlocked."

Pearson noticed my uncertainty, because his cheeks immediately flushed with color. "You have to believe me, Athena. Detective Walters wouldn't."

"Did Walters talk to Denis?"

Pearson nodded. "He said Denis was adamant about not taking the club, and as far as he was concerned, that was the end of it. Maybe if you talked to Denis?"

"Pearson, I can't give your son the third degree. I'm sure your wife would be very upset with me if I did. You need to talk to her and see if she can get Denis to admit what happened."

And frankly, because of Pearson's lies and half-truths, I was having a hard time justifying my continued quest for justice. But then another thought struck me. I looked at Pearson through the glass. "Where did you say the detectives found your golf club?"

"At the murder scene."

"But not near the body."

"Right."

"Do you think Denis could have witnessed the murder? Maybe he dropped the club and ran away."

"I doubt that very highly," Pearson answered. "I'm sure he would've said something."

"So why would he leave the club behind?"

Pearson said nothing.

"Has he ever left a golf club in the woods before?"

"No."

"Let me think for a minute." I began to organize my

thoughts aloud. "Hugo's camera was missing from the crime scene. The police never found it, so we've been assuming that the killer took it to destroy evidence. But what if Denis was playing out in the woods and stumbled upon something he found more interesting?"

"So, you're saying he may have dropped the golf club in exchange for the camera?"

"It would put your club at the scene of the crime."

Pearson gave me a doubtful look. "If Denis took the camera, we would've seen him with it."

"Not if he didn't want it taken away from him." I pressed the phone closer to my ear and leaned in toward the glass. "When you finally saw Denis that morning, what was he doing?"

"It was nearly lunchtime, and he was coming upstairs from the basement. He said he'd been playing hide-and-seek with Niko."

"That's not possible. Niko was with my mother at the food booth all morning." I let that sink in, then said, "Has Denis mentioned anything about a camera?"

Pearson shook his head, but a flash of hope lit up his weary eyes. "I'll bet it's in the basement. Denis likes to hide down there. If you found the camera, would it clear me?"

"If I said yes, it would be pure speculation, but right now, it's the only hope we have."

"It makes sense, Athena. Denis loves taking photos with his cell phone. He'd be intrigued by a professional camera."

"Then we need to find it."

Pearson let out a short breath of relief. "Does that mean you haven't given up on me?"

As much as I wanted to say yes, one question still lingered. If Pearson hadn't taken the bribe money, why was

Pete Harmon so confident about acquiring the land? "Pearson, I need you to be absolutely truthful with me."

"Of course."

"It's about the bribe money." I shifted the phone to my other ear. "We know Tom and Beau accepted Pete's offer. We also know that the other members of the city council were not approached, which means that unless you vote yes for Pete's land acquisition, there's no way Pete will win. And that leads me to my question."

"I know where you're going with this," Pearson said, "and I'll tell you the truth, but you're not going to understand."

I had a sinking feeling as I sat back in my chair. Although I was still holding out hope that Pearson Reed was innocent in the murder of Hugo Lukan, I had to prepare myself for his confession of collusion with Pete Harmon. "I'll try my best to understand. I just want to know why you took the bribe money."

"I didn't accept the bribe money."

"Pearson," I said slowly, "we have the photograph Hugo took of you and Pete in his car. He was handing you an envelope."

"I turned him down, Athena. I told him I would never take his money and I would never vote for his project"— he glanced around, as though afraid someone was listening in—"but there are some things more effective than money."

"What's more effective than money?"

"The power to ruin me."

"I don't understand."

Pearson leaned forward. "I have to vote for Pete's project. If I don't, I'll lose everything."

"How?"

"No one knows this, not even Elissa. I wouldn't have known how to begin to explain it to her." He took a deep breath. "We're broke."

I stared at him in disbelief. "And Elissa doesn't know it?"

"She doesn't know everything. My printing business is failing. Elissa's studios are barely breaking even . . . We were about to lose everything, so I took out a business loan from Tom Silvester at the bank. It was the only thing I could do. No one else would even consider offering such a risky loan."

"Elissa is your partner, Pearson. Why couldn't you tell her?"

"Because she would have felt compelled to sell the Studios. Because I didn't want her to worry. Because, because, because." He looked down, pinching the bridge of his nose, his expression mirroring his pain. "I screwed up, and I couldn't even admit the truth to myself, let alone Elissa. Back then, I was confident that SOD would raise the money. And once that park went up, the Studios would be profitable, and we could finally start digging ourselves out of this hole. I could have sold my business and paid off these loans, and no one would have ever had to know how bad it was."

"So, Tom approved the business loan, knowing how risky it would be?"

"Yes. He knew I was struggling, so he approved the loan. I thought he was being a friend, but I soon learned that I was mistaken. He used the loan as leverage."

"How?"

"Tom found out that I turned down Pete's offer of money, so he told Pete about the loan, and they used it to coerce me. He said he would call it in, and I would be ruined unless I voted to let Pete buy the land."

"Is that why you were arguing at the festival?"

He nodded.

"Last week Case and I followed Tom when he dropped off what I can only assume was the next installment of the bribe money. We followed him to the bank, we followed him to JumboMart to pay Beau a visit, and then we followed him to you. How do you explain that?"

"Tom did pay me a visit last week, but it was only to make sure I was still going to vote Pete's way."

"So, in return for your yes vote, what do you get?"

His shoulders slumped. "Pete will pay off my business loan."

"And what does Tom get in return for pressuring you to vote yes?"

"I don't know the deal they worked out, but I know Tom is planning on leaving the bank after the deal goes through, so I'm assuming he'll be set for life."

I couldn't believe what I was hearing. "How can Pete get away with all that?"

"He's the president of the bank's board of directors. He's bought and sold his way to the top of the food chain, Athena. Believe me, he's got his fingers into everything in this town. I knew it was useless to fight him."

Sonny Talbot had been right. Get rid of one monster, and an even bigger one would take its place. I sat there for a minute thinking over everything Pearson had told me. "What about SOD? How can you be raising money for the new park while voting against it?"

He sighed. "Pete is going to fight SOD. It doesn't matter how much money we raise now. We're going to lose that land."

"Then we'll fight back. You may have given up, Pearson, but I haven't."

"I wish I had your optimism, Athena, but no one can stop Pete Harmon."

"Elissa's going to find out," I told him. "You can't keep this from her any longer."

His eyes were steady, focused on me, but his lower lip trembled, and a tear escaped, rolling down his cheek. "How can I tell the woman I love that I've betrayed her?" He let the phone fall slightly from his ear as one hand brushed away the tear.

"If you're still locked up on Wednesday, can there be a vote?"

He put the phone against his ear again. "No. The voting won't happen."

"Then Pete's proposal will be tabled, right?"

"Until they appoint a new city councilman to take my place. Then Pete will mount another campaign. You can be sure he won't give up. And next time he won't have SOD standing in his way."

"Then I'll go to the newspaper. I'll make sure everyone knows what Pete did to get his yes votes and how he corrupted the city council. Pete will be outed as the monster he is. We'll stop him *and* save the dunes."

"You can't, Athena. The only proof of Pete's bribery plan is in those photos, and believe me, he will know how to explain them away. Remember, Pete has a lot of influence in this town as well as a lot of supporters. People will believe his lies because they want to."

It made me sick to think of Pete getting his hands on that land, but I didn't say a word.

Pearson gazed at me with sad eyes. "Are you going to tell Elissa what I've done?"

"Time's up," a guard behind him said.

"I'm not going to tell her anything until you talk to her."

"Are you taking yourselves off the case then?"

"I don't know what we're going to do."

"And what about the camera? Will you at least look for it?"

"I'll do my best." I pointed my finger at him. "But *you* have to talk to Elissa today and explain everything just like you explained it to me."

"Thank you," he said with relief. "Be expecting a call from Elissa this evening. Just be warned. It's a big basement, and there are a lot of places to hide a camera."

The guard placed the phone on the receiver and helped Pearson to his feet. Pearson left me with a hopeful smile and mouthed the words, *"Thank you."* I watched as he was escorted out of the room, and then I sat for a few moments contemplating our conversation.

As soon as I was out of the building and in the warm, sunny air, I took a deep breath and blew it out, ridding myself of the antiseptic smell and claustrophobic feeling of being in jail. I phoned Case to tell him I was done and then saw him walking toward me, his strong body moving in one fluid, masculine motion. He put his arm around me, and we began walking toward the Jeep.

"How did it go?" I asked him.

"I spoke with Detective Walters. He listened to what I had to say and looked over the list of witnesses, but it doesn't look like Pearson will be released anytime soon."

"Even after you told them everything?"

"Even then. Walters told me that they have enough evidence against Pearson to warrant the murder charge. But at least he did listen. If we could come up with something more substantial, I think he would listen again. How did it go with Pearson?"

After I gave him a rundown on my interview, he said, "So, Pearson thinks his son may have hidden the camera. For what reason?"

"He's a kid, Case. He probably intends to play photographer with it. Remember when we toured the mansion? We saw Denis coming up the staircase. It fits the timeline."

"Shouldn't Denis be able to clear this up?"

"He told Detective Walters he didn't take the golf club. He wasn't asked about the camera, but I'd still like to search for it. Pearson said he'd have Elissa call me after he speaks with her so that she won't be surprised by our request. Then you and I can go over to the Studios and look for it."

"Even if we found the camera, Athena, there's no guarantee that it would be substantial evidence."

"It would verify Pearson's story," I said, "It might even have fingerprints on it. Who knows?"

"Who knows if Pearson is being one hundred percent truthful with you now? He's not even telling his wife the truth."

Normally I would've challenged his opinion on Pearson, but I was starting to doubt myself. "I don't know what to believe anymore."

We stopped at the Jeep. Case opened my door for me as I continued to talk. "I'm worried about the auction. Elissa has only one day to drum up more buyers, and I don't see that happening, not with Pearson in jail."

"You've done all you can," Case reassured me. "I didn't even see you work this hard when *I* was a murder suspect."

As I buckled my seat belt, his words settled in, and I was suddenly overwhelmed by a depressing revelation. "You were telling the truth."

"Excuse me?"

"When you needed my help, you never lied to me. That's why I didn't have to work so hard. I trusted you, and we worked together as a team. Pearson has been deceiving us from the start."

"So, you've crossed over to the dark side?"

"All I'm saying is that maybe it's time I focused solely on helping Elissa with the art auction. The only problem is, how am I going to help her raise twenty thousand dollars?"

"I don't know. Just don't sell the statue." He grinned.

"Maybe I should ask Lila for help. She knows a lot of influential people."

He gave me a skeptical glance as he started the engine. "Do you *really* want to involve her?"

I curled a lock of hair around my finger, thinking hard. "The problem is that we don't have any more options."

"Why don't you talk to your reporter friend? If we can't stop Pete any other way, maybe the reporter can get something in the newspaper about Pete Harmon's past before the council meeting on Wednesday."

"I've already talked to Charlie. He said he'd let me know if he found anything."

Trying to set the investigation aside for a while, I spent the rest of the afternoon working with customers needing advice on shrubs and flowering plants and didn't get home until after six o'clock. After dinner, I spent an hour playing Scrabble with Nicholas, Maia, and Selene, watching the clock in the hopes of hearing from Elissa. I checked the clock again before I wrote my blog. The evening was almost over.

My cell phone dinged with a text message from Case: *Did you hear from Elissa?*

No. Nothing. I don't know what to make of it, I wrote back.

You did what you could. Don't lose sleep over it.

Thanks for the pep talk. I then inserted an emoji of eye-rolling.

Good night, Goddess.

I sat up in bed and began my blog, hoping to calm my mind so I could sleep, but the only thing I could think about was Hugo's camera. It was the only piece of solid evidence we had left. Without it, our investigation was at a dead end.

Dead end. Hmm. Blog topic?

CHAPTER TWENTY-TWO

When Nicholas and I walked into the diner Friday morning, I was surprised to see Case sitting at the counter sipping coffee, listening to my sisters' dissection of my blog.

Nicholas greeted Case with a high five, then said to me, "I'm going to see Yiayiá and Pappoús," and skipped off toward the kitchen. I waved to my grandfather through the pass-through window, and he blew me a kiss.

I slid in next to Case, wanting very much to kiss him good morning and knowing that I didn't dare. All eyes were on us.

"How's it going?" he asked.

"No word from Elissa."

"It'll happen. Don't worry." He took a sip of coffee, looking at me sideways. "On a different topic . . ." He leaned over to say in my ear in a low murmur, "You look good enough to eat."

I dipped my head to hide my smile as a frisson of pleasure raced up my spine.

Then I heard, "Good morning, everyone," and turned to see Delphi walking toward us holding Maguire's hand, looking happier than I'd seen her in weeks. Maia, Selene, and Mama gaped at her for a moment, then Selene and Maia said together, "Good morning to you, too," and smiled back.

"Come have a seat," Mama said, gesturing toward a table.

"I can't stay," Maguire said. "I just wanted to wish you all a good morning."

"Bob offered to drive me here," Delphi said, squeezing his hand. "He's such a gentleman." She stood on tiptoe to kiss him on the cheek. "I'll talk to you later."

"How sweet," I said to Case.

Delphi hopped up onto a stool, still smiling. "Coffee, please."

Mama filled a cup from the pot in her hand and slid it toward Delphi. I could tell by the look on her face that she had something on her mind. "You know, Delphi," she began, "being a police officer is a dangerous job."

Delphi gave her a skeptical look as she poured cream into her cup. "And?"

"And have you considered how you would sleep at night knowing your husband was out there risking his life?"

Delphi rolled her eyes. "Oh, for heaven's sake, Mama, we just started going out."

"And she already has you walking down the aisle," I said.

"Even worse," Selene said. "They're already back from their honeymoon."

As we all laughed, Mama replaced the coffeepot on the warmer and turned with a scowl. "Well, excuse me for worrying about one of my daughters. It's a concern. Mothers are allowed to have concerns about their children, even when they're ungrateful."

An awkward silence followed.

Case cleared his throat. "So, our new sign is coming tomorrow after lunch. Why don't you all take a stroll down later in the afternoon to see it?"

"What a great idea," Selene said with forced joviality.

"Sounds good to me," Maia added. "How about you, Delph?"

She shrugged, clearly unhappy with Mama.

"I won't be there," I said, as Nicholas rejoined us. "The Save Our Dunes art auction is tomorrow. It starts at one o'clock."

I gave them an update on the auction, butterflies fluttering in my stomach just at the thought of the disaster it could be, and then the discussion was tabled as our breakfasts arrived.

Midmorning, I came out to see if I was needed on the sales floor and was stunned to learn that Elissa had come down to speak with Delphi, and that both of them were closeted in the conference room for a coffee grounds reading.

Why hadn't she called me?

I paced in front of the conference room door, waiting

for Elissa to come out, then thought better of it and re-treated to the office. I didn't want to appear to be eaves-dropping.

I was still working in my office when Elissa stuck her head through the doorway. "I just wanted to say hi."

She just wanted to say *hi*? What was going on? Hadn't Pearson talked to her?

Putting on a good face, I said, "Did you come down for some coffee and conversation?"

"Actually, I came to see Delphi." She held up her hand. "I know what you said about not believing her readings, but she's very convincing, and I needed to hear what she had to say."

"It was good news, I hope."

"Mostly." Elissa stepped into the room. Her short dark hair was held back by a red bandanna as though she hadn't even bothered with it, and her eyes had dark circles beneath them. "She said there were trials ahead, but that I'd handle them just fine. She gave me hope that things will work out with Pearson, as well as with the auction."

"I'm glad."

Elissa drew a deep breath. "Pearson was denied bail, Athena."

I came around the desk and gave her a hug. "I'm so sorry."

She began to pace, wringing her hands as worry lines creased her forehead. "He was so distraught when I spoke with him. I feel so bad for everything he's gone through." She turned to me imploringly. "Do you think he's guilty?"

"No," I said emphatically. "Why would you ask that?"

"Because I don't understand what's happening. Who would want to frame my husband? Steal his golf club and use it as a weapon? It just doesn't add up."

"Didn't Pearson tell you his theory about Denis leaving the club in the woods?"

"Denis promised me that he didn't take it there. He didn't even know the golf bag was in the trunk."

"Then who did take it?"

She started pacing again, rubbing her forehead. "I don't know. Maybe someone who plays golf with Pearson and knows that's where he keeps his clubs."

She was reaching.

"What about the camera?" I asked.

"Denis doesn't know anything about a camera, either. He said he was playing hide-and-seek with Niko that morning."

"Elissa," I started, feeling my way along a slippery slope. "Niko was with my mother that morning. Case and I saw Denis coming up the staircase when we were touring the mansion. He could've been coming from the basement. I think you should let me search for the camera down there."

"My son wouldn't have lied to me. He knows this is important."

I wasn't prepared to go to war with her, especially not when she was on the brink of a meltdown. "All I'm saying is that if I can find the camera, we may have evidence to prove Pearson is innocent."

She began to chew her lip, the worry lines back.

I put my hands on her shoulders. "Are you okay?"

"It's just, with everything Pearson told me . . . and now the auction is in jeopardy . . ." She looked down, wiping away tears. "I don't think I'm handling things very well."

"I understand," I told her. "It's a heavy burden. But rest assured, Pearson lied to protect you."

She looked at me with a puzzled expression. "Lied about what?"

Before my mind could catch up with my mouth, I said, "The business loan."

"What business loan?"

I searched her eyes, and as I spoke, I realized my mistake. "The loan Pearson took out on his printing business."

The shocked look on her face made my stomach drop. Had Pearson played me for a fool?

"What did he tell you, Athena?"

"I'm sorry. I may have spoken too soon. Pearson was supposed to talk to you first."

She took my hands. "Be honest with me. *Please*. What did my husband tell you?"

I could've punched Pearson for putting me into such an awkward position. And what could I do but tell her the truth? "Why don't we sit down?"

I led her to the chairs in front of the desk. "Pearson said the business has been failing for some time. He said with all the problems with the auction right now, he hated to burden you by telling you about it."

"He didn't want to *burden* me?" She shook her head, her mouth tight and angry. "What else has he kept from me?"

I took a deep breath and considered where to start. It was a messy situation, but I tried to condense it as much as I could. "Pete Harmon learned about Pearson's business loan from Tom Silvester, and together they used it to threaten your husband."

"Threaten him how?"

"Tom would recall the loan unless Pearson voted for Pete's land proposal."

Elissa gripped the armrests as though she was trying to

keep herself from jumping up. "He was going to vote for Pete's proposal?"

Denis burst into the room cradling one hand. "Oscar bit me!" he cried.

As we both jumped up, Nicholas ran into the office behind him, shaking his head. "He didn't get bitten, Mom. Oscar only snapped at him because he was being rough."

Elissa examined Denis's hand, turning it over to see the palm. "There's no bite mark here, sweetheart. Why did you say you'd been bitten?"

"Because he got mean and tried to bite me."

I turned to Niko. "What happened?"

"Denis was pulling Oscar's tail, so Oscar turned around and snapped at him, but he didn't bite him, honest. I was there. I saw it. Oscar was afraid of Denis. He was trying to get away."

"Denis," Elissa said angrily, "that was unkind of you. No wonder Oscar got angry. You apologize to Niko right now."

Denis shook his head, a stubborn set to his mouth. "No."

"And he stole Oscar's toys," Nicholas said. "We have proof."

"No, I didn't!" Denis shouted.

Elissa said sharply, "You need a time-out, young man. Go wait outside for me. I'll deal with you when we get home."

As soon as both boys were gone, she said, "I'm sorry about Denis's behavior. I hope Oscar will be okay."

I found myself spouting platitudes to ease the situation. "Don't worry. I'm sure it won't happen again. No damage done."

"Thank you," she said in relief. "So much has happened today that I don't know what to focus on first, or what I should do about Pearson."

I put my hand on her shoulder. "The only thing you can do is confront your husband. You deserve to hear the truth from him."

"I don't think I could handle that right now."

"At the very least," I asked, "will you let me search for the camera? It's our only hope to clear him."

"Don't worry about the camera, Athena. Right now, I will believe my son over Pearson."

I didn't know how to convince her otherwise. Denis seemed to be a very adept liar.

She paused at the door. "As far as I'm concerned, the matter is settled. If the detectives want to search the basement, I'll give them full access to it. And if you still want to help, let's focus on the auction."

"Are you going to tell Pearson you know about the loan?"

"I don't know when I'll be seeing him next." Her voice was bitter as she walked away. "I have an auction to run."

As soon as she was gone, I picked up my cell phone and called Case. "Will you meet me on the plaza for lunch? I need to tell you what just happened."

"Of course. Let's make it noon."

"Hey, Thenie?"

I looked up as Delphi walked into the office. "Gotta go," I said to Case. I ended the call and said to my sister, "What's up?"

She sat down opposite me at the desk. "You probably heard that I gave Elissa a reading."

"She told me what you predicted."

Delphi sighed, a miserable look on her face. "Once again, I couldn't bring myself to tell her everything. I just couldn't scare her. I tried to give her a gentle warning instead, but now I need to tell you what I saw."

"Go ahead."

She gazed out the window as if picturing it. "I saw a painting on an easel, and then I saw flashes of light, like lightning flashes coming from above the painting. Then it went all dark except for the flashes, which were blinding."

"What does it mean?"

She turned to look at me. "I'm not sure. All I know is that there's danger ahead and somehow it connects to her painting. Do you see why I couldn't tell her?"

"What you told her was enough, Delphi. You did the right thing." And probably avoided making the situation worse.

She rose and said with another heavy sigh, "Sometimes my gift is a curse."

CHAPTER TWENTY-THREE

When I got to the plaza shortly after noon, Case had already ordered and was waiting in the shade, leaning against the trunk of a large oak tree. "Spinach and goat cheese coming up shortly," he said, pushing himself away from the tree.

"Thanks," I said with a heavy sigh.

"Come here." He put his arm around me and let me lean against his solidness. "Now, tell me what happened."

"You know everything Pearson told me about his business loan and how Tom and Pete were using that against him? Well, he didn't tell Elissa, and I let the cat out of the bag. Now she's furious with him and even went so far as to tell me to forget about the camera. She's choosing to believe her son over her husband."

"Athena, one of them is lying, and there's nothing you can do about that."

"It's infuriating, Case. What if Pearson's son is the key to finding the killer?" I sighed again. "It's all such a mess. But I feel the sorriest for Elissa. Everything is going wrong for her—her husband, her son, the auction . . . her life."

Case was quiet, so I continued. "I told Elissa I wanted to help, and she said the best way was to focus on the auction."

"Then that's what you should do."

"Other than promoting it on social media, I don't know how."

"Order for Case," I heard someone call.

"I'll get it," he said. "You go find us a table."

I spotted a picnic table that had just been vacated and perched on the bench. In a few minutes Case joined me there, setting one plate in front of me and another with his pepperoni pizza on the opposite side of the table.

"I'll get us a couple of waters and be right back," he said, and strode off.

I watched him go, reminding myself of how lucky I was that Case was nothing like Pearson. I knew I could count on Case to be up-front with me, maybe sometimes too much so. But right now, I needed his advice.

"Here you go," he said, handing me an ice-cold bottle of water.

I bit into my pizza and chewed greedily. I hadn't realized how hungry I was until I smelled the cheesy pie.

Case, too, occupied himself with the first few bites, then he wiped his mouth with a napkin and reached for his water. "I think you should go see Lila."

I swallowed hard. "What?"

"You want to help Elissa, right? Then go talk to Lila.

As you said, she knows a lot of influential people. Maybe she can drum up some buyers for the auction."

I put down my slice and wiped my fingers on a napkin. "I'll do it," I said with a smile. "I'll go see Lila after lunch. In fact, I'll text her right now to make sure she's home."

After another good wipe on the napkin, I texted: *Are you home? I need to talk to you.*

There was no reply. I finished chewing a bite of pizza and then heard a *ding*.

I'm home. From Lila.

Okay if I stop by? I asked.

I guess so.

Her reply was chilly, but I was determined. I texted: *I'll be there in twenty minutes.*

I slid my phone into my back pocket and picked up my pizza. "Thanks," I said.

"No problem, partner."

Twenty minutes later, I pulled up the long, circular driveway and parked in front of the big brick mansion. I rang the doorbell and heard it echo inside. In a minute, the door was opened by a tidy-looking woman in a black dress with white collar and cuffs.

"Come in, please." She held out an arm, indicating that I should have a seat in the adjoining room. The room held a long white leather bar, eight matching bar stools at the front, and a massive pool table in the center.

I remembered the white bar very well. The first time we'd ever met Lila Talbot, she'd whisked Case—then known by his alias, Dimitri—into the barroom for drinks and conversation. She had effectively left me to fight her husband alone, shut up in a big conference room with Talbot, his aide, and his lawyer. I pushed that memory aside before I got angry.

I perched on a leather bar stool and waited, counting the bottles reflected in the mirrored backsplash. I finally heard the *click-click* of sharp heels and looked around to see Lila coming down the marble staircase. She was wearing long black yoga pants with black spike heels, and a red tank top over a black exercise bra.

She stopped in the doorway and appraised me. "What do you want, Athena?"

"First, to tell you that there's no hard feelings about what happened the other day."

"No hard feelings on whose part?" She took a seat at the opposite end of the bar, swinging the stool to face me. "I see you came alone. Where's your partner?"

It wasn't my place to apologize for Case, so all I could say was, "Lila, you're a partner, too. I know I haven't been the friendliest to you, and I'm sorry about that. You've been a great help in this investigation. Case wouldn't have brought you on board if he didn't feel the same way."

"Then why isn't he here?"

Again, I didn't want to speak for Case. "I thought it was best if I met with you alone."

In a tense voice, she asked, "Why are you here?"

Given her feelings, my timing was bad. And yet I had no choice if I wanted to help Elissa save the parkland. "I need a favor."

She laughed dryly. "You're kidding."

"You know the art auction is tomorrow."

"Yes. So?"

"So apparently all the big money has pulled out. If we don't get people to come, it'll be a complete failure and SOD won't be able to hand over the money needed to start the park's renovation."

She got off the stool and walked behind the bar, uncorking a bottle of red wine and filling a glass with it, not even making an attempt to be a good hostess and offer me something. "What am I supposed to do about it?"

"You know a lot of influential people. Could you contact them and ask them to come?"

She didn't answer. She simply gazed at the wineglass, swirling the liquid.

"And would you come, too?" I added.

She took a sip of her wine, her eyes narrowing as she studied me. "So now my money and influence are good things." She let that sink in as she put the wine bottle back in its spot. "That's about as two-faced as you can get."

"I never said your money was bad."

"Not to my face, anyway." She looked toward a window edged with stark white curtains. "Well, I'm sorry, but I'm simply too busy to help."

As she walked away with her glass of wine, I slipped off the stool and followed her to the foot of the stairs. "Lila, please," I said as she started up the staircase. "This park is important—to me, to my family, and to the town. It's important that we stop Pete Harmon from destroying that land."

She was approaching the top of the stairs.

"You want the Talbot name to stand for something?" I called. "Then this is your chance. Use your influence. Use your money. Do something great for the people of Sequoia."

"Good-bye, Athena."

"I know you're hurt right now, but if you'd just think about it, you might change your mind."

"Good-*bye*, Athena."

She walked away without a second glance. I looked around at the empty foyer, the big barroom, the massive mansion, and felt a great loneliness sweep over me. After everything that had happened with Lila, all of the ups and downs, the anger, the jealousy, I actually felt sad that this was how it would end between us.

The woman who'd greeted me at the door was nowhere to be found, so I let myself out.

"Well, Lila's help is out," I said to Case over the phone. "She's still hurt."

"That's my fault."

"Don't take all the blame. You did what you had to do. I hurt her, too." I parked my SUV in the public parking lot a block off Greene Street and headed toward Spencer's. "The only thing I can do now to help Elissa is to get on social media and try to drum up support for the auction that way."

"Don't discount that. It's still a help. And while you're doing that, I'm going to work on building a website for our agency. Once our sign is up, people are going to notice us. Who knows? A week from today we may be working on a new case."

I sighed.

"I know, sweetheart," he said. "We haven't finished this one yet, and that's hard to swallow. The truth is, Athena, we may never finish it. It's out of our hands now."

"I know. There's nothing left to do but focus on the auction. I'm going to go online now and blast the social media sites with information. And I still have to write my blog, although that's the last thing I feel like doing."

"I can tell. Maybe you should share your feelings of frustration with your audience and offer ways to cope with them."

"Ha. Maybe I should let them offer *me* ways to cope."

Saturday morning had started out sunny, but by the time Nicholas and I got to the diner, the clouds had rolled in, and the humidity had crept up as though rain was on the horizon. I was surprised to see Case crossing the street toward me, so I waited to walk in with him while Nicholas ran ahead.

"Good morning, Goddess," he said, and bent his head to give me a kiss. "Get any sleep last night?"

"It wasn't a good night. Everything I could possibly worry about kept circulating through my mind in an endless loop. I feel like I let Pearson down, I don't have a good feeling about the auction, and I didn't get many replies to my social media posts. It's going to be a disaster."

"It won't be that bad." He held the door open for me. "Put that aside for the time being and enjoy breakfast with me."

"You sound so optimistic."

"I'm being optimistic for you."

We greeted my family with smiles and hugs, put our orders in at the window, and went to squeeze in at the back booth. By some unspoken agreement, we both sensed we needed the mindless chatter my sisters and mother would provide.

"Good blog topic today, wasn't it?" Selene said to Maia. "About frustrations."

"You should read it, Thenie," Maia said. "Goddess Anon is asking for ways to cope. You've had your share of frustrations. Maybe you can offer some suggestions."

"How do *you* cope with frustrations?" I asked her.

"I do yoga and meditate," Maia said, which led into a discussion with Selene, Delphi, and Mama, who all agreed that the best way to cope was to stay busy. I decided to take their advice.

Fortunately, the garden center was busy all morning, so much so that I ended up working on the sales floor, which helped immensely. At eleven o'clock, I slipped into the office for a well-needed coffee break and found Delphi already there, helping herself to a bottle of water from the mini fridge. She had on a long, bright, full-skirted summer dress with a white gossamer scarf around her neck, looking like she was ready for a picnic.

"I'm coming to the auction," Delphi said. "I told Elissa I wanted to help, and she said I could assist her up front."

I poured creamer into my coffee. "What are you going to do about working here? You can't leave Pops alone."

"Drew is coming in. He said he could be here before one o'clock."

I gave her a long look. "Why are you doing this, Delphi? Elissa doesn't really need your help."

"I need to be there, that's all."

I rubbed my forehead. "It's your vision, isn't it? The flashes, the painting, the black knight . . ."

She scratched her nose.

I sighed. "Fine, but I'm going down early. I'll have to meet you there."

She gave me a thumbs-up and left the office.

At noon, I went home to change into a cheerful yellow-print sundress and forced myself to eat, snacking on hummus and Triscuits with a cup of tea to help calm my nerves. The auction was set to start at one o'clock, and I wanted to get there early, so I set off at twelve fifteen, hoping to burn off some of my nervous energy on the way. Halfway there, I called Case.

"Wouldn't you know it would be a gloomy day," I said as I scanned the gray sky. The dark clouds over the lake were heavy and thick, a precursor to a storm.

"It's not supposed to rain until this evening," he said. "Think positive."

"I'm trying."

"I have to go. The sign installers just arrived. If it doesn't take them too long, I'll join you at the auction."

I hung up and continued my walk, my feet pounding out one thought: *It has to succeed.* But when I arrived, my heart sank at the sight of only a few cars in the parking lot. *It's still early,* I told myself. Half an hour yet to go.

I followed a flagstone path around the mansion to the backyard and gazed around at the once-plain patio. The massive cement area had been transformed into an elegant venue, with giant planters overflowing with flowers on each corner, and in the back, near the house, beautiful heron and egret statues flanking the fountain, its rainbow-colored lights playing on the splashing water. In front of the fountain stood a long table where beverages and appetizers were being offered.

An auctioneer's podium stood up front with a tall

white wooden arch behind it interwoven with blue clematis. Matching blue lanterns outlined the rows of white folding chairs facing the podium and the lake beyond it. It truly was a spectacular transformation, and I was proud to see my designs come to life.

I stood by one of the planters and looked around for Elissa. A technician was setting up a microphone at the podium, and another worker was setting up paintings on easels in front of a long table stacked with more artwork. Only a smattering of people filled the wooden seats, but I recognized some of them from the Greek Merchants Association.

I waved to my friends Barb and Nancy and was about to make my way over to them when someone passed me, rudely brushing my shoulder as he walked by. With a shudder I realized it was Tom Silvester, dressed as though for a business meeting in a suit and tie. He looked over his shoulder at me as he took a seat in the very back row. I felt a wave of anger flash over me. Why was he there?

I spotted Elissa coming out of the mansion's back door and made my way over to her. She finished giving instructions to several members of the Save Our Dunes group, then turned to greet me. "The patio looks beautiful, Athena. To think you donated all this. How can I ever thank you?"

"You don't have to thank me. I just want this to be a success."

She turned with a sigh to look at the empty rows. "The auction is set to start in twenty minutes. Call me crazy, but I'm still holding out hope."

I didn't know what to say other than to offer a lame, "I'm sure more will come."

"Elissa," said a woman behind her, "we need your advice about the appetizers."

"Coming," she said, then turned back to me. "Let me know when Delphi gets here. I have a special job for her. In the meantime, get a drink and have a seat."

Too nervous to sit, I took a walk down toward the lake, stopping short of the sand. The water looked as murky as the sky, where long gray cumulus clouds floated eastward. To my right was the entrance to the forested trail where Hugo's body had been found just a few weeks ago. A heavy weight settled on my shoulders as I was once again faced with the feeling that Hugo's murder would go unsolved.

I turned to go back but stopped short. Next to the fountain stood Pearson Reed.

CHAPTER TWENTY-FOUR

I crossed the long expanse of lawn and strode toward Pearson, blurting tactlessly, "How did you get out of jail?"

He glanced around just as Pete Harmon came strolling toward the patio. He wore a crisp blue suit and a smile, looking like a man who already owned the property.

Pearson looked at me with a sheepish expression. "Pete got me out."

"How?"

"Money and influence. He knew the judge."

I was flummoxed.

My expression must have shown my feelings, because he was quick to offer, "It was a million-dollar bond, Athena. Who else could put up the bail money?"

"Why did he get you out?"

"Why do you think?"

Pete walked up to the fountain, pulled some change from his pocket, and picked out a quarter, tossing it into the water. "Make a wish, Athena."

"What are you doing here?" I knew my utter disgust for the man was evident in my voice.

He used his fingers to comb through his short beard as he studied the surroundings. "Speaking of wishes," he said, ignoring my question, "look at all this effort, and for what?"

"So, you came to gloat," I said. "That's low. Even for you."

He pointed across the lawn. "I'm going to have a brand-new business center built right over there, next to the water, with a big corner office facing the lake. I figured I'd need new artwork for it, so I decided to come." He turned his head to gaze at the empty rows. "By the looks of it, this will be the cheapest way to get it."

My upper lip curled in distaste as I glared at him, unable to find the words to express my contempt.

Pearson glanced around nervously. "You shouldn't be here, Pete. It isn't going to look good for either one of us."

"You don't need to worry about me, my friend," Pete said before walking away.

I watched him take a seat in the front row, right in front of the podium, and felt sick. Looking back at Pearson, I said, "Pete got you out so you could vote at Wednesday's council meeting, didn't he?"

Pearson looked down.

I stepped away from him. It was all I could do not to be physically ill.

I walked to the other side of the patio and texted Case: *Pearson is at the auction. Pete got him out of jail.*

Case replied, *How?*

He talked to a judge. You can figure out why. Pete and Tom are here, too, I informed him.

You're kidding.

I think they came to gloat.

Ten minutes later, as I stood at the table in the back, dipping a ladle into a huge punch bowl, I saw Elissa come out and spot Pearson standing to one side of the patio. She made her way over to him, her expression stormy. They moved away from the chairs and began conversing, Elissa using angry hand gestures, Pearson holding up his hands to calm her. Elissa finally pointed toward the street, her mouth forming the word, *Go!* then turned sharply and stormed off. Pearson watched her for a moment, his shoulders falling, then he turned and started toward the flagstone path.

As Pearson made his way around the house, heading for the street, Delphi came floating up the path past him. She saw me standing at the back by the fountain and came over. "This patio is amazing!" she exclaimed, holding her fingers under the water. "Wow, sis. Well done."

I thanked her and told her Elissa had a job for her. As Delphi went off in search of Elissa, I noted that a few more people had come in, but the seats remained mostly unoccupied. Barb and Nancy waved me over again, so I made my way along the third row to sit beside them, feeling Tom Silvester's eyes on me.

At one o'clock, the auctioneer pounded the gavel. Elissa, Delphi, and two other women took their places near the podium behind a long table, and the auction began.

The first painting was displayed: a slender, graceful woman in a flowing, diaphanous dress, poised in a ballerina move. The bidding started low, silence filling the long gaps in between lackluster bids. I couldn't look at Elissa. I glanced at my sister instead, and she looked back with a sorrowful gaze. With a heavy sigh, I checked my watch, wondering how long until Case joined me, wondering if it was even worth his time to come down.

A second painting was put up with the same tragic results. Marie, the owner of Wear for Art Thou resale shop, took the bid up to two hundred. The auctioneer slowed his rapid-fire patter, repeating his request for bids several times, but the people in the seats looked at their shoes, studied their hands, or checked their phones, embarrassed that they couldn't bid higher.

I recognized the third painting as Elissa's lakeview landscape. The scene showed a similar view to the one in front of me, except in the painting the sun was shining, the water was bright, and there was a feeling of hope. I looked up at the sky and wondered how long until the rain came and brought the doomed auction to an end.

After the bidding stalled at a meager amount, Pete raised his hand and bought the painting. I was so angry I found it difficult to continue watching.

Several more landscapes were slowly and quietly auctioned with the same disappointing results. Thirty minutes into the auction, I estimated that SOD had raised only two thousand dollars. And then Elissa and Delphi put up the painting of the statue of Athena, the largest and most impressive painting of the lot. I crossed my fingers. Nancy reached over and squeezed my hand for support, and Delphi gave me a hopeful smile, while Elissa stood on one side of the painting, her hands balled nervously at her sides.

At the start of the bidding, Pete Harmon swiveled in

his seat to give me an arrogant grin, as if to say, *This one's mine, too.*

No way could I let him win that painting. I'd checked my savings account that morning, knowing I'd be inclined to bid on a few items, but there wasn't much money to spare. Yet in order to keep Pete from winning, I'd bid as high as I could, and hope others did the same.

The auctioneer started at five hundred dollars, and my arm shot up. At five hundred fifty, a second hand went up. At six hundred, a third, and at that point I was outbid. The bidding continued in small increments, but as the price increased, the bids thinned and finally stalled at nine hundred.

As the auctioneer prepared to lift his gavel, Pete Harmon called, "One thousand," and the gavel halted in midair. Pete glanced back at me with a smile. At that amount it was a steal, and he knew it.

"One thousand," the auctioneer called. "Do I hear fifteen hundred?"

No one made a sound.

Then I noticed Delphi trying to catch my attention. She was standing off to the side of the painting motioning with her eyes for me to look up at the mansion.

I swiveled my head to look but didn't see anything unusual. I glanced back at her with a shrug, and she lifted her chin, raising her gaze so I'd look way up. I turned back again, studying the third-floor windows, but still saw nothing.

Clearly annoyed with me, I could see Delphi fidgeting under the table and then heard a ding from my purse.

Delphi had texted. *Top floor. Middle window. The black knight.*

I looked around again, and then I saw a flash in a center window, a window I immediately recognized as Denis's playroom. Another flash followed, and then another.

I glanced back at Delphi and saw her tap the center of her forehead, her third eye. Paintings and flashes. It was just like her vision. But what was making the flash?

I looked up again and saw a small figure standing back behind the glass holding something square and black. As it flashed again, I realized it was a camera. And then a face came into view. I gazed up in shock. Denis had Hugo's camera.

People behind me were swiveling to see what I was staring at, so I turned toward the front once again, giving Delphi a subtle nod.

"One thousand dollars going once," the auctioneer called out.

I put my phone into my purse and slid the purse onto my shoulder, ready to make a quick exit.

"One thousand going twice."

As the auctioneer raised the gavel, I heard a woman's voice from the back call, "Five thousand dollars."

I turned around and saw a large group of people coming from the side of the mansion heading toward the patio, some already filtering into the chairs. And there was Lila directing people into the rows, her attention on the auctioneer as more came in, filling up the empty seats. She looked stunning in a white sundress with long, dangling silver earrings, white sandals, and white sunglasses shielding her eyes. I stared at her in surprise.

"Five thousand, one hundred," Pete called from the front row.

"Seven thousand," Lila shot back. She moved around the rows of chairs to stand by the table in back.

"Seven thousand, one hundred." Pete turned and locked eyes with her.

Lila removed her sunglasses and smiled at him. "Eight thousand."

A gasp went up from the audience. The auctioneer waited.

I scooted out of my seat and walked back to her. "You came," was all I could say.

She put her hands on her hips. "You really thought I'd leave you high and dry?"

"After what you said yesterday, I didn't think you'd show up."

"We're partners, Athena, just like you said. Partners don't leave each other in the lurch. Now, if you'll excuse me, I have a painting to win."

"We have a bid of eight thousand dollars," the auctioneer called. "Eight thousand going once . . ."

"Eight thousand, one hundred," Pete called.

"He's playing games with me," Lila said. "Let's see him play with this." She gave me a wink, then called out, "Ten thousand dollars."

People cheered. I gaped at her in astonishment.

"We have a bid of ten thousand dollars," the auctioneer called. He glanced at Pete, waiting. As the cheers subsided, it seemed as though everyone was holding their breaths until the auctioneer finally said, "Ten thousand going once."

All eyes were on Pete as the auctioneer said, "Ten thousand going twice."

Pete turned in his chair to glare at Lila. When he saw me standing beside her, giving him the same smirk he'd given me earlier, he turned away. He looked at the auctioneer and gave a small shake of his head.

"Sold to the lady in white!" the auctioneer called, banging his gavel.

Amid another loud cheer, I watched Lila stride toward the front, her hips swaying, a triumphant smile on her face, and my whole body sagged in relief. It didn't matter anymore that Tom or Pete was there. Lila had won. Plus, she'd brought her people, and they would bid, too.

I looked at Elissa and saw her beaming from ear to ear. Delphi once again found me with her gaze and lifted her chin toward the house. I nodded my understanding and headed toward the back door. Time to find that camera.

I stopped just outside the door and texted Case again: *How long before you get here?*

Leaving now, he wrote back immediately.

I think Hugo's camera is in the playroom. I'm going up there now.

I'll try to hurry

With my purse over my shoulder, I opened the back door and stepped inside. "Hello?"

Hearing no answer, I made my way across the kitchen and headed up a long hallway to the staircase by the front door. Before I could reach it, Denis came scurrying down the steps, ready to dodge me as I stepped in front of him.

"Denis, were you playing with a camera upstairs?"

"No, Miss Spencer. I have to go. My dad texted me to come outside."

Strange. Hadn't I seen Pearson leave?

Denis dashed around me and ran through the kitchen and out the back door.

I adjusted the purse strap on my shoulder and kept going. The mansion was eerily quiet, the creaking of the old stairs under my feet the only sound. I passed the second floor, climbed another flight to the third-floor hallway and proceeded down the hall to the playroom.

The sky through the window in the back of the room was cloudy and gloomy, allowing just enough light to see without turning on the overhead light. I glanced around for the camera, searching through a toy box and behind furniture, but saw no sign of it. A table sat beneath the window with Denis's bookbag on it. I zipped it open, but the camera wasn't there.

From below came the sound of applause. I looked out the window and saw Elissa and Lila standing at the podium, both beaming with delight. People were on their feet clapping.

I looked around and noticed a pair of doors on the side wall—the forbidden closet Nicholas had told me about. I strode to the closet and gave one of the intricately carved doorknobs a turn, revealing a large, deep storage area behind it. One side held a low pole for hanging smaller-sized clothing and above it was a stack of shelves filled with folded garments. The other side of the closet was filled from top to bottom with shelves taken up with games and toys.

I spotted a thin chain hanging from the ceiling and pulled it, switching on a dim yellow light overhead. I began to search the shelves, starting from the midline and working my way down. I finally spotted the camera on the bottom shelf, hidden behind a jigsaw puzzle. I set the puzzle aside and reached for the camera, only to remember that it might have fingerprints on it. I searched through the clothing and found a shelf of winter items: a scarf; a pair of thick, leather-palmed mittens; and a pair of green knit gloves. I pulled on the gloves, inching the stretchy fabric over my fingers.

The camera itself wasn't large, but the thick, bulky lens had heft to it. I heard a floorboard creak behind me and paused to listen.

"Case?" I called softly but heard no response.

I stepped out of the closet and came face-to-face with Pearson Reed.

CHAPTER TWENTY-FIVE

"What are you doing up here, Athena?"

I hesitated. His expression was unreadable, his gaze unwavering. "I-I was looking for the camera."

"I thought we agreed that it was in the basement."

"I thought so, too, until I saw flashes coming through the window. I looked up and saw Denis through the glass."

Pearson walked up to the closet and peered inside. "Was Denis here when you got here?"

"No," I answered, backing away. I didn't know what to expect from Pearson, but the one thing I had learned was that I couldn't trust him. I moved away from the closet as I spoke. "I saw him coming down the stairs. He told me you wanted him to come outside." My palms were sweating in the gloves. "How did you know I was up here?"

"Denis told me you were in the playroom, although I didn't know if I should believe him." He turned toward me with a sardonic grin. "It seems my son has a tendency to bend the truth." He gave me a puzzled glance. "You're wearing Denis's gloves?"

My heart was racing. "I didn't want to leave fingerprints on the camera."

"Then you found it."

Stall him, Athena. "I saw you and Elissa arguing earlier. I thought you'd left."

"I couldn't leave," he said, "not until I found the camera."

"You searched the basement?"

"I searched, obviously with no luck."

Pearson stepped closer, and I held up my palm to stop him, glad he couldn't see my hands shaking in the gloves. "Stay right there."

He stopped, looking almost frightened. "What's wrong? Don't you believe me?"

His expression was sincere, but as I'd learned, Pearson was a master of false sincerity. "I don't know what to believe right now, but I want you to back over to the window while I get the camera."

Pearson held up his hands in a gesture of surrender and backed up to the window. As I pulled the camera from its hiding place, he said, "I promise you, I had nothing to do with Hugo's murder. Check the photos on the camera. They should verify my story."

"I'm taking this to the detectives," I said. "They can sort it out."

"Please, Athena, I need to know what's on that camera."

"Why?"

He had his hands in the air but took a step closer. "I was on the trail with Hugo during the art fair. He showed me photos of Tom and Beau exchanging money with Pete. He said he wanted my help stopping Pete once and for all. That's all that happened, I swear. Hugo was just trying to help me, but I brushed him off."

"If you know what's on the camera, why do you need to see the photos again?"

"I'm afraid Hugo has a picture of me on that trail." Pearson stepped closer. "If he does, I need to delete it. Please, Athena, you know what the detectives will think if they see it."

"Everything on the camera is evidence, Pearson. I'm not deleting anything."

He gave up with a sigh. "If you don't believe me, check the pictures. And if you're still not convinced, I won't try to stop you from taking the camera to the detectives."

I stood in the doorway studying him. He moved to the orange sofa and sat down, rubbing his eyes as though they were tired.

"I'll check the photos," I said, "but you stay right where you are."

With the gloves still stretched over my fingers, I held the camera in front of me, then pushed the playback button, and a screen came up with thumbnails of photos. I scrolled backward, past pictures that Denis had obviously taken, and scrolled through photos of the festival, scrolled past a video and several more photos until finally photos of Pearson appeared.

I clicked on one of them and saw him dressed as I remembered, in a green golf shirt and khaki pants. As I moved backward through the photos, it quickly became evident that Pearson was not interested in harming Hugo. In fact, he appeared friendly.

Continuing forward, I came across a set of photos of Pete and Tom. The first photo showed the two men talking together near the water. The second showed the men with surprised expressions, looking toward the camera. The next photo showed Tom looking in the direction of the festival as Pete strode toward Hugo. In the following photo, Pete was just yards away from the camera, a furious look on his face. In the last photo before the video, Pete's hands were outstretched, as though reaching for the camera.

I looked up from the screen. "It was Pete Harmon."

"What?" He looked stunned.

"Pete killed Hugo. Tom was there, too. He knew."

Pearson started to reply, but then stopped and cocked his head toward the door. "Did you hear that?" He listened again. "Someone's coming up the stairs."

I listened for a moment before I heard a soft creak of the stairs.

Pearson rose from the couch and ducked out of the room for a moment, then came back seconds later, putting his finger to his lips as he motioned for me to step into the closet. Gripping the camera in one hand, I grabbed my purse and backed inside as Pearson quietly closed the door. I pulled the overhead chain to switch off the light, leaving only the soft glow from the camera's screen. I stayed perfectly still, listening to the wooden stairs creak and finally stop.

"Tom," Pearson called loud enough so I could hear, "what are you doing up here?"

"I was looking for you." His words were muffled, but I could still hear the conversation clearly. "Pete and I want to have a word with you outside."

"Now?"

"Yes, now." Tom's voice was hurried, clipped.

"Sorry. Now's not a good time."

"You've got pressing business up here or what? Let's go."

"I'm not going anywhere. And you can tell Pete that I'm done with this whole mess. I've decided not to vote for his project after all."

"That's not a smart move, Pearson. In fact, it's downright dangerous."

"What do you mean?"

I could see Tom's shadow beneath the door, coming closer to the closet. "Do you know how much you stand to lose if you don't go through with this?"

"I know what I have to lose. But it can't be worse than losing my family."

"Then think about how much *I* stand to lose," Tom said, raising his voice. "You're not going to ruin this for me, Pearson. That's what Hugo was trying to do."

The anger in his tone sent a shiver down my spine. What was he implying?

As the two men continued to argue, I looked down at the camera screen. There was one thing I hadn't yet checked—the video.

I hit the forward button and the video began to play. I turned the volume down until I could barely hear it, then watched as Pete came straight at Hugo, his face dark and angry. I couldn't believe my eyes. Hugo had captured his own attack on camera.

In an instant, Pete's blue T-shirt filled the screen, blurring the image until it went black. Seconds went by before the screen lightened again, and then there seemed to be a jolt. In the next frame, the camera appeared to be tumbling, coming to rest on the ground. Several moments later, Pete could be heard saying, "For God's sake, Tom, what have you done?"

Tom? I glanced up at the door in shock. *Tom* had killed Hugo?

The video stayed motionless for so long I thought it had ended. Then a new image suddenly came into focus, and I stared openmouthed at the sight of Tom dragging Hugo's lifeless body away. The video continued to play, but no one else appeared on the screen.

I looked up as Tom's shadow beneath the door grew larger. "If you ruin this," he said from very close by, "Pete will destroy us both."

"Pete can't hurt us, Tom. I can prove he killed Hugo."

Pearson, no!

"I found Hugo's camera," Pearson continued. "Once I turn it over to the police, Pete will be charged with murder, and his project will be dead. No vote. No more threats."

With shaking hands, I set the camera by my feet, pulled out my phone, and typed a quick message to Case: *Call 911.*

"Where's the camera?" I heard Tom say.

"In a safe spot."

"I know it's in this room. I saw camera flashes coming from the window. Get it for me now." He was demanding now, his voice threatening.

"What do you need it for?"

"Let's not do this the hard way, Pearson. Just give me the camera."

Pearson's voice shook as he said, "I think you'd better leave now."

A thundering *crack* rang out, and then something slammed into the closet door. I jumped back, nearly dropping my phone. At first, I thought Tom was trying to break the door down, but I then realized the two men were struggling.

I looked around the dark closet, but there was nowhere to hide. Toys, board games—nothing I could use to defend myself, either. I heard a loud *crash* and prayed that someone in the backyard would hear the men fighting.

And then everything went silent. I froze, afraid to draw a breath, fearful of making a sound. I heard a slight movement outside the closet, and my skin prickled with dread.

All of a sudden, my cell phone dinged in my hand. My heart thudded against my ribs as I stared at the door, waiting to be discovered. For what seemed an eternity, I stayed there, frozen, but nothing happened. Carefully, I raised the phone and felt along the side for the button to silence it before it dinged again. But before I could reach it, another *ding* sounded, and the screen lit up with a text.

It was from Delphi. *I told you. Just like in my vision, blinding flashes.*

"Athena?" I heard Tom say, drawing out my name. "Is that you?"

His shadow grew nearer. I squeezed the phone in fear.

"Come out, Athena," Tom said, as though talking to a child. "All I want is the camera."

As the doorknob slowly turned, part of Delphi's text message jumped off the screen: *Blinding flashes.*

It gave me an idea.

I dropped the phone and grabbed the camera off the floor just as the closet door swung open. Tom stood in front of me, legs splayed, smiling like the cat who'd caught the canary. "Look what we have here."

Hands shaking violently, I aimed the camera and took his picture. The flash went off in the darkness, momentarily blinding him. Clutching the camera, I dashed past him, past Pearson's prone body, out of the room, and down the staircase, only to see Pete Harmon on the second-floor landing.

I glanced back and saw Tom standing at the top of the stairs. "Going somewhere?" he asked. He pressed his hand against his ribs as he drew a breath. A wince of pain flashed across his dark features, telling me that Pearson had put up a good fight. Still, Tom gave me a smile, letting me know he was still in control. "Do you want Pete to escort you up here, or do you want to come up all by yourself?"

I glared at him defiantly, ready to hold my own.

"I thought you told me everything was taken care of," Pete said to Tom.

"She has Hugo's camera," Tom answered, still holding his side.

Pete shook his head in disgust. "You screwed up my project right from the start. Why did I ever think I could trust you? Now here's another mess you've made."

"There's no time to argue now. We just need to get the camera and get out of here."

Pete nodded his head toward me. "What are you going to do about her?"

I looked over the banister, hoping for a way to escape, but the drop was too far. "Pete," I said, patting the camera, "the evidence is all here. You're not the killer. All you have to do is let me go, and Tom takes the rap. If you harm me, you'll be arrested, too."

"Forget it, Athena," Tom said from the top of the stairs.

I turned my attention back to Pete. "Listen to reason. Just let me go. You'll be cleared. You'll still have a good reputation."

Pete started up the stairs. "You're very convincing, but I'm still going to need that camera."

I put the strap around my neck and wrapped my fingers around the banister, preparing for a struggle. When Pete drew near enough to reach me, I pulled my foot back and aimed for his face, narrowly missing his jaw. It was enough of a shock to throw him off balance and give me a chance to escape. But as I prepared to charge past him, I felt fingers grasp the camera strap at the back of my neck and yank the heavy camera against my throat. I gagged from the pressure and clawed at the strap, my vision blurring.

"Tom, let her go," Pete commanded. "There are people everywhere."

Tom pulled the strap tighter. His breath was loud in my ear. "It's too late for that."

Desperately trying to tug the strap away from my throat, I gasped for breath and felt the blood pulse in my eyes as I watched Pete back away and turn to hurry down the stairwell. He was leaving me to die.

I tried to reach behind me and scratch Tom's face, but my strength was fading. My legs gave way, and I felt the jolt as my spine hit the steps hard. As everything began to go black, I heard a yell and felt the strap suddenly loosen around my neck.

Gulping air into my starved lungs, I turned to see Pearson above me, trying to drag Tom away, both men falling backward and hitting the stairs hard. My entire body shook as I tried to pull myself up by the wooden rails. I knew Pearson was in for another fight, this time in a weakened condition, no match for Tom's brute strength. I had to get downstairs and call for help.

Then I heard Pearson cry out, "No!" and turned to see Tom with his fist pulled back, gathering his strength to lay one final blow. Pearson kicked him in the ribs, causing Tom to double over in pain. He lost his balance and fell backward down the stairs. I moved quickly, hugging my body into the railing as Tom landed next to me and continued to tumble, until he collapsed onto the second-floor landing.

Pearson fell back onto his elbows, wincing in pain. He was bleeding from the nose and mouth, and there was a dark purple bruise under his eye, but he was alive.

The front door opened, and I heard, "Police!" I turned to see Bob Maguire, flanked by a troop of policemen who poured into the house, weapons drawn.

I pointed to where Tom was struggling to get up. "He killed Hugo!"

As several officers charged up the stairs toward him, I called, "His name is Tom Silvester. All the evidence is here on this camera. And Pete Harmon was his accomplice."

"We'll take care of it." Maguire snapped directions into his shoulder radio, then hurried up the stairs to help me to my feet. "Are you okay?"

"I've been better," I answered shakily. I turned to gaze up the staircase at Pearson, who was sitting on the top step, holding his head. "That's Pearson Reed. He's going to need medical attention."

And then I heard a familiar deep voice call, "Athena!"

I turned to see Case taking the stairs two at a time, his face tight with worry. I was so relieved to see him, my eyes welled with tears as I fell into his arms. "I'm all right," I said, burrowing into his solid chest. "I'm all right, but Pete got away."

"No, he didn't." Case smoothed back strands of hair from my face. "The police caught him outside."

At that my emotions took over, and I wept with relief.

"It's okay, sweetheart," Case said, hugging me against him. "It's over."

It *was* over. After weeks of frustrations, worries, and dead ends, we'd finally brought the case to a close. I wiped away my tears and carefully removed the camera from around my neck. "It's all here, Case. All the evidence. We did it."

He handed the camera to Maguire, then pulled me in close and stroked my hair. "*You* did it, Athena."

Sunday was a glorious morning. The sun was out, the sky was a crystal-clear blue, and Hugo's murder was finally solved. And though my back ached, my throat was bruised, and my neck was sore, I was in a supremely good mood.

Nicholas and I walked into the Parthenon and were greeted warmly by grateful diners. The ladies of the Red Hat Society even stood and removed their hats, while others stopped to shake my hand and offer congratulations.

I could feel myself glowing as my son and I joined my

sisters at their booth. Mama was pouring coffee, Maia and Selene were arguing about something insignificant, and my yiayiá and pappoús came out from the kitchen to offer their praise in Greek and wrap me in fierce hugs. Delphi walked in with Bob Maguire and sat at the adjacent booth, Bob giving me a kind nod before returning his attention to his new girlfriend. I checked my watch, expecting Case at any moment.

After being treated by the EMTs, I'd spent the previous evening with Case at the police station helping Maguire and the detectives piece together the whole story. We'd been happily informed that Tom had already been charged with murder and Pete had been charged with accessory to murder. Detective Walters had actually thanked us for our work in solving the case, a rare honor, and the detectives who'd been reluctant to accept our help asked Case for a business card.

Now I looked around at the diners eating casually—my sisters rolling their eyes at something Mama said, Nicholas perusing the menu, and Bob and Delphi holding hands across their table—and I had to suppress a disappointed sigh. Just like that, the diner had returned to business as usual.

I wasn't sure exactly what I'd expected from my family, maybe a request for a recounting of how I'd bravely fought off Tom and Pete on the staircase, preserving the evidence on the camera, and securing my title of Goddess of Greene Street once again, or maybe what had happened was already old news.

I heard a *ding* and checked my phone.

It was Case. *Can't meet up at the diner. Got a call from a potential client.*

It seemed as though even Case had moved on without any further ado.

It was the same way at Spencer's. I greeted Drew and my dad as usual, gave Nicholas a kiss, and headed off to the office to do my morning work. No fuss, no bother. Just business as usual.

At ten o'clock, my dad came into the office holding the newspaper, with Delphi right behind him. "You made the news," Dad announced.

I took the paper and unfolded it. *KILLER CAUGHT!* the banner headline read. I skimmed the article, relieved to see that Hugo's reputation had been restored. He was lauded for trying to halt the Harmon land deal and mourned for losing his life over it. There was a nice write-up by Charlie Bolt of Hugo's life accomplishments, including how he'd uncovered Pete's underhanded dealings years before. I hoped Jewel would see the article.

"Look!" Delphi said. "Right here. 'Athena Spencer, affectionately known as the Goddess of Greene Street, is being credited for catching Thomas L. Silvester, now charged with the murder of Hugo Lukan.'" She put her arm around me and gave me a hug. "My famous sister."

Below the two-column article, Delphi pointed out another headline that read: *HARMON PROJECT DEAD*.

As I read the headline out loud, I heard from the doorway, "Well, I would hope so."

I glanced up as Elissa walked in with a smile, the dark circles under her eyes gone. Dad and Delphi greeted her and then slipped out to leave us alone in the office.

She gave me a hug. "I'm so glad you're okay."

"Thanks to Pearson. He really came through, Elissa. How's he doing?"

"A few bumps and bruises, but he'll be fine."

"And the auction?" I asked. "Did we raise enough money to save the dunes?"

"More than enough. Thanks to you and Lila, we'll have a signed check ready for the city council by Wednesday. I don't even know how to thank you for everything you've done for us."

I offered Elissa a seat and sat across from her, a thought suddenly occurring to me. "I think I know how you can thank me. Have you dedicated the new park yet?"

After sharing my idea with Elissa, she shared something personal with me. "Pearson and I had a lot to discuss last night. He apologized for lying to me, and I made him promise never to keep secrets from me again. I don't know if I fully trust him yet, but I'm hopeful we can work things out."

"I'm glad to hear that."

"Denis and I had a long talk, too." Elissa opened her purse and removed several shiny, metallic items, including a star toy. "I think these belong to Oscar. Denis will be coming over later to apologize to you and Niko."

"I'm glad to hear that, too."

Elissa smiled as she rose. "Maybe once all this hoopla blows over, you and I can go out for a cup of coffee and have a normal conversation."

"I think things have already blown over," I said, walking her out of the office. "By the looks of it, everything is back to business as usual."

We walked up the short hallway where I could hear a low murmur of voices coming from the conference room. I stopped to look inside, and a cheer went up. There stood Case and Lila, Delphi and Maguire, Nicholas, my parents, all three of my sisters, and my aunts, uncles, and cousins, all crowded around the conference table.

"Look, Mom!" Nicholas cried, as my mom and dad held up a big, three-layer frosted cake for me to see. On top of the vanilla frosting written in bright strawberry pink were the words, *Three Cheers for the Goddess of Greene Street.*

Okay, so it wasn't business as usual.

My mouth opened in surprise as I gazed from the cake to the smiling faces around the table. "I don't know what to say!"

"Sas efxaristó would be nice," Mama said.

"That means 'thank you,'" Nicholas told the group, puffing out his chest with pride.

"Athena," Maguire said, "I think you and everyone here will be happy to know that both Tom Silvester and Pete Harmon were denied bail this morning. They'll be cooling their heels in jail for a long time." He waited until the clapping stopped to add, "And I'm sorry, but I have to get back to work. So *adío.*" He glanced at Mama. "Did I say that right?"

She gave Maguire the once-over before finally cracking a smile. "You said it exactly right, *agapitó agóri.*" *Dear boy.*

"Mom," Nicholas called, "say cheese!" I looked over to see him holding a cell phone. He snapped a picture of me surrounded by my friends and family, then handed the phone to Case and ran around the table to stand beside me. "Take our picture now!"

Case obliged and then began to snap photos of everyone in the room.

"I think I know what I want for my birthday, Mom," Nicholas told me. "A professional camera."

Case glanced at me with a smile as he handed the phone back to Niko. "Well, isn't that an *interesting* idea."

"Athena?"

I turned to see Elissa standing behind me. "Maybe this would be a good time to share the news?"

I gave her the go-ahead and clapped my hands to get everyone's attention.

"The Save Our Dunes group has secured enough funds to halt any future outside development," she announced. "In fact, because of the incredible success of our auction, the city can begin renovating the park immediately."

Another round of applause filled the room. "And I would like to thank a very special person for making that happen." Elissa turned toward Lila. "Lila Talbot, on be-half of SOD, I am recommending that the city dedicate the park to you."

As everyone clapped again, tears welled in Lila's eyes. She clasped her hands together and looked up as though already reading the sign. "The Lila Talbot Park," she said reverently.

"Or just Talbot Park," I suggested.

"Talbot Park," Lila repeated. "What a perfect way to save the Talbot name. I love it."

As everyone began to talk, and my mother started cut-ting the cake into slices, Case came up and put an arm around me. "Did I surprise you?"

I smiled up at him. "You did. I thought I was already old news."

"No way," he said, and tilted his head down to give me a kiss.

Lila edged her way in beside Case. "Surprise!"

"Yes, this was a surprise," I said, glancing at all the happy faces around me. "Lila, I can't thank you enough for coming to the auction yesterday. You really saved the day."

"Thank you," she said. "And that's not all that happened yesterday. I'm happy to announce that Case and I are back on speaking terms." She gave him a nudge. "He called me last night to apologize. Oh, and by the way, I brought the painting of *The Statue of Athena* over to the Greene Street office this morning and found the perfect place for it on that big blank wall in the reception area. Wait until you see it."

"You're donating the painting to our detective agency?" I asked.

With an impatient sigh, Lila put her hands on her hips. "Don't look so surprised. I'm a very generous person."

"You *are* a generous person," I said. "Thank you."

"And wait until you see the new sign above the entrance," Case said. "We are officially in business as the Greene Street Detective Agency."

"So." Lila put her arm around Case's waist and my shoulders and hugged us to her. "Are we partners again?"

Case looked at me for confirmation.

"Partners," I said.

"Now," Lila continued, "about the two offices—"

Drew leaned in the doorway. "Athena, there's someone here to see you. She said it's important."

"Hold that thought," I said to Lila. I followed Drew out to the front, where a young, redheaded woman was waiting by the checkout counter.

"Athena Spencer?"

"That's me."

"It's a pleasure to meet you." She shook my hand. "Abby Knight Salvare. Bloomers Flower Shop. Have I got a case for you."

Keep reading for a special excerpt . . .

Single mom Athena Spencer is back in Michigan, work-
ing at her family's garden center, raising a pet racoon,
and digging up clues in the smart new mystery series by
the **New York Times** *bestselling author of the Flower*
Shop Mysteries . . .

A BIG FAT GREEK MURDER
By Kate Collins

The entire family has been put to work when a big fat
Greek wedding rehearsal is booked at the Parthenon. All
hands are needed for rolling grape leaves, layering *mous-*
saka, and keeping the bride calm. But then the groom
goes MIA, and there's far more to worry about than just
whether Yiayiá's lemon rice soup has gone cold.

No matter how tangy the *tzatziki*, everyone's appetite is
ruined when the groom is found dead, a pair of scissors
planted in his back. When the bride accuses Athena's sister Selene, a hairstylist, of seducing and stabbing her fi-
ancé, it's all-out war—and it's up to Athena to dig up the
dirt on the suspects and nip suspicions in the bud . . .

***Look for* A BIG FAT GREEK MURDER,**
on sale now!

IT'S ALL GREEK TO ME
by Goddess Anon

This has to be a fast post because I'm due at a re-hearsal dinner in an hour, and I have yet to change. Lucky me, you say? Sounds like a good time? "Humbug" is my reply. Getting all dolled up after a day of work so I can spend my evening pretending to be overjoyed for a happy couple is not my idea of a good time. Lest ye forget, I was once one-half of a so-called "happy couple."

It won't be easy for me to watch the soon-to-be-wed duo entwine arms, sip champagne, and promise to be loyal to each other forever because I know that forever is a long, long time.

I realize it seems I've soured on marriage, but I haven't completely given up. I keep hoping to find my Prince Charming out there somewhere. But who knows where that will be? Surely not here in my small Michigan hometown. I can't even find a decent white wine, let alone

*a white knight—unless my luck is changing. I don't be-
lieve in miracles, but there does seem to be a certain
magic in the air lately. Who knows? Maybe it could happen tonight.*

*Look at the time, and I still don't have a clue as to
what I should wear. How does one attract a white knight?
Black, perhaps?*

*Till tomorrow, this is Goddess Anon bidding you adío.
P.S. That's Greek for good-bye. Wish me luck!*

CHAPTER ONE

Friday

I posted the blog, closed my laptop, and turned in my chair to look at the small bedroom closet overflowing with clothes from my former life. Somewhere in that mess was the dress I'd be wearing to the rehearsal dinner.

A white knight. *Hmm.* Dark wavy hair, strong jaw, soulful eyes that seem to look through me, melt me like butter . . . and there was Case Donnelly once again creeping into my thoughts. After inviting him to meet me for a drink after the rehearsal dinner, and his nonchalant excuse, I cursed myself for taking the chance. A white knight was out there somewhere for me, but clearly it wasn't Case Donnelly.

I took a deep breath and began the hunt for my black dress.

Fifteen minutes later, after one last look in the bathroom mirror, I kissed my ten-year-old son, Nicholas, good-bye, blew a kiss at my youngest sister, Delphi, who'd stayed home to babysit, grabbed my purse and a light-weight coat, and hurried out to my white SUV for the ten-minute ride to the Parthenon, my grandparents' diner.

My phone rang through the car's speakers, and I tapped a button to answer, "Hello."

"Thenie, it's Dad. I need your help."

"I'm almost at the Parthenon, Pops. What's up?"

"Mrs. Bird is out back pecking at the new rose bushes and demanding to see you, Delphi is babysitting your son, and I've got a line of customers out the door. I know you promised your mother that you'd help out at the diner, but I could really use your help."

"Might I mention again that we need seasonal employ-ees?"

"You can lecture me when you get here."

"I can't make it right now, Pops. I'll call Delphi. She can bring Nicholas with her."

"Thanks, but we need a landscape consultant or we're going to lose Mrs. Bird's business."

"Let Delphi ring up the customers. You can handle Mrs. Bird."

"That's not the answer I was looking for."

"I'll be there as soon as I can, Pops."

Landscape consultant was on the opposite end of the spectrum from my former job as a newspaper reporter in Chicago. The vibrant tourist town of Sequoia was equally distant on the spectrum from the bustling Windy City that my son and I used to call home. The two cities shared the same water, but the breeze blowing east from Lake Michigan felt different. It smelled different, fresher per-haps.

If circumstances hadn't forced me to move back into the big family home, I'd still be running around the city, interviewing people and sitting at a computer until late at night to turn in my "noteworthy" articles. Instead, I was able to be outdoors working with plants and flowers and the cheerful people who came to our garden center to buy them. And at last, after one month of working in the office, learning the ins and outs of the business end of the operation, my dad felt I was ready to try my hand at landscape design. Turned out, I loved it.

I parked my car in the public lot on the block behind Greene Street and scurried up the alley. I entered through a back gate in the high fence and made my way to the outdoor eating area. With white wrought-iron tables and chairs, a concrete patio floor painted Grecian blue, white Greek-style columns on each corner, and blue-and-white lights strung around the entire perimeter, Yiayiá and Pappoús could not have made it look cozier or more inviting.

At least I thought so. But the guests didn't seem to be enjoying it. In fact, there was a distinctly unhappy *vibe* in the air, as Delphi would say. My mother was standing in front of the kitchen door, worrying the thick gold Greek bracelet she was never without. As I approached, my feet already hurting, Mama said, "It's not good, Athena. The groom-to-be hasn't shown up, and no one can reach him. What are you wearing?"

My mother had on black slacks with a Grecian blue blouse, or, as Mama referred to blue, "the color of the Ionian Sea." Unfortunately, I hadn't gotten the memo, so I was the oddball in my short black dress and strappy black heels. And no prince in sight. "I didn't know there was a dress code."

I glanced around at the tables, full of worried, whispering guests. "Maybe he got cold feet. Did he show up for the rehearsal?"

"They're having the wedding rehearsal after the dinner because some of the family members had to work."

"Why such a big crowd for a rehearsal dinner?" I asked. "Usually it's just for the wedding party."

"The Blacks decided to include the families of the wedding party," Mama said. "They're wealthy, and they pay very well. I wasn't about to question them on their decision."

I scanned the area, making mental notes. The wedding party was gathered at the head table, where Mandy, the bride-to-be, in a yellow silk dress, was being consoled not only by her bridesmaids, but also her parents and my oldest sister, Selene. Mitchell, the bride's twin brother and best man, stood directly behind them, checking his watch and looking perturbed, while maid of honor Tonya stood off to the side, talking quietly on her phone.

"What about the groom's parents?" I asked. "Have they heard from him?"

"His parents aren't here," Mama said. "Apparently, they declined the invitation."

My sister Maia joined us, breathless with news. "I just heard that two of Brady's groomsmen have gone to his apartment to see what the holdup is. He lives down the road, so it shouldn't take long—and aren't those my heels, Athena? And why are you so dressed up?"

Mama licked her thumb to wipe away a smudge from under Maia's eye, causing my sister to roll her head to the side. "Never mind about her outfit," Mama said, "and good for those brave boys. Yiayiá and Pappoús will be pleased. You know how upset they get if their food gets cold. Hold *still*, Maia."

That was so typical of our Greek family—more concerned about the guests missing a meal than the bride-to-be missing her groom.

Submitting to my mother's ministrations, Maia rolled her eyes, while I tried to hide my smile with a cough.

Maia was born after me; we were the two middle sisters of four, all named after Greek goddesses—Selene after the moon goddess, me after Athena, goddess of war and wisdom, and Maia after goddess of the fields. The exception was our youngest sister, Delphi, who was named in honor of the Oracle of Delphi. Stymied that she wasn't a "goddess," Delphi had long ago decided that she had the gift of foresight and was a true modern-day oracle. The remarkable thing was that sometimes she got her predictions right.

Also remarkable was how much Maia, Selene, and Delphi looked like our mother, shortish in stature, with fuller curves, lots of curly black hair, and typical Greek features. I, on the other hand, took after my father's English side of the family, inheriting his light brown hair, slender body, oval face, and softer features. In family photos, I was the gawky, pale-skinned girl in the back row standing beside the tall, pale-skinned man.

Selene broke away from the inconsolable bride and headed in our direction, an exasperated look on her face—coincidentally, the same expression Mama was wearing. Because she was also part of the wedding party, Selene wore a black-and-white sheath dress and heels instead of the waitress outfit.

"Selene," Mama said, "go back and ask the bride's mother whether we should serve the appetizers now. These poor people have to eat something."

"I just came from there," Selene replied, looking even

more exasperated than before. "I don't think they're in any mood to—"

Mama gave her "the look," and Selene did an about-face, slipping away obediently.

My grandmother joined our little group then, asking if she and Pappoús should start serving the lemon rice soup known as *avgolemono* (pronounced "ahv-lemono").

"No, Yiayiá," I said. "We're waiting for the groom to arrive."

"Still?" she asked in her high, raspy voice. "But the people need food."

Maia looked at me, trying to suppress another eye roll. I couldn't help but laugh, rubbing my grandmother's back to calm her down.

"Why you laugh?" Yiayiá asked with a scowl. Standing at a mere five feet high, she wore a black blouse, a long, full, black-print cotton skirt, and thick-soled black shoes. The only brightness in her outfit was a blue—excuse me—Ionian Sea–colored scarf that wrapped around her white hair, wound into its usual tight knot at the back of her head.

"It shouldn't be long, Mama," my mother said to her, shooting us a glare. "We expect them at any moment."

"*Endáksi,*" she said with a sigh and a shrug. *Okay.* Wearing her usual world-weary expression, she headed back into the kitchen to share the news with Pappoús.

Suddenly, the two absent groomsmen came jogging around the corner of the restaurant, out of breath and wild-eyed. "Brady," one gasped, holding his side, "he's been hurt. Badly."

"Taken," the second groomsmen said, bending over to gulp air, "to the hospital."

As the guests rose to their feet in concern, the bride

gathered her full skirt and ran toward the two men, grabbing onto the shirt front of one. "Trevor, is Brady dead?"

In between gulps of air, Trevor replied, "He was—unconscious—when the paramedics—took him away."

Mandy took a step backward as though she'd been pushed. "Then he's alive?"

"We don't know," Patrick, the other groomsman said, "We found him on his apartment floor with a pair of—"

"Patrick," Trevor snapped, giving a subtle nod in Mandy's direction.

"With a pair of what?" Mandy cried, grabbing his shirt front again. "Tell me. With *what*?"

Trevor's chin began to tremble, and a tear ran down his cheek. "Scissors in his back."

There was a collective gasp. My mother made the sign of the cross. Maia's mouth dropped open. Selene froze in place. I spotted Tonya, the bridesmaid who'd been on the cell phone, turn to give the other bridesmaids a knowing look, and I instantly filed it away.

"The police are on their way, Mandy," Patrick said. "They'll be able to tell you more."

The bride-to-be collapsed in a puddle of yellow silk, sobbing hysterically, "Brady's dead. I know he's dead. What will I do? Oh my God, what will I do?"

Her parents helped her to her chair and sat on either side of her, rubbing her hands, while her brother strode toward the two groomsmen to have a whispered conference. My mother hurried over to talk to the bride's mother, who was consoling her distraught daughter. That was when I spotted Selene, her face ashen, slip around the guests and disappear into the kitchen.

Before I could follow her, Mama returned to say quietly to us, "I just spoke with Mandy and her parents.

They're going to stay here until the police arrive. Maia, go tell Yiayiá and Pappoús we'll start serving the soup afterward."

"Maia, wait!" I called, as she started toward the kitchen. "Mama, no one is going to stay for dinner. This is supposed to be a celebration."

"But they must eat!" she cried. "Think of all the food waiting for them."

"Athena is right, Mama," Maia said. "They've just had horrible news. They're not going to sit down and dine now."

Mama put her hand over her forehead. "Then go tell your grandparents that, Maia."

"I'll tell them," I said, and headed inside to deliver the message and find out why Selene had slipped away.

"Yiayiá, Pappoús, the dinner has been canceled," I announced. "The groom was taken to the hospital with a serious injury."

Pappoús stopped stirring the soup, and Yiayiá straightened, putting one hand on her lower back. Almost in unison they said, "But the people have to eat!"

"It's not appropriate to serve food when there's been a calamity," I explained.

"Calamity is right," Yiayiá said grumpily, eyeing all the food.

"The groom is injured, sure," Pappoús said in his thick Greek accent, "but what about the others?"

"They'll be going home soon." I glanced around but didn't see my sister. "Yiayiá, did you see Selene come through the kitchen?"

"She's sitting out there by herself," Yiayiá replied, nodding her head toward the swinging doors to the diner.

"Maybe you can talk to her. She won't tell me what's wrong."

I found my sister in a booth in the empty diner, staring blankly into space. She had scooted to the far end, with her back to the wall and her feet hanging off the edge. I slid in opposite her and reached for her hand.

"What's wrong, Selene? You look like you just lost your best friend."

Her gaze shifted to mine, and I saw fear in her eyes. Just as she was about to speak, my mother stepped into the room and clapped her hands. "Girls, the police are here. They want everyone outside except for Yiayiá and Pappoús. *Páme!*"

As soon as Mama left, Selene bent her head and sobbed. I hadn't seen my oldest sister cry since we were children, and it startled me. Selene had always been strong and bold, the fearless firstborn, a role model for her sisters. Now she wept as though her heart was broken.

"Selene, what is it?"

"Stay with me, Athena," she sobbed, reaching for my hand. "Don't leave my side."

"I won't, but tell me why."

"The scissors in Brady's back? I think they're mine."

Connect with Us

Visit us online at
KensingtonBooks.com
to read more from your favorite authors, see books
by series, view reading group guides, and more.

Join us on social media

for sneak peeks, chances to win books and prize packs,
and to share your thoughts with other readers.

facebook.com/kensingtonpublishing
twitter.com/kensingtonbooks

Tell us what you think!

To share your thoughts, submit a review,
or sign up for our eNewsletters, please visit:
KensingtonBooks.com/TellUs.